They found it behind a coffin on the bottom shelf—a simple crawl space. "Down there," said Bod. "We go down there."

Scarlett found herself suddenly enjoying the adventure rather less. She said, "We can't see down there. It's dark."

"I don't need light," said Bod. "Not while I'm in the graveyard."

"I do," said Scarlett. "It's dark."

Bod thought about the reassuring things that he could say, like "there's nothing bad down there," but the tales of hair turning white and people never returning meant that he could not have said them with a clear conscience, so he said, "I'll go down. You wait for me up here."

Scarlett frowned. "You shouldn't leave me," she said.

"I'll go down," said Bod, "and I'll see who's there, and I'll come back and tell you all about it."

The Graveyard Book

NEIL GAIMAN

WITH ILLUSTRATIONS BY DAVE McKEAN

HARPER

An Imprint of HarperCollinsPublishers

Library of Congress Cataloging-in-Publication Data

Gaiman, Neil.

The graveyard book / Neil Gaiman ; with illustrations by Dave McKean. — 1st ed.

p. cm.

Summary: Nobody Owens is a normal boy, except that he has been raised by ghosts and other denizens of the graveyard.

ISBN 978-0-06-053094-5

[1. Dead—Fiction. 2. Supernatural—Fiction. 3. Cemeteries—Fiction.] I. McKean, Dave, ill. II. Title.

PZ7.G1273Gr 2008   2008013860

[Fic]—dc22   CIP

                                            AC

Typography by Hilary Zarycky

10 11 12 13 14   LP/CW   10 9 8 7 6 5 4 3

❖

First paperback edition, 2010

Rattle his bones
Over the stones
It's only a pauper
Who nobody owns

The Graveyard Book

CHAPTER ONE

How Nobody Came to the Graveyard

THERE WAS A HAND IN the darkness, and it held a knife.

The knife had a handle of polished black bone, and a blade finer and sharper than any razor. If it sliced you, you might not even know you had been cut, not immediately.

The knife had done almost everything it was brought to that house to do, and both the blade and the handle were wet.

The street door was still open, just a little, where the knife and the man who held it had slipped in, and wisps of

nighttime mist slithered and twined into the house through the open door.

The man Jack paused on the landing. With his left hand he pulled a large white handkerchief from the pocket of his black coat, and with it he wiped off the knife and his gloved right hand which had been holding it; then he put the handkerchief away. The hunt was almost over. He had left the woman in her bed, the man on the bedroom floor, the older child in her brightly colored bedroom, surrounded by toys and half-finished models. That only left the little one, a baby barely a toddler, to take care of. One more and his task would be done.

He flexed his fingers. The man Jack was, above all things, a professional, or so he told himself, and he would not allow himself to

smile until the job was completed.

His hair was dark and his eyes were dark and he wore black leather gloves of the thinnest lambskin.

The toddler's room was at the very top of the house. The man Jack walked up the stairs, his feet silent on the carpeting. Then he pushed open the attic door, and he walked in. His shoes were black leather, and they were polished to such a shine that they looked like

dark mirrors: you could see the moon reflected in them, tiny and half full.

The real moon shone through the casement window. Its light was not bright, and it was diffused by the mist, but the man Jack would not need much light. The moonlight was enough. It would do.

He could make out the shape of the child in the crib, head and limbs and torso.

The crib had high, slatted sides to prevent the child from getting out. Jack leaned over, raised his right hand, the one holding the knife, and he aimed for the chest . . .

. . . and then he lowered his hand. The shape in the crib was a teddy bear. There was no child.

The man Jack's eyes were accustomed to the dim moonlight, so he had no desire to turn on an electric light. And light was not that important, after all. He had other skills.

The man Jack sniffed the air. He ignored the scents that had come into the room with him, dismissed the scents that he could safely ignore, honed in on the smell of the thing he had come to find. He could smell the child: a milky smell, like chocolate chip cookies, and the sour tang of a wet, disposable, nighttime diaper. He could smell the baby shampoo in its hair, and something small and rubbery—*a toy*, he thought, and then, *no, something to suck*—that the child had been carrying.

The child had been here. It was here no longer. The man Jack followed his nose down the stairs through the middle of the tall, thin house. He inspected the bathroom, the kitchen, the airing cupboard, and, finally, the downstairs hall, in which there was nothing to be seen but the family's bicycles, a pile of empty shopping bags, a fallen diaper, and the stray tendrils of fog that had insinuated themselves into the hall from the open door to the street.

The man Jack made a small noise then, a grunt that contained in it both frustration and also satisfaction. He slipped the knife into its sheath in the inside pocket of his long coat, and he stepped out into the street. There was moonlight, and there were streetlights, but the fog stifled everything, muted light and muffled sound and made the night shadowy and treacherous. He looked down the hill towards the light of the closed shops, then up the street, where the last high houses wound up the hill on their way to the darkness of the old graveyard.

The man Jack sniffed the air. Then, without hurrying, he began to walk up the hill.

Ever since the child had learned to walk he had been his mother's and father's despair and delight, for there never was such a boy for wandering, for climbing up things, for getting into and out of things. That night, he had been woken by the sound of something on the floor beneath him falling with a crash. Awake, he soon became bored, and had begun looking for a way out of his crib. It had

10

high sides, like the walls of his playpen downstairs, but he was convinced that he could scale it. All he needed was a step . . .

He pulled his large, golden teddy bear into the corner of the crib, then, holding the railing in his tiny hands, he put his foot onto the bear's lap, the other foot up on the bear's head, and he pulled himself up into a standing position, and then he half-climbed, half-toppled over the railing and out of the crib.

He landed with a muffled thump on a small mound of furry, fuzzy toys, some of them presents from relations from his first birthday, not six months gone, some of them inherited from his older sister. He was surprised when he hit the floor, but he did not cry out: if you cried they came and put you back in your crib.

He crawled out of the room.

Stairs that went up were tricky things, and he had not yet entirely mastered them. Stairs that went down however, he had discovered, were fairly simple. He did them sitting down, bumping from step to step on his well-padded bottom.

He sucked on his *nummer*, the rubber pacifier his mother had just begun to tell him that he was getting too old for.

His diaper had worked itself loose on his journey on his bottom down the stairs, and when he reached the last step, when he reached the little hall and stood up, the diaper fell off. He stepped out of it. He was only wearing a child's nightshirt. The stairs that led back up to his room and his family were steep, but the door to the street was open and inviting. . . .

The child stepped out of the house a little hesitantly. The fog wreathed around him like a long-lost friend. And then, uncertainly at first, then with increasing speed and confidence, the boy tottered up the hill.

The fog was thinner as you approached the top of the hill. The half-moon shone, not as bright as day, not by any means, but enough to see the graveyard, enough for that.

Look.

You could see the abandoned funeral chapel, iron doors padlocked, ivy on the sides of the spire, a small tree growing out of the guttering at roof level.

You could see stones and tombs and vaults and memorial plaques. You could see the occasional dash or scuttle of a rabbit or a vole or a weasel as it slipped out of the undergrowth and across the path.

You would have seen these things, in the moonlight, if you had been there that night.

You might not have seen a pale, plump woman, who walked the path near the front gates, and if you had seen her, with a second, more careful glance you would have realized that she was only moonlight, mist, and shadow. The plump, pale woman was there, though. She walked the path that led through a clutch of half-fallen tombstones towards the front gates.

The gates were locked. They were always locked at four in the afternoon in winter, at eight at night in summer. Spike-topped iron railings ran around part of the cemetery, a high brick wall around the rest of it. The bars of the gates were closely spaced: they would have stopped a grown man from getting through, even stopped a ten-year-old child . . .

"Owens!" called the pale woman, in a voice that might have been the rustle of the wind through the long grass. "Owens! Come and look at this!"

She crouched down and peered at something on the ground, as a patch of shadow moved into the moonlight, revealing itself to be a grizzled man in his mid-forties. He looked down at his wife, and then looked at what she was looking at, and he scratched his head.

"Mistress Owens?" he said, for he came from a more formal age than our own. "Is that what I think it is?"

And at that moment the thing he was inspecting seemed to catch sight of Mrs. Owens, for it opened its mouth, letting the rubber nipple it was sucking fall to the ground, and it reached out a small, chubby fist, as if it were trying for all the world to hold on to Mrs. Owens's pale finger.

"Strike me silly," said Mr. Owens, "if that isn't a baby."

"Of course it's a baby," said his wife. "And the question is, what is to be done with it?"

"I daresay that is a question, Mistress Owens," said her husband. "And yet, it is not *our* question. For this here baby is unquestionably alive, and as such is nothing to do with us, and is no part of our world."

"Look at him smile!" said Mrs. Owens. "He has the sweetest of smiles," and with one insubstantial hand she stroked the child's sparse blond hair. The little boy giggled with delight.

A chilly breeze blew across the graveyard, scattering the fog in the lower slopes of the place (for the graveyard covered the whole of the top of the hill, and its paths wound up the hill and down and back upon themselves). A rattling: someone at the main gate of the graveyard was pulling and shaking it, rattling the old gates and the heavy padlock and chain that held them.

"There now," said Owens, "it's the babe's family, come to bring him back to the loving bosom. Leave the little man be," he added, because Mrs. Owens was putting her insubstantial arms around the toddler, smoothing, stroking.

Mrs. Owens said, "He dun't look like nobody's family, that one." The man in the dark coat had given up on rattling the main gates and was now examining the smaller side gate. It, too, was well-locked. There had been some vandalism in the graveyard the previous year, and the council had Taken Steps.

"Come on, Mistress Owens. Leave it be. There's a dear," said Mr. Owens, when he saw a ghost, and his mouth dropped open, and he found himself unable to think of anything to say.

You might think—and if you did, you would be right—that Mr. Owens should not have taken on so at seeing a ghost, given that Mr. and Mrs. Owens were themselves

14

dead and had been for a few hundred years now, and given that the entirety of their social life, or very nearly, was spent with those who were also dead. But there was a difference between the folk of the graveyard and *this*: a raw, flickering, startling shape the grey color of television static, all panic and naked emotion which flooded the Owenses as if it was their own. Three figures, two large, one smaller, but only one of them was in focus, was more than an outline or a shimmer. And the figure said, *My baby! He is trying to harm my baby!*

A clattering. The man outside was hauling a heavy metal garbage can across the alley to the high brick wall that ran around that part of the graveyard.

"Protect my son!" said the ghost, and Mrs. Owens thought it was a woman. Of course, the babe's mother.

"What did he do to you?" asked Mrs. Owens, but she was not certain that the ghost could hear her. *Recently dead, poor love*, she thought. It's always easier to die gently, to wake in due time in the place you were buried, to come to terms with your death and to get acquainted with the other inhabitants. This creature was nothing but alarm and fear for her child, and her panic, which felt to the Owenses like a low-pitched screaming, was now attracting attention, for other pale figures were coming from all over the graveyard.

"Who are you?" Caius Pompeius asked the figure. His headstone was now only a weathered lump of rock, but two thousand years earlier he had asked to be laid to rest on the mound beside the marble shrine, rather than to have his body sent back to Rome, and he was one of the most senior citizens of the graveyard. He took his responsibilities extremely seriously. "Are you buried here?"

"Of course she's not! Freshly dead by the look of her." Mrs. Owens put an arm around the woman-shape and spoke to it privately, in a low voice, calm and sensible.

There was a thump and a crash from the high wall beside the alley. The garbage can had fallen. A man clambered up onto the top of the wall, a dark outline against the mist-smudged streetlights. He paused for a moment, then climbed down the other side, holding on to the top of the wall, legs dangling, then let himself fall the last few feet, down into the graveyard.

"But my dear," Mrs. Owens said to the shape, now all that was left of the three shapes that had appeared in the graveyard. "He's living. We're not. Can you imagine . . ."

The child was looking up at them, puzzled. It reached for one of them, then the other, finding nothing but air. The woman-shape was fading fast.

"Yes," said Mrs. Owens, in response to something that no one else had heard. "If we can, then we will." Then she turned to the man beside her. "And you, Owens? Will you be a father to this little lad?"

"Will I what?" said Owens, his brow crinkling.

"We never had a child," said his wife. "And his mother wants us to protect him. Will you say yes?"

The man in the black coat had tripped in the tangle of ivy and half-broken headstones. Now he got to his feet

16

and walked forward more carefully, startling an owl which rose on silent wings. He could see the baby and there was triumph in his eyes.

Owens knew what his wife was thinking when she used that tone of voice. They had not, in life and in death, been married for over two hundred and fifty years for nothing. "Are you certain?" he asked. "Are you sure?"

"Sure as I ever have been of anything," said Mrs. Owens.

"Then yes. If you'll be its mother, I'll be its father."

"Did you hear that?" Mrs. Owens asked the flickering shape in the graveyard, now little more than an outline, like distant summer lightning in the shape of a woman. It said something to her that no one else could hear, and then it was gone.

"She'll not come here again," said Mr. Owens. "Next time she wakes it'll be in her own graveyard, or wherever it is she's going."

Mrs. Owens bent down to the baby and extended her arms. "Come now," she said, warmly. "Come to Mama."

To the man Jack, walking through the graveyard towards them on a path, his knife already in his hand, it seemed as if a swirl of mist had curled around the child, in the moonlight, and that the boy was no longer there: just damp mist and moonlight and swaying grass.

He blinked and sniffed the air. Something had happened, but he had no idea what it was. He growled in the back of his throat, like a beast of prey, angry and frustrated.

"Hullo?" called the man Jack, wondering if perhaps the

child had stepped behind something. His voice was dark and rough, and there was an odd edge to it, as if of surprise or puzzlement at hearing himself speak.

The graveyard kept its secrets.

"Hello?" he called, again. He hoped to hear a baby cry or utter a half-word, or to hear it move. He did not expect what he actually heard, a voice, silky smooth, saying,

"Can I help you?"

The man Jack was tall. This man was taller. The man Jack wore dark clothes. This man's clothes were darker. People who noticed the man Jack when he was about his business—and he did not like to be noticed—were troubled, or made uncomfortable, or found themselves unaccountably scared. The man Jack looked up at the stranger, and it was the man Jack who was troubled.

"I was looking for someone," said the man Jack, slipping his right hand back into his coat pocket, so the knife was hidden, but there if he needed it.

"In a locked graveyard, at night?" said the stranger.

"It was just a baby," said the man Jack. "I was just passing, when I heard a baby cry, and I looked through the gates and I saw him. Well, what would anyone do?"

"I applaud your public-spiritedness," said the stranger. "Yet if you managed to find this child, how were you planning to get out of here with it? You can't climb back over the wall holding a baby."

"I would have called until someone let me out," said the man Jack.

18

A heavy jingling of keys. "Well, that would have been me, then," said the stranger. "I would have had to let you out." He selected one large key from the key ring, said "Follow me."

The man Jack walked behind the stranger. He took his knife from his pocket. "Are you the caretaker, then?"

"Am I? Certainly, in a manner of speaking," said the stranger. They were walking towards the gates and, the man Jack was certain, away from the baby. But the caretaker had the keys. A knife in the dark, that was all it would take, and then he could search for the child all through the night, if he needed to.

He raised the knife.

"If there *was* a baby," said the stranger, without looking back, "it wouldn't have been here in the graveyard. Perhaps you were mistaken. It's unlikely that a child would have come in here, after all. Much more likely that you heard a nightbird, and saw a cat, perhaps, or a fox. They declared this place an official nature reserve, you know, thirty years ago, around the time of the last funeral. Now think carefully, and tell me you are *certain* that it was a child that you saw."

The man Jack thought.

The stranger unlocked the side gate. "A fox," he said. "They make the most uncommon noises, not unlike a person crying. No, your visit to this graveyard was a misstep, sir. Somewhere the child you seek awaits you, but he is not here." And he let the thought sit there, in the man

19

Jack's head for a moment, before he opened the gate with a flourish. "Delighted to have made your acquaintance," he said. "And I trust that you will find everything you need out there."

The man Jack stood outside the gates to the graveyard. The stranger stood inside the gate, and he locked it again, and put the key away.

"Where are you going?" asked the man Jack.

"There are other gates than this," said the stranger. "My car is on the other side of the hill. Don't mind me. You don't even have to remember this conversation."

"No," said the man Jack, agreeably. "I don't." He remembered wandering up the hill, that what he had thought to be a child had turned out to be a fox, that a helpful caretaker had escorted him back out to the street. He slipped his knife into its inner sheath. "Well," he said. "Good night."

"A good night to you," said the stranger whom Jack had taken for a caretaker.

The man Jack set off down the hill, in pursuit of the infant.

From the shadows, the stranger watched Jack until he was out of sight. Then he moved through the night, up and up, to the flat place below the brow of the hill, a place dominated by an obelisk and a flat stone set into the ground dedicated to the memory of Josiah Worthington, local brewer, politician and later baronet, who had, almost three hundred years before, bought the old cemetery and the land around it, and given it to the city in perpetuity.

He had reserved for himself the best location on the hill—a natural amphitheater, with a view of the whole city and beyond—and had insured that the graveyard endured as a graveyard, for which the inhabitants of the graveyard were grateful, although never quite as grateful as Josiah Worthington, Bart., felt they should have been.

There were, all told, some ten thousand souls in the graveyard, but most of them slept deep, or took no interest in the night-to-night affairs of the place, and there were less than three hundred of them up there, in the amphitheater, in the moonlight.

The stranger reached them as silently as the fog itself, and he watched the proceedings unfold, from the shadows, and he said nothing.

Josiah Worthington was speaking. He said, "My dear madam. Your obduracy is quite, is . . . well, can't you see how ridiculous this is?"

"No," said Mrs. Owens. "I can't."

She was sitting, cross-legged, on the ground, and the living child was sleeping in her lap. She cradled its head with her pale hands.

"What Mistress Owens is trying to say, sir, begging your honor's pardon," said Mr. Owens, standing beside her, "is that she dun't see it that way. She sees it as doing her duty."

Mr. Owens had seen Josiah Worthington in the flesh back when they were both alive, had in fact made several pieces of fine furniture for the Worthington manor house, out near Inglesham, and was still in awe of him.

21

"Her *duty*?" Josiah Worthington, Bart., shook his head, as if to dislodge a strand of cobweb. "Your *duty*, ma'am, is to the graveyard, and to the commonality of those who form this population of discarnate spirits, revenants and suchlike wights, and your *duty* thus is to return the creature as soon as possible to its natural home—which is not here."

"His mama gave the boy to me," said Mrs. Owens, as if that was all that needed to be said.

"My dear woman . . ."

"I am not your dear woman," said Mrs. Owens, getting to her feet. "Truth to tell, I don't even see why I am even here, talking to you fiddle-pated old dunderheads, when this lad is going to wake up hungry soon enough—and where am I going to find food for him in this graveyard, I should like to know?"

"Which," said Caius Pompeius, stiffly, "is precisely the point. What *will* you feed him? How *can* you care for him?"

Mrs. Owens's eyes burned. "I can look after him," she said, "as well as his own mama. She already gave him to me. Look: I'm holding him, aren't I? I'm touching him."

"Now, see reason, Betsy," said Mother Slaughter, a tiny old thing, in the huge bonnet and cape that she had worn in life and been buried wearing. "Where would he live?"

"Here," said Mrs. Owens. "We could give him the Freedom of the Graveyard."

Mother Slaughter's mouth became a tiny O. "But," she said. Then she said, "But I never."

"Well, why not? It en't the first time we'd've given the Freedom of the Graveyard to an outsider."

"That is true," said Caius Pompeius. "But *he* wasn't alive."

And with that, the stranger realized that he was being drawn, like it or not, into the conversation and, reluctantly, he stepped out of the shadows, detaching from them like a patch of darkness. "No," he agreed. "I am not. But I take Mrs. Owens's point."

Josiah Worthington said, "You do, Silas?"

"I do. For good or for evil—and I firmly believe that it is for good—Mrs. Owens and her husband have taken this child under their protection. It is going to take more than just a couple of good-hearted souls to raise this child. It will," said Silas, "take a graveyard."

"And what of food, and the rest of it?"

"I can leave the graveyard and return. I can bring him food," said Silas.

"That's all very well you saying that," said Mother Slaughter. "But you comes and you goes and nobody keeps track of you. If you went off for a week, the boy could die."

"You are a wise woman," said Silas. "I see why they speak so highly of you." He couldn't push the minds of the dead as he could the living, but he could use all the tools of flattery and persuasion he possessed, for the dead are not immune to either. Then he came to a decision. "Very well. If Mr. and Mrs. Owens will be his parents, I shall be his guardian. I shall remain here, and if I need to leave I shall ensure that someone takes my place, bringing the

23

child food and looking after him. We can use the crypt of the chapel," he added.

"But," expostulated Josiah Worthington. "But. A human child. A living child. I mean. I mean, *I mean*. This is a graveyard, not a nursery, blast it."

"Exactly," said Silas, nodding. "A very good point, Sir Josiah. I couldn't have put it better myself. And for that reason, if for no other, it is vital that the child be raised with as little disruption as possible to the, if you'll forgive the expression, the *life* of the graveyard." With that he strolled over to Mrs. Owens, and he looked down at the infant asleep in her arms. He raised an eyebrow. "Does he have a name, Mrs. Owens?"

"Not that his mother told me," she said.

"Well, then," said Silas. "His old name won't be of much use to him now, anyway. There are those out there who mean him harm. Suppose we pick a name for him, eh?"

Caius Pompeius stepped over and eyed the child. "He looks a little like my proconsul, Marcus. We could call him Marcus."

Josiah Worthington said, "He looks more like my head gardener, Stebbins. Not that I'm suggesting Stebbins as a name. The man drank like a fish."

"He looks like my nephew Harry," said Mother Slaughter, and it seemed then as if the whole graveyard was about to join in, each inhabitant offering his or her own comparisons between the infant and someone long forgotten, when Mrs. Owens broke in.

"He looks like nobody but himself," said Mrs. Owens, firmly. "He looks like nobody."

"Then Nobody it is," said Silas. "Nobody Owens."

It was then that, as if responding to the name, the child opened its eyes wide in wakefulness. It stared around it, taking in the faces of the dead, and the mist, and the moon. Then it looked at Silas. Its gaze did not flinch. It looked grave.

"And what kind of a name is Nobody?" asked Mother Slaughter, scandalized.

"His name. And a good name," Silas told her. "It will help to keep him safe."

"I don't want trouble," said Josiah Worthington. The infant looked up at him and then, hungry or tired or simply missing his home, his family, his world, he screwed up his tiny face and began to cry.

"Leave us," said Caius Pompeius to Mrs. Owens. "We will discuss this further without you."

Mrs. Owens waited outside the funeral chapel. It had been decreed over forty years before that the building, in appearance a small church with a spire, was a listed building of historical interest. The town council had decided that it would cost too much to renovate it, a little chapel in an overgrown graveyard that had already become unfashionable, so they had padlocked it, and waited for it to fall down. Ivy covered it, but it was solidly built, and it would not fall down this century.

The child had fallen asleep in Mrs. Owens's arms. She rocked it gently, sang to it an old song, one her mother had sung to her when she was a baby herself, back in the days when men had first started to wear powdered wigs. The song went,

Sleep my little babby-oh
Sleep until you waken
When you're grown you'll see the world
If I'm not mistaken.
Kiss a lover,
Dance a measure,
Find your name
and buried treasure . . .

And Mrs. Owens sang all that before she discovered that she had forgotten how the song ended. She had a feeling that the final line was something in the way of "and some hairy bacon," but that might have been another song altogether, so she stopped and instead she sang him the one about the Man in the Moon who came down too soon, and after that she sang, in her warm country voice, a more recent song about a lad who put in his thumb and pulled out a plum, and she had just started a long ballad about a young country gentleman whose girlfriend had, for no particular reason, poisoned him with a dish of spotted eels, when Silas came around the side of the chapel, carrying a cardboard box.

"Here we go, Mistress Owens," he said. "Lots of good things for a growing boy. We can keep it in the crypt, eh?"

The padlock fell off in his hand and he pulled open the iron door. Mrs. Owens walked inside, looking dubiously at the shelves, and at the old wooden pews tipped up against a wall. There were mildewed boxes of old parish records in one corner, and an open door that revealed a Victorian flush toilet and a basin, with only a cold tap, in the other.

The infant opened his eyes and stared.

"We can put the food here," said Silas. "It's cool, and the food will keep longer." He reached into the box, pulled out a banana.

"And what would that be when it was at home?" asked Mrs. Owens, eyeing the yellow and brown object suspiciously.

"It's a banana. A fruit, from the tropics. I believe you peel off the outer covering," said Silas, "like so."

The child—Nobody—wriggled in Mrs. Owens's arms, and she let it down to the flagstones. It toddled rapidly to Silas, grasped his trouser-leg and held on.

Silas passed it the banana.

Mrs. Owens watched the boy eat. "Ba-na-na," she said, dubiously. "Never heard of them. Never. What's it taste like?"

"I've absolutely no idea," said Silas, who consumed only one food, and it was not bananas. "You could make up a bed in here for the boy, you know."

"I'll do no such thing, with Owens and me having a

lovely little tomb over by the daffodil patch. Plenty of room in there for a little one. Anyway," she added, concerned that Silas might think she was rejecting his hospitality, "I wouldn't want the lad disturbing you."

"He wouldn't."

The boy was done with his banana. What he had not eaten was now smeared over himself. He beamed, messy and apple-cheeked.

"Narna," he said, happily.

"What a clever little thing he is," said Mrs. Owens. "And such a mess he's made! Why, attend, you little wriggler . . ." and she picked the lumps of banana from his clothes and his hair. And then, "What do you think they'll decide?"

"I don't know."

"I can't give him up. Not after what I promised his mama."

"Although I have been a great many things in my time," said Silas, "I have never been a mother. And I do not plan to begin now. But I *can* leave this place . . ."

Mrs. Owens said simply, "I cannot. My bones are here. And so are Owens's. I'm never leaving."

"It must be good," said Silas, "to have somewhere that you belong. Somewhere that's home." There was nothing wistful in the way he said this. His voice was drier than deserts, and he said it as if he were simply stating something unarguable. Mrs. Owens did not argue.

"Do you think we will have long to wait?"

"Not long," said Silas, but he was wrong about that.

28

Up in the amphitheater on the side of the hill, the debate continued. That it was the Owenses who had got involved in this nonsense, rather than some flibbertigibbet johnny-come-latelies, counted for a lot, for the Owenses were respectable and respected. That Silas had volunteered to be the boy's guardian had weight—Silas was regarded with a certain wary awe by the graveyard folk, existing as he did on the borderland between their world and the world they had left. But still, but still . . .

A graveyard is not normally a democracy, and yet death is the great democracy, and each of the dead had a voice, and an opinion as to whether the living child should be allowed to stay, and they were each determined to be heard, that night.

It was late autumn when the daybreak was long in coming. Although the sky was still dark, cars could now be heard starting up further down the hill, and as the living folk began to drive to work through the misty night-black morning, the graveyard folk talked about the child that had come to them, and what was to be done. Three hundred voices. Three hundred opinions. Nehemiah Trot, the poet, from the tumbled northwestern side of the graveyard, had begun to declaim his thoughts on the matter, although what they were no person listening could have said, when something happened; something to silence each opinionated mouth, something unprecedented in the history of that graveyard.

A huge white horse, of the kind that the people who

know horses would call a "grey," came ambling up the side of the hill. The pounding of its hooves could be heard before it was seen, along with the crashing it made as it pushed through the little bushes and thickets, through the brambles and the ivy and the gorse that had grown up on the side of the hill. The size of a Shire horse it was, a full nineteen hands or more. It was a horse that could have carried a knight in full armor into combat, but all it carried on its naked back was a woman, clothed from head to foot in grey. Her long skirt and her shawl might have been spun out of old cobwebs.

Her face was serene, and peaceful.

They knew her, the graveyard folk, for each of us encounters the Lady on the Grey at the end of our days, and there is no forgetting her.

The horse paused beside the obelisk. In the east the sky was lightening gently, a pearlish, pre-dawn luminescence that made the people of the graveyard uncomfortable and made them think about returning to their comfortable homes. Even so, not a one of them moved. They were watching the Lady on the Grey, each of them half-excited, half-scared. The dead are not superstitious, not as a rule, but they watched her as a Roman Augur might have watched the sacred crows circle, seeking wisdom, seeking a clue.

And she spoke to them.

In a voice like the chiming of a hundred tiny silver bells she said only, "The dead should have charity." And she smiled.

The horse, which had been contentedly ripping up and masticating a clump of thick grass, stopped then. The lady touched the horse's neck, and it turned. It took several huge, clattering steps, then it was off the side of the hill and cantering across the sky. Its thunderous hooves became an early rumble of distant thunder, and in moments it was lost to sight.

That, at least, was what the folk of the graveyard who had been on the hillside that night claimed had happened.

The debate was over and ended, and, without so much as a show of hands, had been decided. The child called Nobody Owens would be given the Freedom of the Graveyard.

Mother Slaughter and Josiah Worthington, Bart., accompanied Mr. Owens to the crypt of the old chapel, and they told Mrs. Owens the news.

She seemed unsurprised by the miracle. "That's right," she said. "Some of them dun't have a ha'porth of sense in their heads. But *she* does. Of course she does."

Before the sun rose on a thundering grey morning the child was fast asleep in the Owenses' fine little tomb (for Master Owens had died the prosperous head of the local cabinetmaker's guild, and the cabinetmakers had wanted to ensure that he was properly honored).

Silas went out for one final journey before the sunrise. He found the tall house on the side of the hill, and he examined the three bodies he found there, and he studied

31

the pattern of the knife-wounds. When he was satisfied he stepped out into the morning's dark, his head churning with unpleasant possibilities, and he returned to the graveyard, to the chapel spire where he slept and waited out the days.

In the little town at the bottom of the hill the man Jack was getting increasingly angry. The night had been one that he had been looking forward to for so long, the culmination of months—of years—of work. And the business of the evening had started so promisingly—three people down before any of them had even had a chance to cry out. And then . . .

Then it had all gone so maddeningly wrong. Why on earth had he gone up the hill when the child had so obviously gone *down* the hill? By the time he had reached the bottom of the hill, the trail had gone cold. Someone must have found the child, taken it in, hidden it. There was no other explanation.

A crack of thunder rang out, loud and sudden as a gunshot, and the rain began in earnest. The man Jack was methodical, and he began to plan his next move—the calls he would need to pay on certain of the townsfolk, people who would be his eyes and ears in the town.

He did not need to tell the Convocation he had failed.

Anyway, he told himself, edging under a shopfront as the morning rain came down like tears, he had not failed. Not yet. Not for years to come. There was plenty of time. Time to tie up this last piece of unfinished business.

Time to cut the final thread.

It was not until the police sirens sounded and first a police car, then an ambulance, then an unmarked police car with a siren blaring, sped past him on their way up the hill that, reluctantly, the man Jack turned up the collar of his coat, put his head down, and walked off into the morning. His knife was in his pocket, safe and dry inside its sheath, protected from the misery of the elements.

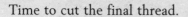

CHAPTER TWO

The New Friend

BOD WAS A QUIET child with sober grey eyes and a mop of tousled, mouse-colored hair. He was, for the most part, obedient. He learned how to talk, and, once he had learned, he would pester the graveyard folk with questions. "Why amn't I allowed out of the graveyard?" he would ask,

or "How do *I* do what *he* just did?" or "Who lives in here
The adults would do their best to answer his questions, but
their answers were often vague, or confusing, or contradic-
tory, and then Bod would walk down to the old chapel and
talk to Silas.

He would be there waiting at sunset, just before Silas
awakened.

His guardian could always be counted upon to explain
matters clearly and lucidly and as simply as Bod needed in
order to understand.

"You aren't allowed out of the graveyard—it's *aren't*, by
the way, not *amn't*, not these days—because it's only in
the graveyard that we can keep you safe. This is where you
live and this is where those who love you can be found.
Outside would not be safe for you. Not yet."

"*You* go outside. You go outside every night."

"I am infinitely older than you, lad. And I am safe wherever I am."

"I'm safe there too."

"I wish that that were true. But as long as you stay here,
you *are* safe."

Or,

"How could you do that? Some skills can be attained by
education, and some by practice, and some by time. Those
skills will come if you study. Soon enough you will master
Fading and Sliding and Dreamwalking. But some skills cannot be mastered by the living, and for those you must wait
a little longer. Still, I do not doubt that you will acquire

37

even those, in time.

"You were given the Freedom of the Graveyard, after all," Silas would tell him. "So the Graveyard is taking care of you. While you are here, you can see in the darkness. You can walk some of the ways that the living should not travel. The eyes of the living will slip from you. I too was given the Freedom of the Graveyard, although in my case it comes with nothing but the right of abode."

"I want to be like you," said Bod, pushing out his lower lip.

"No," said Silas, firmly. "You do not."

Or,

"Who lies there? You know, Bod, in many cases it is written on the stone. Can you read yet? Do you know your alphabet?"

"My what?"

Silas shook his head, but said nothing. Mr. and Mrs. Owens had never been much for reading when they were alive, and there were no alphabet books in the graveyard.

The next night, Silas appeared at the front of the Owenses' cozy tomb carrying three large books—two of them brightly colored alphabet books (A is for Apple, B is for Ball) and a copy of *The Cat in the Hat*. He also had paper and a packet of wax crayons. Then he walked Bod around the graveyard, placing the boy's small fingers on the newest and clearest of the headstones and the plaques, and taught Bod how to find the letters of the alphabet when they appeared, beginning with the sharp steeple of the capital *A*.

Silas gave Bod a quest—to find each of the twenty-six letters in the graveyard—and Bod finished it, proudly, with the discovery of Ezekiel Ulmsley's stone, built into the side of the wall in the old chapel. His guardian was pleased with him.

Every day Bod would take his paper and crayons into the graveyard and he would copy names and words and numbers as best he could, and each night, before Silas would go off into the world, Bod would make Silas explain to him what he had written, and make him translate the snatches of Latin which had, for the most part, baffled the Owenses.

A sunny day: bumblebees explored the wildflowers that grew in the corner of the graveyard, dangling from the gorse and the bluebells, droning their deep lazy buzz, while Bod lay in the spring sunlight watching a bronze-colored beetle wandering across the stone of G⁰· Reeder, his wife, Dorcas, and their son Sebastian *(Fidelis ad Mortem)*. Bod had copied down their inscription and now he was only thinking about the beetle when somebody said,

"Boy? What're you doing?"

Bod looked up. There was someone on the other side of the gorse bush, watching him.

"Nuffing," said Bod. He stuck out his tongue.

The face on the other side of the gorse bush crumpled into a gargoyle, tongue sticking out, eyes popping, then returned to girl.

"That was good," said Bod, impressed.

"I can make really good faces," said the girl. "Look at this one." She pushed her nose up with one finger, creased her mouth into a huge, satisfied smile, squinted her eyes, puffed out her cheeks. "Do you know what that was?"

"No."

"It was a pig, silly."

"Oh." Bod thought. "You mean, like *P* is for Pig?"

"Of course like that. Hang on."

She came around the gorse bush and stood next to Bod, who got to his feet. She was a little older than he was, a little taller, and was dressed in bright colors, yellow and pink and orange. Bod, in his grey winding sheet, felt dowdy and drab.

"How old are you?" said the girl. "What are you doing here? Do you live here? What's your name?"

"I don't know," said Bod.

"You don't know your name?" said the girl. "'Course you do. Everybody knows their own name. Fibber."

"I know my name," said Bod. "And I know what I'm doing here. But I don't know the other thing you said."

"How old you are?"

Bod nodded.

"Well," said the girl, "what was you when you was last birthday?"

"I didn't," said Bod. "I never was."

"Everybody gets birthdays. You mean you never had cake or candles or stuff?"

Bod shook his head. The girl looked sympathetic. "Poor

thing. I'm five. I bet you're five too."

Bod nodded enthusiastically. He was not going to argue with his new friend. She made him happy.

Her name was Scarlett Amber Perkins, she told him, and she lived in a flat with no garden. Her mother was sitting on a bench by the chapel at the bottom of the hill, reading a magazine, and she had told Scarlett to be back in half an hour, and to get some exercise, and not to get into trouble or talk to strangers.

"I'm a stranger," pointed out Bod.

"You're not," she said, definitely. "You're a little boy." And then she said, "And you're my friend. So you can't be a stranger."

Bod smiled rarely, but he smiled then, hugely and with delight. "I'm your friend," he said.

"What's your name?"

"Bod. It's short for Nobody."

She laughed then. "Funny sort of a name," she said. "What are you doing now?"

"ABCs," said Bod. "From the stones. I have to write them down."

"Can I do it with you?"

For a moment Bod felt protective—the gravestones were *his*, weren't they?—and then he realized how foolish he was being, and he thought that there were things that might be more fun done in the sunlight with a friend. He said, "Yes."

They copied down names from tombstones, Scarlett

helping Bod pronounce unfamiliar names and words, Bod telling Scarlett what the Latin meant, if he already knew, and it seemed much too soon when they heard a voice further down the hill shouting, "Scarlett!"

The girl thrust the crayons and paper back at Bod. "I got to go," she said.

"I'll see you next time," said Bod. "Won't I?"

"Where do you live?" she asked.

"Here," he said. And he stood and watched her as she ran down the hill.

On the way home Scarlett told her mother about the boy called Nobody who lived in the graveyard and had played with her, and that night Scarlett's mother mentioned it to Scarlett's father, who said that he believed that imaginary friends were a common phenomenon at that age, and nothing at all to be concerned about, and that they were fortunate to have a nature reserve so near.

After that initial meeting, Scarlett never saw Bod first. On days when it was not raining one of her parents would bring her to the graveyard. The parent would sit on the bench and read while Scarlett would wander off the path, a splash of fluorescent green or orange or pink, and explore. Then, always sooner rather than later, she would see a small, grave face and grey eyes staring up at her from beneath a mop of mouse-colored hair, and then Bod and she would play—hide-and-seek, sometimes, or climbing things, or being quiet and watching the rabbits behind the old chapel.

Bod would introduce Scarlett to some of his other friends. That she could not see them did not seem to matter. She had already been told firmly by her parents that Bod was imaginary and that there was nothing at all wrong with that—her mother had, for a few days, even insisted on laying an extra place at the dinner table for Bod—so it came as no surprise to her that Bod also had imaginary friends. He would pass on their comments to her.

"Bartleby says that thou dost have a face like unto a squishèd plum," he would tell her.

"So does he. And why does he talk so funny? Doesn't he mean squashed tomato?"

"I don't think that they had tomatoes when he comes from," said Bod. "And that's just how they talk then."

Scarlett was happy. She was a bright, lonely child, whose mother worked for a distant university teaching people she never met face-to-face, grading English papers sent to her over the computer, and sending messages of advice or encouragement back. Her father taught particle physics, but there were, Scarlett told Bod, too many people who wanted to teach particle physics and not enough people who wanted to learn it, so Scarlett's family had to keep moving to different university towns, and in each town her father would hope for a permanent teaching position that never came.

"What's particle physics?" asked Bod.

Scarlett shrugged. "Well," she said. "There's atoms, which is things that is too small to see, that's what we're all made of. And there's things that's smaller than atoms, and that's particle physics."

Bod nodded and decided that Scarlett's father was probably interested in imaginary things.

Bod and Scarlett wandered the graveyard together every weekday afternoon, tracing names with their fingers, writing them down. Bod would tell Scarlett whatever he knew of the inhabitants of the grave or mausoleum or tomb, and she would tell him stories that she had been read or learned, and sometimes she would tell him about the world outside, about cars and buses and television and aeroplanes (Bod had seen them flying high overhead, had thought them loud silver birds, but had never been curious about them until now). He in his turn would tell her about the days when the people in the graves had been alive—how Sebastian Reeder had been to London Town and had seen the Queen, who had been a fat woman in a fur cap who had glared at everyone and spoke no English. Sebastian Reeder could not remember which queen she had been, but he did not think she had been queen for very long.

"When was this?" Scarlett asked.

"He died in 1583, it says on his tombstone, so before then."

"Who is the oldest person here. In the whole graveyard?" asked Scarlett.

Bod frowned. "Probably Caius Pompeius. He came here a hundred years after the Romans first got here. He told me about it. He liked the roads."

"So he's the oldest?"

"I think so."

"Can we make a little house in one of those stone houses?"

"You can't get in. It's locked. They all are."

"Can *you* get in?"

"Of course."

"Why can't I?"

"The graveyard," he explained. "I got the Freedom of the Graveyard. It lets me go places."

"I want to go in the stone house and make little houses."

"You can't."

"You're just mean."

"Not."

"Meany."

"Not."

Scarlett put her hands into the pocket of her anorak and walked down the hill without saying good-bye, convinced that Bod was holding out on her, and at the same time suspecting that she was being unfair, which made her angrier.

That night, over dinner, she asked her mother and father if there was anyone in the country before the Romans came.

"Where did you hear about the Romans?" asked her father.

"Everybody knows," said Scarlett, with withering scorn. "Was there?"

"There were Celts," said her mother. "They were here first. They go back before the Romans. They were the people that the Romans conquered."

On the bench beside the old chapel, Bod was having a similar conversation.

"The oldest?" said Silas. "Honestly, Bod, I don't know. The oldest in the graveyard that I've encountered is Caius Pompeius. But there were people here before the Romans came. Lots of them, going back a long time. How are your letters coming along?"

"Good, I think. When do I learn joined-up letters?"

Silas paused. "I have no doubt," he said, after a moment's reflection, "that there are, among the many talented individuals interred here, at least a smattering of teachers. I shall make inquiries."

Bod was thrilled. He imagined a future in which he could read everything, in which all stories could be opened and discovered.

When Silas had left the graveyard to go about his own affairs, Bod walked to the willow tree beside the old chapel, and called Caius Pompeius.

The old Roman came out of his grave with a yawn. "Ah. Yes. The living boy," he said. "How are you, living boy?"

Bod said, "I do very well, sir."

"Good. I am pleased to hear it." The old Roman's hair was pale in the moonlight, and he wore the toga in which he had been buried, with, beneath it, a thick woolen vest and leggings because this was a cold country at the edge of the world, and the only place colder was Caledonia to the North, where the men were more animal than human and covered in orange fur, and were too savage even to be conquered by the Romans, so would soon be walled off in their perpetual winter.

"Are you the oldest?" asked Bod.

"The oldest in the graveyard? I am."

"So you were the first to be buried here?"

A hesitation. "Almost the first," said Caius Pompeius. "Before the Celts there were other people on this island. One of them was buried here."

"Oh." Bod thought for a moment. "Where's his grave?"

Caius pointed up the hill.

"He's up at the top," said Bod.

Caius shook his head.

"Then what?"

The old Roman reached down and he ruffled Bod's hair. "In the hill," he said. "Inside it. I was first brought here by my friends, followed in their turn by the local officials and the mimes, who wore the wax faces of my wife, taken by a fever in Camulodonum, and my father, killed in a border skirmish in Gaul. Three hundred years after my death a farmer, seeking a new place to graze his sheep, discovered the boulder that covered the entrance, and rolled it away, and went down, thinking there might be treasure. He came out a little later, his dark hair now as white as mine . . ."

"What did he see?"

Caius said nothing, then, "He would not speak of it. Or

ever return. They put the boulder back, and in time, they forgot. And then, two hundred years ago, when they were building the Frobisher vault, they found it once more. The young man who found the place dreamed of riches, so he told no one, and he hid the doorway behind Ephraim Pettyfer's casket, and went down one night, unobserved, or so he thought."

"Was his hair white when he came up?"

"He did not come up."

"Um. Oh. So, who is buried down there?"

Caius shook his head. "I do not know, young Owens. But I felt him, back when this place was empty. I could feel something waiting even then, deep in the hill."

"What was he waiting for?"

"All I could feel," said Caius Pompeius, "was the waiting."

Scarlett was carrying a large picture book, and she sat next to her mother on the green bench near the gates, and she read her book while her mother inspected an educational supplement. She enjoyed the spring sunshine and she did her best to ignore the small boy who waved at her first from behind an ivy-covered monument, then, when she had resolved to no longer look at the monument, the boy popped up—literally, like a jack-in-a-box—from behind a tombstone (Joji G. Shoji, d. 1921, *I was a stranger and you took me in*). He gestured towards her, frantically. She ignored him.

Eventually she put her book down on the bench.

"Mummy? I'm going for a walk, now."

"Stay on the path, dear."

She stayed on the path until she was round the corner, and she could see Bod waving at her from further up the hill. She made a face at him.

"I've found things out," said Scarlett.

"Me too," said Bod.

"There were people before the Romans," she said. "Way back. They lived, I mean, when they died they put them underground in these hills, with treasure and stuff. And they were called barrows."

"Oh. Right," said Bod. "That explains it. Do you want to come and see one?"

"Now?" Scarlett looked doubtful. "You don't really know where one is, do you? And you know I can't always follow you where you go." She had seen him slip through walls, like a shadow.

In reply, he held up a large, rusted, iron key. "This was in the chapel," he said. "It should open most of the gates up there. They used the same key for all of them. It was less work."

She scrambled up the hillside beside him.

"You're telling the truth?"

He nodded, a pleased smile dancing at the corners of his lips. "Come on," he said.

It was a perfect spring day, and the air was alive with birdsong and bee hum. The daffodils bustled in the breeze and here and there on the side of the hill a few early tulips nodded. A blue powdering of forget-me-nots and fine, fat yellow primroses punctuated the green of the slope as the two children walked up the hill toward the Frobishers' little mausoleum.

It was old and simple in design, a small, forgotten stone house with a metal gate for a door. Bod unlocked the gate with his key, and they went in.

"It's a hole," said Bod. "Or a door. Behind one of the coffins."

They found it behind a coffin on the bottom shelf—a simple crawl space. "Down there," said Bod. "We go down there."

Scarlett found herself suddenly enjoying the adventure rather less. She said, "We can't see down there. It's dark."

"I don't need light," said Bod. "Not while I'm in the graveyard."

"I do," said Scarlett. "It's dark."

Bod thought about the reassuring things that he could say, like "there's nothing bad down there," but the tales of hair turning white and people never returning meant that he could not have said them with a clear conscience, so he said, "I'll go down. You wait for me up here."

Scarlett frowned. "You shouldn't leave me," she said.

"I'll go down," said Bod, "and I'll see who's there, and I'll come back and tell you all about it."

He turned to the opening, bent down, and clambered through on his hands and knees. He was in a space big enough to stand up in, and he could see steps cut into the stone. "I'm going down the steps now," he said.

"Do they go down a long way?"

"I think so."

"If you held my hand and told me where I was walking," she said, "then I could come with you. If you make sure I'm okay."

"Of course," said Bod, and before he had finished speaking the girl was coming through the hole on her hands and her knees.

"You can stand up," Bod told her. He took her hand. "The steps are just here. If you put a foot forward you can find it. There. Now I'll go first."

"Can you really see?" she asked.

"It's dark," said Bod. "But I can see."

He began to lead Scarlett down the steps, deep into the hill, and to describe what he saw to her as they went. "It's steps down," he said. "Made of stone. And there's stone all above us. Someone's made a painting on the wall."

"What kind of painting?"

"A big hairy C is for Cow, I think. With horns. Then something that's more like a pattern, like a big knot. It's sort of carved in the stone too, not just painted, see?" and he took her fingers and placed them onto the carved knot-work.

"I can feel it!" she said.

"Now the steps are getting bigger. We are coming out into some kind of big room, now, but the steps are still going. Don't move. Okay, now I am between you and the room. Keep your left hand on the wall."

They kept going down. "One more step and we are on the rock floor," said Bod. "It's a bit uneven."

The room was small. There was a slab of stone on the ground, and a low ledge in one corner, with some small objects on it. There were bones on the ground, very old bones indeed, although below where the steps entered the room Bod could see a crumpled corpse, dressed in the remains of a long brown coat—the young man who had dreamed of riches, Bod decided. He must have slipped and fallen in the dark.

The noise began all about them, a rustling slither, like a snake twining through dry leaves. Scarlett's grip on Bod's hand was harder.

"What's that? Do you see anything?"

"No."

Scarlett made a noise that was half gasp and half wail, and Bod saw something, and he knew without asking that she could see it too.

There was a light at the end of the room, and in the light a man came walking, walking through the rock, and Bod heard Scarlett choking back a scream.

The man looked well-preserved, but still like something that had been dead for a long while. His skin was painted (Bod thought) or tattooed (Scarlett thought) with purple designs and patterns. Around his neck hung a necklace of sharp, long teeth.

"I am the master of this place!" said the figure, in words so ancient and gutteral that they were scarcely words at all.

"I guard this place from all who would harm it!"

His eyes were huge in his head. Bod realized it was because he had circles drawn around them in purple, making his face look like an owl's.

"Who are you?" asked Bod. He squeezed Scarlett's hand as he said it.

The Indigo Man did not seem to have heard the question. He looked at them fiercely.

"Leave this place!" he said in words that Bod heard in his head, words that were also a gutteral growl.

"Is he going to hurt us?" asked Scarlett.

"I don't think so," said Bod. Then, to the Indigo Man, he said, as he had been taught, "I have the Freedom of the Graveyard and I may walk where I choose."

There was no reaction to this by the Indigo Man, which puzzled Bod even more because even the most irritable inhabitants of the graveyard had been calmed by this statement. Bod said, "Scarlett, can you *see* him?"

"Of course I can see him. He's a big scary tattooey man and he wants to kill us. Bod, make him go away!"

Bod looked at the remains of the gentleman in the brown coat. There was a lamp beside him, broken on the rocky floor. "He ran away," said Bod aloud. "He ran because he was scared. And he slipped or he tripped on the stairs and he fell off."

"Who did?"

"The man on the floor."

Scarlett sounded irritated now, as well as puzzled and

scared. "What man on the floor? It's too dark. The only man I can see is the tattooey man."

And then, as if to make quite sure that they knew that he was there, the Indigo Man threw back his head and let out a series of yodeling screams, a full-throated ululation that made Scarlett grip Bod's hand so tightly that her fingernails pressed into his flesh.

Bod was no longer scared, though.

"I'm sorry I said they were imaginary," said Scarlett. "I believe now. They're real."

The Indigo Man raised something over his head. It looked like a sharp stone blade. "All who invade this place will die!" he shouted, in his gutteral speech. Bod thought about the man whose hair had turned white after he had discovered the chamber, how he would never return to the graveyard or speak of what he had seen.

"No," said Bod. "I think you're right. I think this one is."

"Is what?"

"Imaginary."

"Don't be stupid," said Scarlett. "I can see it."

"Yes," said Bod. "And *you* can't see dead people." He looked around the chamber. "You can stop now," he said. "We know it's not real."

"I will feast on your liver!" screamed the Indigo Man.

"No, you won't," said Scarlett, with a huge sigh. "Bod's right." Then she said, "I think maybe it's a scarecrow."

"What's a scarecrow?" asked Bod.

"It's a thing farmers put in fields to scare crows."

54

"Why would they do that?" Bod quite liked crows. He thought they were funny, and he liked the way they helped to keep the graveyard tidy.

"I don't know exactly. I'll ask Mummy. But I saw one from a train and I asked what it was. Crows think it's a real person. It's just a made-up thing, that looks like a person, but it's not. It's just to scare the crows away."

Bod looked around the chamber. He said, "Whoever you are, it isn't working. It doesn't scare us. We know it isn't real. Just stop."

The Indigo Man stopped. It walked over to the rock slab and it lay down on it. Then it was gone.

For Scarlett the chamber was once more swallowed by the darkness. But in the darkness, she could hear the twining sound again, getting louder and louder, as if something were circling the round room.

Something said, WE ARE THE SLEER.

The hairs on the back of Bod's neck began to prickle. The voice in his head was something very old and very dry, like the scraping of a dead twig against the window of the chapel, and it seemed to Bod that there was more than one voice there, that they were talking in unison.

"Did you hear that?" he asked Scarlett.

"I didn't hear anything, just a slithery noise. It made me feel strange. All prickly in my tummy. Like something horrible is going to happen."

"Nothing horrible is going to happen," said Bod. Then, to the chamber, he said, "What are you?"

55

WE ARE THE SLEER. WE GUARD AND WE PROTECT.

"What do you protect?"

THE RESTING PLACE OF THE MASTER. THIS IS THE HOLIEST OF ALL HOLY PLACES, AND IT IS GUARDED BY THE SLEER.

"You can't touch us," said Bod. "All you can do is scare."

The twining voices sounded petulant. FEAR IS A WEAPON OF THE SLEER.

Bod looked down at the ledge. "Are those the treasures of your master? An old brooch, a cup, and a little stone knife? They don't look like much."

THE SLEER GUARDS THE TREASURES. THE BROOCH, THE GOBLET, THE KNIFE. WE GUARD THEM FOR THE MASTER, WHEN HE RETURNS. IT COMES BACK. IT ALWAYS COMES BACK.

"How many of you are there?"

But the Sleer said nothing. The inside of Bod's head felt as if it were filled with cobwebs, and he shook it, trying to clear it. Then he squeezed Scarlett's hand. "We should go," he said.

He led her past the dead man in the brown coat—and honestly, thought Bod, if he hadn't got scared and fallen the man would have been disappointed in his hunt for treasure. The treasures of ten thousand years ago were not the treasures of today. Bod led Scarlett carefully up the steps, through the hill, into the jutting black masonry of the Frobisher mausoleum.

Late spring sunlight shone through the breaks in the masonry and through the barred door, shocking in its brightness, and Scarlett blinked and covered her eyes at the suddenness of the glare. Birds sang in the bushes, a bumble-bee droned past, everything was surprising in its normality.

Bod pushed open the mausoleum door, and then locked it again behind them.

Scarlett's bright clothes were covered in grime and cob-webs, and her dark face and hands were pale with dust.

Further down the hill somebody—quite a few some-bodies—was shouting. Shouting loudly. Shouting franti-cally.

Someone called, "Scarlett? Scarlett Perkins?" and Scarlett said "Yes? Hello?" and before she and Bod had a chance to discuss what they had seen, or to talk about the Indigo Man, there was a woman in a fluorescent yellow jacket with POLICE on the back demanding to know if she was okay, and where she had been, and if someone had tried to kidnap her, and then the woman was talking on a radio, letting them know that the child had been found.

Bod slipped along beside them as they walked down the hill. The door to the chapel was open, and inside both of Scarlett's parents were waiting, her mother in tears, her father worriedly talking to people on a mobile phone, along with another policewoman. No one saw Bod as he waited in the corner.

The people kept asking Scarlett what had happened to her, and she answered, as honestly as she could, told them about a boy called Nobody who took her deep inside a hill where a purple tattoo man appeared in the dark, but he was really a scarecrow. They gave her a chocolate bar and they wiped her face and asked if the tattooed man had ridden a motorbike, and Scarlett's mother and father, now that they were relieved and not afraid for her any longer were angry with themselves and with her, and they told each other that it was the other one's fault for letting their little girl play in a cemetery, even if it was a nature reserve, and that the world was a very dangerous place these days, and if you didn't keep your eyes on your children every second you could not imagine what awful things they would be plunged into. Especially a child like Scarlett.

Scarlett's mother began sobbing, which made Scarlett cry, and one of the policewomen got into an argument with Scarlett's father, who tried to tell her that he, as a taxpayer, paid her wages, and she told him that she was a taxpayer too and probably paid *his* wages, while Bod sat in the shadows in the corner of the chapel, unseen by anyone, not even Scarlett, and watched and listened until he could take no more.

It was twilight in the graveyard by now, and Silas came and found Bod, up near the amphitheater, looking out over the town. He stood beside the boy and he said nothing, which was his way.

"It wasn't her fault," said Bod. "It was mine. And now she's in trouble."

"Where did you take her?" asked Silas.

"Into the middle of the hill, to see the oldest grave. Only there isn't anybody in there. Just a snaky thing called a Sleer who scares people."

"Fascinating."

They walked back down the hill together, watched as the old chapel was locked up once more and the police and Scarlett and her parents went off into the night.

"Miss Borrows will teach you joined-up letters," said Silas. "Have you read *The Cat in the Hat* yet?"

"Yes," said Bod. "Ages ago. Can you bring me more books?"

"I expect so," said Silas.

"Do you think I'll ever see her again?"

"The girl? I very much doubt it."

But Silas was wrong. Three weeks later, on a grey afternoon, Scarlett came to the graveyard, accompanied by both her parents.

They insisted that she remain in sight at all times, although they trailed a little behind her. Scarlett's mother occasionally exclaimed about how morbid this all was and how fine and good it was that they would soon be leaving it behind forever.

When Scarlett's parents began to talk to each other, Bod said, "Hello."

"Hi," said Scarlett, very quietly.

"I didn't think I'd see you again."

"I told them I wouldn't go with them unless they brought me back here one last time."

"Go where?"

"Scotland. There's a university there. For Dad to teach particle physics."

They walked on the path together, a small girl in a bright orange anorak and a small boy in a grey winding sheet.

"Is Scotland a long way away?"

"Yes," she said.

"Oh."

"I hoped you'd be here. To say good-bye."

"I'm always here."

"But you aren't dead, are you, Nobody Owens?"

"'Course not."

"Well, you can't stay here all your life. Can you? One day you'll grow up and then you will have to go and live in the world outside."

He shook his head. "It's not safe for me out there."

"Who says?"

"Silas. My family. Everybody."

She was silent.

Her father called, "Scarlett! Come on, love. Time to go. You've had your last trip to the graveyard. Now let's go home."

Scarlett said to Bod, "You're brave. You are the bravest person I know, and you are my friend. I don't care if you *are* imaginary." Then she fled down the path back the way they had come, to her parents and the world.

CHAPTER THREE

The Hounds of God

ONE GRAVE IN EVERY graveyard belongs to the ghouls. Wander any graveyard long enough and you will find it—waterstained and bulging, with cracked or broken stone, scraggly grass or rank weeds about it, and a feeling, when you reach it, of abandonment. It may be colder than the other gravestones, too, and the name on the stone is all too often impossible to read. If there is a statue on the grave it will be headless or so scabbed with fungus and lichens as to look like a fungus itself. If one grave in a graveyard looks like a target for petty vandals, that is the ghoul-gate. If the grave makes you want to be somewhere else, that is the ghoul-gate.

There was one in Bod's graveyard.

There is one in every graveyard.

Silas was leaving.

Bod had been upset by this when he had first learned about it. He was no longer upset. He was furious.

"But *why?*" said Bod.

"I told you. I need to obtain some information. In order to do that, I have to travel. To travel, I must leave here. We have already been over all this."

"What's so important that you have to go away?" Bod's six-year-old mind tried to imagine something that could make Silas want to leave him, and failed. "It's not fair."

His guardian was unperturbed. "It is neither fair nor unfair, Nobody Owens. It simply is."

Bod was not impressed. "You're meant to look after me. You *said.*"

"As your guardian I have responsibility for you, yes. Fortunately, I am not the only individual in the world willing to take on this responsibility."

"Where are you going anyway?"

"Out. Away. There are things I need to uncover that I cannot uncover here."

Bod snorted and walked off, kicking at imaginary stones. On the northwestern side of the graveyard things had become very overgrown and tangled, far beyond the ability of the groundskeeper or the Friends of the Graveyard to tame, and he ambled over there, and woke a family of Victorian children who had all died before their tenth birthdays, and they played at hide-and-go-seek in the moonlight in the ivy-twined jungle. Bod tried to pretend

65

that Silas was not leaving, that nothing was going to change, but when the game was done and he ran back to the old chapel, he saw two things that changed his mind.

The first thing he saw was a bag. It was, Bod knew the moment he laid eyes on it, Silas's bag. It was at least a hundred and fifty years old, a thing of beauty, black leather with brass fittings and a black handle, the kind of bag a Victorian doctor or undertaker might have carried, containing every implement that might have been needed. Bod had never seen Silas's bag before, he had not even known that Silas had a bag, but it was the sort of bag that could only have belonged to Silas. Bod tried to peek inside it, but it was closed with a large brass padlock. It was too heavy for him to lift.

That was the first thing.

The second thing was sitting on the bench by the chapel.

"Bod," said Silas. "This is Miss Lupescu."

Miss Lupescu was not pretty. Her face was pinched and her expression was disapproving. Her hair was grey, although her face seemed too young for grey hair. Her front teeth were slightly crooked. She wore a bulky mackintosh and a man's tie around her neck.

"How do you do, Miss Lupescu?" said Bod.

Miss Lupescu said nothing. She sniffed. Then she looked at Silas and said, "So. This is the boy." She got up from her seat and walked all around Bod, nostrils flared, as if she were sniffing him. When she had made a complete circuit, she said, "You will report to me on waking, and before you go to sleep. I have rented a room in a house over there." She pointed to a roof just visible from where they stood. "However, I shall spend my time in this graveyard. I am here as a historian, researching the history of old graves. You understand, boy? *Da?*"

"Bod," said Bod. "It's Bod. Not boy."

"Short for Nobody," she said. "A foolish name. Also, Bod is a pet name. A nickname. I do not approve. I will call you 'boy.' You will call me 'Miss Lupescu.'"

Bod looked up at Silas, pleadingly, but there was no sympathy on Silas's face. He picked up his bag and said, "You will be in good hands with Miss Lupescu, Bod. I am sure that the two of you will get on."

"We won't!" said Bod. "She's horrible!"

"That," said Silas, "was a very rude thing to say. I think you should apologize, don't you?"

Bod didn't, but Silas was looking at him and Silas was carrying his black bag, and about to leave for no one knew how long, so he said, "I'm sorry, Miss Lupescu."

At first she said nothing in reply. She merely sniffed. Then she said, "I have come a long way to look after you, boy. I hope you are worth it."

Bod could not imagine hugging Silas, so he held out his hand and Silas bent over and gently shook it, engulfing Bod's small, grubby hand with his huge, pale one. Then, lifting his black leather bag as if it were weightless, he walked down the path and out of the graveyard.

Bod told his parents about it.

"Silas has gone," he said.

"He'll be back," said Mr. Owens, cheerfully. "Don't you worry your head about that, Bod. Like a bad penny, as they say."

Mrs. Owens said, "Back when you were born he promised us that if he had to leave, he would find someone else to bring you food and keep an eye on you, and he has. He's so reliable."

Silas had brought Bod food, true, and left it in the crypt each night for him to eat, but this was, as far as Bod was concerned, the least of the things that Silas did for him. He gave advice, cool, sensible, and unfailingly correct; he knew more than the graveyard folk did, for his nightly excursions into the world outside meant that he was able to describe a world that was current, not hundreds of years out of date; he was unflappable and dependable, had been there every night of Bod's life, so the idea of the little chapel without its only inhabitant was one that Bod found difficult to conceive of; most of all, he made Bod feel safe.

Miss Lupescu also saw her job as more than bringing Bod food. She did that too, though.

"What is that?" asked Bod, horrified.

"Good food," said Miss Lupescu. They were in the crypt. She had put two plastic containers on the tabletop, and opened the lids. She pointed to the first: "Is beetroot-barley-stew-soup." She pointed to the second. "Is salad. Now, you eat both. I make them for you."

Bod stared up at her to see if this was a joke. Food from

Silas mostly came in packets, purchased from the kind of places that sold food late at night and asked no questions. No one had ever brought him food in a plastic container with a lid before. "It smells horrible," he said.

"If you do not eat the stew-soup soon," she said, "it will be more horrible. It will be cold. Now eat."

Bod was hungry. He took a plastic spoon, dipped it into the purple-red stew, and he ate. The food was slimy and unfamiliar, but he kept it down.

"Now the salad!" said Miss Lupescu, and she unpopped the top of the second container. It consisted of large lumps of raw onion, beetroot, and tomato, all in a thick vinegary dressing. Bod put a lump of beetroot into his mouth and started to chew. He could feel the saliva gathering, and realized that if he swallowed it, he would throw it back up. He said, "I can't eat this."

"Is good for you."

"I'll be sick."

They stared at each other, the small boy with tousled, mousy hair, the pinched pale woman with not a silver hair out of place. Miss Lupescu said, "You eat one more piece."

"I can't."

"You eat one more piece now, or you stay here until you have eaten it all."

Bod picked out a piece of vinegary tomato, chewed it, and choked it down. Miss Lupescu put the tops back on the containers and replaced them in the plastic shopping bag. She said, "Now, lessons."

It was high summer. It would not get fully dark until almost midnight. There were no lessons in high summer— the time that Bod spent awake he spent in an endless warm twilight in which he would play or explore or climb.

"Lessons?" he said.

"Your guardian felt it would be good for me to teach you things."

"I have teachers. Letitia Borrows teaches me writing and words, and Mr. Pennyworth teaches me his Compleat Educational System for Younger Gentlemen with Additional Material for Those Post Mortem. I do geography and everything. I don't *need* more lessons."

"You know everything, then, boy? Six years old, and already you know everything."

"I didn't say that."

Miss Lupescu folded her arms. "Tell me about ghouls," she said.

Bod tried to remember what Silas had told him about ghouls over the years. "Keep away from them," he said.

"And that is all you know? *Da?* Why do you keep away from them? Where do they come from? Where do they go? Why do you not stand near a ghoul-gate? Eh, boy?"

Bod shrugged and shook his head.

"Name the different kinds of people," said Miss Lupescu. "Now."

Bod thought for a moment. "The living," he said. "Er. The dead." He stopped. Then, ". . . Cats?" he offered, uncertainly.

"You are ignorant, boy," said Miss Lupescu. "This is bad. And you are content to be ignorant, which is worse. Repeat after me, there are the living and the dead, there are day-folk and night-folk, there are ghouls and mist-walkers, there are the high hunters and the Hounds of God. Also, there are solitary types."

"What are you?" asked Bod.

"I," she said sternly, "am Miss Lupescu."

"And what's Silas?"

She hesitated. Then she said, "He is a solitary type."

Bod endured the lesson. When Silas taught him things it was interesting. Much of the time Bod didn't realize he had been taught anything at all. Miss Lupescu taught in lists, and Bod could not see the point to it. He sat in the crypt, aching to be out in the summer's twilight, under the ghost moon.

When the lesson was done, in the foulest of moods, he fled. He looked for playmates, but found no one and saw nothing but a large grey dog, which prowled the grave-stones, always keeping its distance from him, slipping between gravestones and through shadows.

The week got worse.

Miss Lupescu continued to bring Bod things she had cooked for him: dumplings swimming in lard; thick reddish-purple soup with a lump of sour cream in it; small, cold boiled potatoes; cold garlic-heavy sausages; hardboiled eggs in a grey unappetizing liquid. He ate as little as he could get away with. The lessons continued: for two days

71

she taught him nothing but ways to call for help in every language in the world, and she would rap his knuckles with her pen if he slipped up, or forgot. By the third day she was firing them at him,

"French?"

"*Au secours.*"

"Morse Code?"

"S-O-S. Three short dots, three long ones, three short ones again."

"Night-Gaunt?"

"This is stupid. I don't remember what a night-gaunt *is*."

"They have hairless wings, and they fly low and fast. They do not visit this world, but they fly the red skies above the road to Ghûlheim."

"I'm never going to need to know this."

Her mouth pinched in tighter. All she said was, "Night-Gaunt?"

Bod made the noise in the back of his throat that she had taught him—a guttural cry, like an eagle's call. She sniffed. "Adequate," she said.

Bod could not wait until the day that Silas returned.

He said, "There's a big grey dog in the graveyard sometimes. It came when you did. Is it your dog?"

Miss Lupescu straightened her tie. "No," she said.

"Are we done?"

"For today. You will read the list I give you tonight and remember it for tomorrow."

Miss Lupescu's lists were printed in pale purple ink on

white paper, and they smelled odd. Bod took the new list up onto the side of the hill and tried to read the words, but his attention kept sliding off it. Eventually he folded it up and placed it beneath a stone.

No one would play with him that night. No one wanted to play or to talk, to run and climb beneath the huge summer moon.

He went down to the Owenses' tomb to complain to his parents, but Mrs. Owens would not hear a word said against Miss Lupescu, on, as far as Bod was concerned, the unfair grounds that Silas had chosen her, while Mr. Owens simply shrugged and started telling Bod about his days as a young apprentice cabinetmaker, and how much he would have loved to have learned about all the useful things that Bod was learning, which was, as far as Bod was concerned, even worse.

"Aren't you meant to be studying, anyway?" asked Mrs. Owens, and Bod squeezed his fists together and said nothing.

He stomped off into the graveyard, feeling unloved and underappreciated.

Bod brooded on the injustice of it all, and wandered through the graveyard kicking at stones. He spotted the dark grey dog, and called to it to see if it would come over and play with him, but it kept its distance, and Bod, frustrated, threw a clump of mud towards it, which broke on a nearby gravestone, and scattered earth everywhere. The big dog gazed at Bod reproachfully, then stepped away into the shadows, and was gone.

The boy walked back down the southwest side of the hill, avoiding the old chapel: he did not want to see the place that Silas wasn't. Bod stopped beside a grave that looked the way he felt: it was beneath an oak that had once been struck by lightning, and now was just a black trunk, like a sharp talon coming out of the hill; the grave itself was waterstained and cracked, and above it was a memorial stone on which a headless angel hung, its robes looking like a huge and ugly tree-fungus.

Bod sat down on a clump of grass, and felt sorry for himself, and hated everybody. He even hated Silas, for going away and leaving him. Then he closed his eyes, and curled into a ball on the grass, and drifted into a dreamless sleep.

Down the street and up the hill came the Duke of Westminster, the Honorable Archibald Fitzhugh, and the Bishop of Bath and Wells, slipping and bounding from shadow to shadow, lean and leathery, all sinews and cartilage, wearing raggedy clothes all a-tatter, and they bounded and loped and skulked, leapfrogging over dustbins, keeping to the dark side of hedges.

They were small, like full-size people who had shrunk in the sun; they spoke to each other in undertones, saying things like, "If Your Grace has any more blooming idea of where we is than us do, I'd be grateful if he'd say so. Otherwise, he should keep his big offal-hole shut," and "All I'm saying, Your Worship, is that I knows there's a graveyard near to here, I can smell it," and "If you could smell it then I should be able to smell it, 'cos I've got a better nose than you have, Your Grace."

All this as they dodged and wove their way through suburban gardens. They avoided one garden ("Psst!" hissed the Honorable Archibald Fitzhugh. "Dogs!") and ran along the top of the garden wall, scampering over it like rats the size of children. Down into the high street, and up the road to the top of the hill. And then they were at the graveyard wall, and they went up it like squirrels up a tree, and they sniffed the air.

"'Ware dog," said the Duke of Westminster.

"Where? I dunno. Somewhere around here. Doesn't smell like a proper dog anyway," said the Bishop of Bath and Wells.

"Somebody couldn't smell this graveyard neither," said the Honorable Archibald Fitzhugh. "Remember? It's just a dog."

The three of them leapt down from the wall to the ground, and they ran, using their arms as much as their legs to propel themselves through the graveyard, to the ghoul-gate by the lightning tree.

And beside the gate, in the moonlight, they paused.

"What's this when it's at home, then?" asked the Bishop of Bath and Wells.

"Lumme," said the Duke of Westminster.

Bod woke then.

The three faces staring into his could have been those

of mummified humans, fleshless and dried, but their features were mobile and interested—mouths that grinned to reveal sharp, stained teeth; bright beady eyes; clawed fingers that moved and tapped.

"Who are you?" Bod asked.

"*We*," said one of the creatures—they were, Bod realized, only a little bigger than he was—"is most important folk, we is. This here is the Duke of Westminster."

The biggest of the creatures gave a bow, saying, "Charmed, I'm sure."

". . . and this is the Bishop of Bath and Wells—"

The creature, which grinned sharp teeth and let a pointed tongue of improbable length waggle between them, did not look like Bod's idea of a bishop: its skin was piebald and it had a large spot across one eye, making it look almost piratical. ". . . and I 'ave the honor to be ther 'onorable Harchibald Fitzhugh. Hat your service."

The three creatures bowed as one. The Bishop of Bath and Wells said, "Now me lad, what's your story, eh? And don't tell any porkies, remember as how you're talkin' to a bishop."

"You tell him, Your Worship," said the other two.

So Bod told them. He told them how no one liked him or wanted to play with him, how no one appreciated him or cared, and how even his guardian had abandoned him.

"Blow me down," said the Duke of Westminster, scratching his nose (a little dried-up thing that was mostly nostrils). "What you need is to go somewhere the people would appreciate you."

"There isn't anywhere," said Bod. "And I'm not allowed out of the graveyard."

"You needs an 'ole world of friends and playfellows," said the Bishop of Bath and Wells, wiggling his long tongue. "A city of delights, of fun and magic, where you would be appreciated, not ignored."

Bod said, "The lady who's looking after me. She makes horrible food. Hard-boiled egg soup and things."

"Food!" said the Honorable Archibald Fitzhugh. "Where *we're* going the food's the best in the whole world. Makes me tum rumble and me mouf water just thinking about it."

"Can I come with you?" asked Bod.

"Come with us?" said the Duke of Westminster. He sounded shocked.

"Don't be like that, Yer Grace," said the Bishop of Bath and Wells. "'Ave a blinking 'eart. Look at the little mite. 'Asn't 'ad a decent meal in 'e don't know 'ow long."

"I vote to take him," said the Honorable Archibald Fitzhugh. "There's good grub back at our place." He patted his stomach to show just how good the food was.

"So. You game for adventure?" asked the Duke of Westminster, won over by the novel idea. "Or do you want to waste the rest of your life *here*?" and with bony fingers he indicated the graveyard and the night.

Bod thought of Miss Lupescu and her awful food and her lists and her pinched mouth.

"I'm game," he said.

His three new friends might have been his size, but they were far stronger than any child, and Bod found himself picked up by the Bishop of Bath and Wells and held high above the creature's head, while the Duke of Westminster grabbed a handful of mangy-looking grass, shouted what sounded like *"Skagh! Thegh! Khavagah!"* and pulled. The stone slab that covered the grave swung open like a trapdoor, revealing a darkness beneath.

"Quick now," said the duke, and the Bishop of Bath and Wells tossed Bod into the dark opening, then leapt in after him, followed by the Honorable Archibald Fitzhugh and then, with one agile bound, by the Duke of Westminster, who, as soon as he was inside, called out, *"Wegh Khârados!"* to close the ghoul-gate, and the stone crashed down above them.

Bod fell, tumbling through the darkness like a lump of marble, too startled to be scared, wondering how deep the hole beneath that grave could possibly be, when two strong hands caught him beneath the armpits and he found himself swinging forward through the pitch-blackness.

Bod had not experienced total darkness for many years. In the graveyard, he saw as the dead see, and no tomb or grave or crypt was truly dark to him. Now he was in utter darkness, feeling himself being pitched forward in a sequence of jerks and rushes, the wind rushing past him. It was frightening, but it was also exhilarating.

And then there was light, and everything changed.

The sky was red, but not the warm red of a sunset.

This was an angry, glowering red, the color of an infected wound. The sun was small and seemed like it was old and distant. The air was cold and they were descending a wall. Tombstones and statues jutted out of the side of the wall, as if a huge graveyard had been upended, and, like three wizened chimpanzees in tattered black suits that did up in the back, the Duke of Westminster, the Bishop of Bath and Wells, and the Honorable Archibald Fitzhugh were swinging from statue to stone, dangling Bod between them as they went, tossing him from one to another, never missing him, always catching him with ease, without even looking.

Bod tried to look up, to see the grave through which they had entered this strange world, but he could see nothing but headstones.

He wondered if each of the graves they were swinging past was a door for the kind of people who were carrying him. . . .

"Where are we going?" he asked, but his voice was whipped away by the wind.

They went faster and faster. Up ahead of them Bod saw a statue swing up, and another two creatures came catapulting out into this crimson-skied world, just like the ones that carried Bod. One wore a raggedy silken gown that looked like it had once been white, the other wore a stained grey suit too large for it, the sleeves of which were shredded into shadowy tatters. They spotted Bod and his three new friends and made for them, dropping twenty feet with ease.

The Duke of Westminster gave a guttural squawk and pretended to be scared, and Bod and the three of them swung down the wall of graves with the two new creatures in pursuit. None of them seemed to get tired or out of breath, under that red sky, with the burnt-out sun gazing down at them like a dead eye, but eventually they fetched up on the side of a huge statue of a creature whose whole face seemed to have become a fungoid growth. Bod found himself being introduced to the 33rd President of the United States and the Emperor of China.

"This is Master Bod," said the Bishop of Bath and Wells. "He's going to become one of us."

"He's in search of a good meal," said the Honorable Archibald Fitzhugh.

"Well, you're guaranteed fine dining when you becomes one of us, young lad," said the Emperor of China.

"Yup," said the 33rd President of the United States.

Bod said, "I become one of you? You mean, I'll turn into you?"

"Smart as a whip, sharp as a tack, you'd have to get up pretty late at night to put anything past this lad," said the Bishop of Bath and Wells. "Indeed. One of us. As strong, as fast, as unconquerable."

"Teeth so strong they can crush any bones, and tongue sharp and long enough to lick the marrow from the deepest marrowbone or flay the flesh from a fat man's face," said the Emperor of China.

"Able to slip from shadow to shadow, never seen, never

suspected. Free as air, fast as thought, cold as frost, hard as nails, dangerous as, as *us*," said the Duke of Westminster.

Bod looked at the creatures. "But what if I don't *want* to be one of you?" he said.

"Don't *want* to? Of course you *wants* to! What could be finer? I don't think there's a soul in the universe doesn't want to be *just* like us."

"We've got the best city—"

"Ghûlheim," said the 33rd President of the United States.

"The best life, the best food—"

"Can you imagine," interrupted the Bishop of Bath and Wells, "how fine a drink the black ichor that collects in a leaden coffin can be? Or how it feels to be more important than kings and queens, than presidents or prime ministers or heroes, to be *sure* of it, in the same way that people are more important than brussels sprouts?"

Bod said, "What *are* you people?"

"Ghouls," said the Bishop of Bath and Wells. "Bless me, somebody wasn't paying attention, was he? We're ghouls."

"Look!"

Below them, a whole troupe of the little creatures were bouncing and running and leaping, heading for the path below them, and before he could say another word, he was snatched up by a pair of bony hands and was flying through the air in a series of jumps and lurches, as the creatures headed down to meet the others of their kind.

The wall of graves was ending, and now there was a

road, and nothing but a road, a much-trodden path across a barren plain, a desert of rocks and bones, that wound towards a city high on a huge red rock hill, many miles away.

Bod looked up at the city, and was horrified: an emotion engulfed him that mingled repulsion and fear, disgust and loathing, all tinged with shock.

Ghouls do not build. They are parasites and scavengers, eaters of carrion. The city they call Ghûlheim is something they found, long ago, but did not make. No one knows (if anyone human ever knew) what kind of creatures it was that made those buildings, who honeycombed the rock with tunnels and towers, but it is certain that no one but the ghoul-folk could have wanted to stay there, or even to approach that place.

Even from the path below Ghûlheim, even from miles away, Bod could see that all of the angles were wrong—that the walls sloped crazily, that it was every nightmare he had ever endured made into a place, like a huge mouth of jutting teeth. It was a city that had been built just to be abandoned, in which all the fears and madnesses and revulsions of the creatures who built it were made into stone. The ghoul-folk had found it and delighted in it and called it home.

Ghouls move fast. They swarmed along the path through the desert more swiftly than a vulture flies and Bod was carried along by them, held high overhead by a pair of strong ghoul arms, tossed from one to another, feeling sick, feeling dread and dismay, feeling stupid.

Above them in the sour red skies, things were circling on huge black wings.

"Careful," said the Duke of Westminster. "Tuck him away. Don't want the night-gaunts stealing him. Bloody stealers."

"Yar! We hates stealers!" shouted the Emperor of China.

Night-gaunts, in the red skies above Ghûlheim . . . Bod took a deep breath, and shouted, just as Miss Lupescu had taught him. He made a call like an eagle's cry, in the back of his throat.

One of the winged beasts dropped towards them, circled lower, and Bod made the call again, until it was stifled by hard hands clamping over his mouth. "Good idea, calling 'em down," said the Honorable Archibald Fitzhugh, "but trust me, they aren't edible until they've been rotting for at least a couple of weeks, and they just causes trouble. No love lost between our side and theirs, eh?"

The night-gaunt rose again in the dry desert air, to rejoin its fellows, and Bod felt all hope vanish.

The ghouls sped on towards the city on the rocks, and Bod, now flung unceremoniously over the stinking shoulders of the Duke of Westminster, was carried with them.

The dead sun set, and two moons rose, one huge and pitted and white, which seemed, as it rose, to be taking up half the horizon, although it shrank as it ascended, and a smaller moon, the bluish-green color of the veins of mold in a cheese, and the arrival of this moon was an occasion of celebration for the ghoul-folk. They stopped marching and made a camp beside the road.

One of the new members of the band—Bod thought it might have been the one he had been introduced to as "the famous writer Victor Hugo"—produced a sack which turned out to be filled with firewood, several pieces still with the hinges or brass handles attached, along with a metal cigarette lighter, and soon made a fire, around which all the ghoul-folk sat and rested. They stared up at the greenish-blue moon, and scuffled for the best places by the fire, insulting each other, sometimes clawing or biting.

"We'll sleep soon, then set off for Ghûlheim at moon-set," said the Duke of Westminster. "It's just another nine or ten hours' run along the way. We should reach it by next moonrise. Then we'll have a party, eh? Celebrate you being made into one of us!"

"It doesn't hurt," said the Honorable Archibald Fitzhugh, "not so as you'd notice. And after, think how happy you'll be."

They all started telling stories, then, of how fine and wonderful a thing it was to be a ghoul, of all the things they had crunched up and swallowed down with their powerful teeth. Impervious they were to disease or illness, said one of them. Why, it didn't matter what their dinner had died of, they could just chomp it down. They told of the places they had been, which mostly seemed to be catacombs and plague-pits. ("Plague-pits is good eatin'," said the Emperor of China, and everyone agreed.) They told

Bod how they had got their names and how he, in his turn, once he had become a nameless ghoul, would be named as they had been.

"But I don't want to become one of you," said Bod.

"One way or another," said the Bishop of Bath and Wells, cheerily, "you'll become one of us. The other way is messier, involves being digested, and you're not really around very long to enjoy it."

"But that's not a good thing to talk about," said the Emperor of China. "Best to be a ghoul. We're afraid of nuffink!"

And all the ghouls around the coffin-wood fire howled at this statement, and growled and sang and exclaimed at how wise they were, and how mighty, and how fine it was to be scared of nothing.

There was a noise then, from the desert, from far away, a distant howl, and the ghouls gibbered and they huddled closer to the flames.

"What was that?" asked Bod.

The ghouls shook their heads. "Just something out there in the desert," whispered one of them. "Quiet! It'll hear us!"

And all the ghouls were quiet for a bit, until they forgot about the thing in the desert, and began to sing ghoul-song, filled with foul words and worse sentiments, the most popular of which were simply lists of which rotting body parts were to be eaten, and in what order.

"I want to go home," said Bod, when the last of the bits in the song had been consumed. "I don't want to be here."

"Don't take on so," said the Duke of Westminster. "Why, you little coot, I promise you that as soon as you're one of us, you'll not ever remember as you even *had* a home."

"I don't remember anything about the days before I was a ghoul," said the famous writer Victor Hugo.

"Nor I," said the Emperor of China, proudly.

"Nope," said the 33rd President of the United States.

"You'll be one of a select band, of the cleverest, strongest, bravest creatures ever," bragged the Bishop of Bath and Wells.

Bod was unimpressed by the ghouls' bravery or their wisdom. They were strong, though, and inhumanly fast, and he was in the center of a troupe of them. Making a break for it would have been impossible. They would be able to catch up with him before he could cover a dozen yards.

Far off in the night something howled once more, and the ghouls moved closer to the fire. Bod could hear them sniffling and cursing. He closed his eyes, miserable and homesick: he did not want to become one of the ghouls. He wondered how he would ever be able to sleep when he was this worried and hopeless and then, almost to his surprise, for two or three hours, he slept.

A noise woke him—upset, loud, close. It was someone saying, "Well, where *is* they? Eh?" He opened his eyes to see the Bishop of Bath and Wells shouting at the Emperor of China. It seemed that a couple of the members of their group had disappeared in the night, just vanished, and no one had an explanation. The rest of the ghouls were on edge. They packed up their camp quickly, and the 33rd President of the United States picked Bod up and bundled him over his shoulder.

The ghouls scrabbled back down the rocky cliffs to the road, beneath a sky the color of bad blood, and they headed towards Ghûlheim. They seemed significantly less exuberant this morning. Now they seemed—at least to Bod, as he was bounced along—to be running away from something.

Around midday, with the dead-eyed sun high overhead, the ghouls stopped, and huddled. Ahead of them, high in the sky, circling on the hot air currents, were the night-gaunts, dozens of them, riding the thermals.

The ghouls divided into two factions: there were those who felt that the vanishing of their friends was meaning-less, and those who believed that something, probably the night-gaunts, was out to get them. They came to no agreement, except for a general agreement to arm them-selves with rocks to throw at the night-gaunts should they descend, and they filled the pockets of their suits and robes with pebbles from the desert floor.

Something howled, off in the desert to their left, and the ghouls eyed each other. It was louder than the night before, and closer, a deep, wolfish howl.

"Did you hear that?" asked the Lord Mayor of London.

"Nope," said the 33rd President of the United States.

"Me neither," said the Honorable Archibald Fitzhugh.

The howl came again.

"We got to get home," said the Duke of Westminster, hefting a large stone.

The nightmare city of Ghûlheim sat on a high rocky outcrop ahead of them, and the creatures loped down the road towards it.

"Night-gaunts coming!" shouted the Bishop of Bath and Wells. "Throw stones at the bleeders!"

Bod's view of things was upside down at this point, bouncing up and down on the back of the 33rd President of the United States, gritty sand from the path blown up into his face. But he heard cries, like eagle cries, and once again Bod called for help in Night-Gaunt. No one tried to stop him this time, but he was not sure that anyone could have heard him over the cries of the night-gaunts, or the oaths and curses of the ghoul-folk as they pitched and flung their stones into the air.

Bod heard the howling again: now it came from their right.

"There's dozens of the blooming blinkers," said the Duke of Westminster, gloomily.

The 33rd President of the United States handed Bod over to the famous writer Victor Hugo, who threw the boy into his sack and put it over his shoulder. Bod was just glad the sack smelled of nothing worse than dusty wood.

"They're retreating!" shouted a ghoul."Look at 'em go!"

"Don't you worry, boy," said a voice that sounded to Bod like the Bishop of Bath and Wells, near the sack.

"There won't be any of this nonsense when we get you to Ghûlheim. It's impenetrable, is Ghûlheim."

Bod could not tell if any of the ghouls had been killed or injured fighting the night-gaunts. He suspected, from the imprecations of the Bishop of Bath and Wells, that several more of the ghouls might have run off.

"Quickly!" shouted someone who was probably the Duke of Westminster, and the ghouls set off at a run. Bod, in the sack, was uncomfortable, being painfully slammed against the famous writer Victor Hugo's back and occasionally banged on the ground. To make his time in the sack even more uncomfortable there were still several lumps of wood, not to mention sharp screws and nails, in there with him, the final remnants of the coffin-based firewood. A screw was just under his hand, digging into him.

Despite being jogged and jounced, jolted and jarred with every one of his captor's steps, Bod managed to grasp the screw in his right hand. He felt the tip of it, sharp to the touch. He hoped, deep inside. Then he pushed the screw into the fabric of the sack behind him, working the sharp end in, then pulling it back, and making another hole a little way below the first.

From behind, he could hear something howl once more and it occurred to him that anything that could terrify the ghoul-folk must itself be even more terrifying than he could imagine, and for a moment he stopped stabbing with the screw—what if he fell from the sack into the jaws of some evil beast? But at least if he died, thought Bod, he would have died as himself, with all his memories, knowing who his parents were, who Silas was, even who Miss Lupescu was.

That was good.

He attacked the sacking with his brass screw again, jabbing and pushing until he'd made another hole in the fabric.

"Come on, lads," shouted the Bishop of Bath and Wells. "Up the steps and then we're home, all safe in Ghûlheim!"

"Hurrah, Your Worship!" called someone else, probably the Honorable Archibald Fitzhugh.

Now the motion of his captors had changed. It was no longer a forward motion: now it was a sequence of movements, up and along, up and along.

Bod pushed at the sacking with his hand to try and make an eye-hole. He looked out. Above, the drear red sky, below . . .

. . . he could see the desert floor, but it was now hundreds of feet below him. There were steps stretching out behind them, but steps made for giants, and the ochre rock wall to his right. Ghûlheim, which Bod could not see from where he was, had to be above them. To his left was a sheer drop. He was going to have to fall straight down, he decided, onto the steps, and he would just hope that the ghouls wouldn't notice that he was making his break for it in their desperation to be home and safe. He saw night-gaunts high in the red sky, hanging back, circling.

He was pleased to see there were no other ghouls

behind him: the famous writer Victor Hugo was bringing up the rear, and no one was behind him to alert the ghouls to the hole that was growing in the sack. Or to see Bod if he fell out.

But there was something else. . . .

Bod was bounced onto his side, away from the hole. But he had seen something huge and grey, on the steps beneath, pursuing them. He could hear an angry growling noise.

Mr. Owens had an expression for two things he found equally unpleasant: "I'm between the Devil and the Deep Blue Sea," he would say. Bod had wondered what this meant, having seen, in his life in the graveyard, neither the Devil nor the Deep Blue Sea.

I'm between the ghouls and the monster, he thought.

And as he thought it, sharp canine teeth caught at the sacking, pulled at it until the fabric tore along the rips Bod had made, and the boy tumbled down on the rock stairs, where a huge grey animal, like a dog but far larger, growled and drooled, and stood over him, an animal with flaming eyes and white fangs and huge paws. It panted and it stared at Bod.

Ahead of him the ghouls had stopped. "Bloody Nora!" said the Duke of Westminster. "That hellhound's got the blinking boy!"

"Let it have him," said the Emperor of China. "Run!"

"Yikes!" said the 33rd President of the United States.

The ghouls ran up the steps. Bod was now certain that

the steps had been carved by giants, for each step was higher than he was. As they fled, the ghouls paused only to turn and make rude gestures at the beast and possibly also at Bod.

The beast stayed where it was.

It's going to eat me, Bod thought bitterly. *Smart, Bod.* And he thought of his home in the graveyard, and now he could no longer remember why he had ever left. Monster dog or no monster dog, he had to get back home once more. There were people waiting for him.

He pushed past the beast, jumped down to the next step four feet below, fell his height, landed on his ankle, which twisted underneath him, painfully, and he dropped, heavily, onto the rock.

He could hear the beast running, jumping down towards him, and he tried to wriggle away, to pull himself up onto his feet, but his ankle was useless, now, numb and in pain, and before he could stop himself, he fell again. He fell off the step, away from the rock wall, out into space, off the cliff-side, where he dropped—a nightmarish tumble down distances that Bod could not even imagine. . . .

And as he fell, he was certain he heard a voice coming from the general direction of the grey beast. And it said, in Miss Lupescu's voice, "Oh, Bod!"

It was like every dream of falling he had ever had, a scared and frantic drop through space, as he headed towards the ground below. Bod felt as though his mind was only big enough for one huge thought, so, *That big dog was actually Miss Lupescu*, and, *I'm going to hit the rock floor and splat*, competed in his head for occupation.

Something wrapped itself about him, falling at the same speed he was falling, and then there was the loud flapping of leathery wings and everything slowed. The ground no longer seemed to be heading towards him at the same speed.

The wings flapped harder. They lifted slightly and now the only thought in Bod's head was *I'm flying!* And he was. He turned his head. Above him was a dark brown head, perfectly bald, with deep eyes that looked as if they were polished slabs of black glass.

Bod made the screeching noise that means "Help," in Night-Gaunt, and the night-gaunt smiled and made a deep hooting noise in return. It seemed pleased.

A swoop and a slow, and they touched down on the desert floor with a thump. Bod tried to stand up, and his ankle betrayed him once again, sent him stumbling down into the sand. The wind was high, and the sharp desert sand blew hard, stinging Bod's skin.

The night-gaunt crouched beside him, its leathery wings folded on its back. Bod had grown up in a graveyard and was used to images of winged people, but the angels on the headstones looked nothing like this.

And now, bounding toward them across the desert floor in the shadow of Ghûlheim, a huge grey beast, like an enormous dog.

The dog spoke, in Miss Lupescu's voice.

It said, "This is the third time the night-gaunts have saved your life, Bod. The first was when you called for help, and they heard. They got the message to me, telling me where you were. The second was around the fire last night, when you were asleep: they were circling in the darkness, and heard a couple of the ghouls saying that you were ill-luck for them and that they should beat your brains in with a rock and put you somewhere they could find you again, when you were properly rotted down, and then they would eat you. The night-gaunts dealt with the matter silently. And now this."

"Miss Lupescu?"

The great dog-like head lowered towards him, and for one mad, fear-filled moment, he thought she was going to take a bite out of him, but her tongue licked the side of his face, affectionately. "You hurt your ankle?"

"Yes. I can't stand on it."

"Let's get you onto my back," said the huge grey beast that was Miss Lupescu.

She said something in the night-gaunt's screeching tongue and it came over, held Bod up while he put his arms around Miss Lupescu's neck.

"Hold my fur," she said. "Hold tight. Now, before we go, say . . ." and she made a high screeching noise.

"What does it mean?"

"Thank you. Or good-bye. Both."

Bod screeched as best as he could, and the night-gaunt made an amused chuckle. Then it made a similar noise, and it spread its great leathery wings, and it ran into the desert wind, flapping hard, and the wind caught it and carried it aloft, like a kite that had begun to fly.

"Now," said the beast that was Miss Lupescu, "hold on tightly." And she began to run.

"Are we going to the wall of graves?"

"To the ghoul-gates? No. Those are for ghouls. I am a Hound of God. I travel my own road, into Hell and out of it." And it seemed to Bod as if she ran even faster then.

The huge moon rose and the smaller mold-colored moon and they were joined by a ruby-red moon, and the grey wolf ran at a steady lope beneath them across the desert of bones. She stopped by a broken clay building like an enormous beehive, built beside a small rill of water that came bubbling out of the desert rock, splashed down into a tiny pool and was gone again. The grey wolf put her head down and drank, and Bod scooped water up in his hands, drinking the water in a dozen tiny gulps.

"This is the boundary," said the grey wolf that was Miss Lupescu, and Bod looked up. The three moons had gone. Now he could see the Milky Way, see it as he had never seen it before, a glimmering shroud across the arch of the sky. The sky was filled with stars.

"They're beautiful," said Bod.

"When we get you home," said Miss Lupescu, "I teach you the names of the stars and their constellations."

"I'd like that," admitted Bod.

Bod clambered onto her huge, grey back once more

and he buried his face in her fur and held on tightly, and it seemed only moments later that he was being carried—awkwardly, as a grown woman carries a six-year-old boy—across the graveyard, to the Owenses' tomb.

"He's hurt his ankle," Miss Lupescu was saying.

"Poor little soul," said Mistress Owens, taking the boy from her, and cradling him in her capable, if insubstantial arms. "I can't say I didn't worry, for I did. But he's back now, and that's all that matters."

And then he was perfectly comfortable, beneath the earth, in a good place, with his head on his own pillow, and a gentle, exhausted darkness took him.

Bod's left ankle was swollen and purple. Doctor Trefusis (1870–1936, *May He Wake to Glory*) inspected it and pronounced it merely sprained. Miss Lupescu returned from a journey to the chemist's with a tight ankle bandage, and Josiah Worthington, Bart., who had been buried with his ebony walking cane, insisted on lending it to Bod, who had too much fun leaning on the stick and pretending to be one hundred years old.

Bod limped up the hill and retrieved a folded piece of paper from beneath a stone.

The Hounds of God

he read. It was printed in a purple ink, and was the first item on a list.

Those that men call Werewolves or Lycanthropes call themselves the Hounds of God, as they claim their transformation is a gift from their creator, and they repay the gift with their tenacity, for they will pursue an evildoer to the very gates of Hell.

Bod nodded.

Not just evildoers, he thought.

He read the rest of the list, committing it to memory as best he could, then went down to the chapel, where Miss Lupescu was waiting for him with a small meat pie and a huge bag of chips she had bought from the fish-and-chips shop at the bottom of the hill, and another pile of purple-inked duplicated lists.

The two of them shared the chips, and once or twice, Miss Lupescu even smiled.

Silas came back at the the end of the month. He carried his black bag in his left hand and he held his right arm stiffly. But he was Silas, and Bod was happy to see him, and even happier when Silas gave him a present, a little model of the Golden Gate Bridge in San Francisco.

It was almost midnight, and it was still not fully dark. The three of them sat at the top of the hill, with the lights of the city glimmering beneath them.

"I trust that all went well in my absence," said Silas.

"I learned a lot," said Bod, still holding his Bridge. He pointed up into the night sky. "That's the Big Bear and her son, the Little Bear. That's Draco the Dragon,

97

snaking between them."

"Very good," said Silas.

"And you?" asked Bod. "Did you learn anything, while you were away?"

"Oh yes," said Silas, but he declined to elaborate.

"I also," said Miss Lupescu, primly. "I also learned things."

"Good," said Silas. An owl hooted in the branches of an oak tree. "You know, I heard rumors, while I was away," said Silas, "that some weeks ago you both went somewhat further afield than I would have been able to follow. Normally, I would advise caution, but, unlike some, the ghoul-folk have short memories."

Bod said, "It's okay. Miss Lupescu looked after me. I was never in any danger."

Miss Lupescu looked at Bod, and her eyes shone, then she looked at Silas.

"There are so many things to know," she said. "Perhaps I come back next year, in high summer also, to teach the boy again."

Silas looked at Miss Lupescu, and he raised an eyebrow a fraction. Then he looked at Bod.

"I'd like that," said Bod.

CHAPTER FOUR

The Witch's Headstone

THERE WAS A WITCH buried at the edge of the grave-yard, it was common knowledge. Bod had been told to keep away from that corner of the world by Mrs. Owens as far back as he could remember.

"Why?" he asked.

"T'aint healthy for a living body," said Mrs. Owens. "There's damp down that end of things. It's practically a marsh. You'll catch your death."

Mr. Owens himself was more evasive and less imagina-tive. "It's not a good place," was all he said.

The graveyard proper ended at the bottom of the west side of the hill, beneath the old apple tree, with a fence of rust-brown iron railings, each topped with a small, rusting spearhead, but there was a wasteland beyond that, a mass of nettles and weeds, of brambles and autumnal rubbish, and Bod, who was, on the whole, obedient, did not push between the railings, but he went down there and looked

through. He knew he wasn't being told
the whole story, and it irritated him.

Bod went back up the hill, to the little
chapel near the entrance to the graveyard, and he waited until it got dark. As
twilight edged from grey to purple there
was a noise in the spire, like a fluttering of
heavy velvet, and Silas left his resting place in the
belfry and clambered headfirst down the spire.

"What's in the far corner of the graveyard?"
asked Bod. "Past Harrison Westwood, Baker of
this Parish, and his wives, Marion and Joan?"

"Why do you ask?" said his guardian, brushing
the dust from his black suit with ivory fingers.

Bod shrugged. "Just wondered."

"It's unconsecrated ground," said Silas. "Do you
know what that means?"

"Not really," said Bod.

Silas walked across the path without disturbing
a fallen leaf, and sat down on the bench beside
Bod. "There are those," he said, in his silken
voice, "who believe that all land is sacred. That it
is sacred before we come to it, and sacred after.
But here, in your land, they blessed the churches
and the ground they set aside to bury people in,
to make it holy. But they left land unconsecrated
beside the sacred ground, Potter's Fields to bury

the criminals and the suicides or those who were not of the faith."

"So the people buried in the ground on the other side of the fence are bad people?"

Silas raised one perfect eyebrow. "Mm? Oh, not

at all. Let's see, it's been a while since I've been down that way. But I don't remember anyone particularly evil. Remember, in days gone by you could be hanged for stealing a shilling. And there are always people who find their lives have become so unsupportable they believe the best thing they could do would be to hasten their transition to another plane of existence."

"They kill themselves, you mean?" said Bod. He was about eight years old, wide-eyed and inquisitive, and he was not stupid.

"Indeed."

"Does it work? Are they happier dead?"

"Sometimes. Mostly, no. It's like the people who believe they'll be happy if they go and live somewhere else, but who learn it doesn't work that way. Wherever you go, you take yourself with you. If you see what I mean."

"Sort of," said Bod.

Silas reached down and ruffled the boy's hair.

Bod said, "What about the witch?"

"Yes. Exactly," said Silas. "Suicides, criminals, and witches. Those who died unshriven." He stood up, a midnight shadow in the twilight. "All this talking," he said, "and I have not even had my breakfast. While you will be late for lessons." In the twilight of the graveyard there was a silent implosion, a flutter of velvet darkness, and Silas was gone.

The moon had begun to rise by the time Bod reached Mr. Pennyworth's mausoleum, and Thomes Pennyworth (*here he lyes in the certainty of the moft glorious refurrection*) was already waiting, and was not in the best of moods.

"You are late," he said.

"Sorry, Mr. Pennyworth."

Pennyworth tutted. The previous week Mr. Pennyworth had been teaching Bod about Elements and Humors, and Bod had kept forgetting which was which. He was expecting a test, but instead Mr. Pennyworth said, "I think it is time to spend a few days on practical matters. Time is passing, after all."

"Is it?" asked Bod.

"I am afraid so, young Master Owens. Now, how is your Fading?"

Bod had hoped he would not be asked that question.

"It's all right," he said. "I mean. You know."

"No, Master Owens. I do not know. Why do you not demonstrate for me?"

Bod's heart sank. He took a deep breath, and did his best, squinching up his eyes and trying to fade away.

Mr. Pennyworth was not impressed.

"Pah. That's not the kind of thing. Not the kind of thing at all. Slipping and Fading, boy, the way of the dead. Slip through shadows. Fade from awareness. Try again."

Bod tried harder.

"You're as plain as the nose on your face," said Mr. Pennyworth. "And your nose is remarkably obvious. As is the rest of your face, young man. As are you. For the sake of all that is holy, empty your mind. Now. You are an empty alleyway. You are a vacant doorway. You are nothing. Eyes

105

will not see you. Minds will not hold you. Where you are is nothing and nobody."

Bod tried again. He closed his eyes and imagined himself fading into the stained stonework of the mausoleum wall, becoming a shadow on the night and nothing more. He sneezed.

"Dreadful," said Mr. Pennyworth, with a sigh. "Quite dreadful. I believe I shall have a word with your guardian about this." He shook his head. "So. The humors. List them."

"Um. Sanguine. Choleric. Phlegmatic. And the other one. Um, Melancholic, I think."

And so it went, until it was time for Grammar and Composition with Miss Letitia Borrows, Spinster of this Parish (*Who Did No Harm to No Man all the Dais of Her Life. Reader, Can You Say Lykewise?*). Bod liked Miss Borrows, and the coziness of her little crypt, and that she could all-too-easily be led off the subject.

"They say there's a witch in uncons—unconsecrated ground," he said.

"Yes, dear. But you don't want to go over there."

"Why not?"

Miss Borrows smiled the guileless smile of the dead. "They aren't our sort of people," she said.

"But it *is* the graveyard, isn't it? I mean, I'm allowed to go there if I want to?"

"That," said Miss Borrows, "would not be advisable."

Bod was obedient, but curious, and so, when lessons

106

were done for the night, he walked past Harrison Westwood, Baker, and family's memorial, a broken-armed angel, but did not climb down the hill to the Potter's Field. Instead he walked up the side of the hill to where a picnic some thirty years before had left its mark in the shape of a large apple tree.

There were some lessons that Bod had mastered. He had eaten a bellyful of unripe apples, sour and white-pipped, from the tree some years before, and had regretted it for days, his guts cramping and painful while Mrs. Owens lectured him on what not to eat. Now he always waited until the apples were ripe before eating them, and never ate more than two or three a night. He had finished the last of the apples the week before, but he liked the apple tree as a place to think.

He edged up the trunk, to his favorite place in the crook of two branches, and looked down at the Potter's Field below him, a brambly patch of weeds and unmown grass in the moonlight. He wondered whether the witch would be old and iron-toothed and travel in a house on chicken legs, or whether she would be thin and sharp-nosed and carry a broomstick.

Bod's stomach growled and he realized that he was getting hungry. He wished he had not devoured all the apples on the tree. That he had left just one . . .

He glanced up, and thought he saw something. He looked once, looked twice to be certain: an apple, red and ripe.

Bod prided himself on his tree-climbing skills. He swung himself up, branch by branch, and imagined he was Silas, swarming smoothly up a sheer brick wall. The apple, the red of it almost black in the moonlight, hung just out of reach. Bod moved slowly forward along the branch, until he was just below the apple. Then he stretched up, and the tips of his fingers touched the perfect apple.

He was never to taste it.

A snap, loud as a hunter's gun, as the branch gave way beneath him.

A flash of pain woke him, sharp as ice, the color of slow thunder, down in the weeds that summer's night.

The ground beneath him seemed relatively soft, and oddly warm. He pushed a hand down and felt something like warm fur beneath him. He had landed on the grass-pile, where the graveyard's groundskeeper threw the cuttings from the mower, and it had broken his fall. Still, there was a pain in his chest, and his leg hurt as if he had landed on it first and twisted it.

Bod moaned.

"Hush-a-you-hush-a-boy," said a voice from behind him. "Where did you come from? Dropping like a thunderstone. What way is that to carry on?"

"I was in the apple tree," said Bod.

"Ah. Let me see your leg. Broken like the tree's limb, I'll be bound." Cool fingers prodded his left leg. "Not broken. Twisted, yes, sprained perhaps. You have the Devil's own luck, boy, falling into the compost. 'Tain't the end of the world."

"Oh, good," said Bod. "Hurts, though."

He turned his head, looked up and behind him. She was older than him, but not a grown-up, and she looked neither friendly nor unfriendly. Wary, mostly. She had a face that was intelligent and not even a little bit beautiful.

"I'm Bod," he said.

"The live boy?" she asked.

Bod nodded.

"I thought you must be," she said. "We've heard of you, even over here, in the Potter's Field. What do they call you?"

"Owens," he said. "Nobody Owens. Bod, for short."

"How-de-do, young Master Bod."

Bod looked her up and down. She wore a plain white shift. Her hair was mousy and long, and there was something of the goblin in her face—a sideways hint of a smile that seemed to linger, no matter what the rest of her face was doing.

"Were you a suicide?" he asked. "Did you steal a shilling?"

"Never stole nuffink," she said, "Not even a handkerchief. Anyway," she said, pertly, "the suicides is all over there, on the other side of that hawthorn, and the gallows-birds are in the blackberry-patch, both of them. One was a coiner, t'other a highwayman, or so he says, although if you ask me I doubt he was more than a common footpad and nightwalker."

"Ah," said Bod. Then, suspicion forming, tentatively, he said, "They say a witch is buried here."

She nodded. "Drownded and burnded and buried here without as much as a stone to mark the spot."

"You were drowned *and* burned?"

She settled down on the hill of grass-cuttings beside him, and held his throbbing leg with her chilly hands. "They come to my little cottage at dawn, before I'm proper awake, and drags me out onto the Green. 'You're a witch!' they shouts, fat and fresh-scrubbed all pink in the morning, like so many pigwiggins scrubbed clean for market day. One by one they gets up beneath the sky and tells of milk gone sour and horses gone lame, and finally Mistress Jemima gets up, the fattest, pinkest, best-scrubbed of them all, and tells how as Solomon Porritt now cuts her dead and instead hangs around the washhouse like a wasp about a honeypot, and it's all my magic, says she, that made him so and the poor young man must be bespelled. So they strap me to the cucking stool and forces it under the water of the duckpond, saying if I'm a witch I'll neither drown nor care, but if I am not a witch I'll feel it. And Mistress Jemima's father gives them each a silver groat to hold the stool down under the foul green water for a long time, to see if I'd choke on it."

"And did you?"

"Oh yes. Got a lungful of water. It done for me."

"Oh," said Bod. "Then you weren't a witch after all."

The girl fixed him with her beady ghost-eyes and smiled

110

a lopsided smile. She still looked like a goblin, but now she looked like a pretty goblin, and Bod didn't think she would have needed magic to attract Solomon Porritt, not with a smile like that. "What nonsense. Of course I was a witch. They learned that when they untied me from the cucking stool and stretched me on the Green, nine-parts dead and all covered with duckweed and stinking pond-muck. I rolled my eyes back in my head, and I cursed each and every one of them there on the village Green that morning, that none of them would ever rest easily in a grave. I was surprised at how easily it came, the cursing. Like dancing it was, when your feet pick up the steps of a new measure your ears have never heard and your head don't know, and they dance it till dawn." She stood, and twirled, and kicked, and her bare feet flashed in the moonlight. "That was how I cursed them, with my last gurgling pond-watery breath. And then I expired. They burned my body on the Green until I was nothing but blackened charcoal, and they popped me in a hole in the Potter's Field without so much as a headstone to mark my name," and it was only then that she paused, and seemed, for a moment, wistful.

"Are any of them buried in the graveyard, then?" asked Bod.

"Not a one," said the girl, with a twinkle. "The Saturday after they drownded and toasted me, a carpet was delivered to Master Porringer, all the way from London Town, and it was a fine carpet. But it turned out there was more in that carpet than strong wool and good weaving, for it carried the plague in its pattern, and by Monday five of them were coughing blood, and their skins were gone as black as mine when they hauled me from the fire. A week later and it had taken most of the village, and they threw the bodies all promiscuous in a plague pit they dug outside of the town, that they filled in after."

"Was everyone in the village killed?"

She shrugged. "Everyone who watched me get drownded and burned. How's your leg now?"

"Better," he said. "Thanks."

Bod stood up, slowly, and limped down from the grass-pile. He leaned against the iron railings. "So were you always a witch?" he asked. "I mean, before you cursed them all?"

"As if it would take witchcraft," she said with a sniff, "to get Solomon Porritt mooning round my cottage."

Which, Bod thought, but did not say, was not actually an answer to the question, not at all.

"What's your name?" he asked.

"Got no headstone," she said, turning down the corners of her mouth. "Might be anybody. Mightn't I?"

"But you must have a name."

"Liza Hempstock, if you please," she said tartly. Then she said, "It's not that much to ask, is it? Something to mark my grave. I'm just down there, see? With nothing but nettles to show where I rest." And she looked so sad, just for a moment, that Bod wanted to hug her. And then it came to him, as he squeezed between the railings of the

112

fence. He would find Liza Hempstock a headstone, with her name upon it. He would make her smile.

He turned to wave good-bye as he began to clamber up the hill, but she was already gone.

There were broken lumps of other people's stones and statues in the graveyard, but, Bod knew, that would have been entirely the wrong sort of thing to bring to the grey-eyed witch in the Potter's Field. It was going to take more than that. He decided not to tell anyone what he was planning, on the not entirely unreasonable basis that they would have told him not to do it.

Over the next few days his mind filled with plans, each more complicated and extravagant than the last. Mr. Pennyworth despaired.

"I do believe," he announced, scratching his dusty mustache, "that you are getting, if anything, worse. You are not Fading. You are *obvious*, boy. You are difficult to miss. If you came to me in company with a purple lion, a green elephant, and a scarlet unicorn astride which was the King of England in his Royal Robes, I do believe that it is you and you alone that people would stare at, dismissing the others as minor irrelevancies."

Bod simply stared at him, and said nothing. He was wondering whether there were special shops in the places where the living people gathered that sold only headstones, and if so how he could go about finding one, and Fading was the least of his problems.

He took advantage of Miss Borrows's willingness to be diverted from the subjects of Grammar and Composition to the subject of anything else at all to ask her about money—how exactly it worked, how one used it to get things one wanted. Bod had a number of coins he had found over the years (he had learned that the best place to find money was to go, afterwards, to wherever court-ing couples had used the grass of the graveyard as a place to cuddle and snuggle and kiss and roll about. He would often find metal coins on the ground, in the place where they had been) and he thought perhaps he could finally get some use from them.

"How much would a headstone be?" he asked Miss Borrows.

"In my time," she told him, "they were fifteen guineas. I do not know what they would be today. More, I imagine. Much, much more."

Bod had two pounds and fifty-three pence. It would, he was quite certain, not be enough.

It had been four years, almost half a lifetime, since Bod had visited the Indigo Man's tomb, but he still remem-bered the way. He climbed to the top of the hill, until he was above the whole town, above even the top of the apple tree, above even the steeple of the little chapel, up where the Frobisher mausoleum stood like a rotten tooth. He slipped down into it, behind the coffin, and down and down and still further down, down to the tiny stone steps cut into the center of the hill, and those he descended until he reached the stone chamber. It was dark in that tomb, dark as a tin mine, but Bod saw as the dead see and the room gave up its secrets to him.

The Sleer was coiled around the wall of the barrow. He could feel it. It was as he remembered it, an invisible thing, all smoky tendrils and hate and greed. This time, however, he was not afraid of it.

FEAR US, whispered the Sleer. FOR WE GUARD THINGS PRECIOUS AND NEVER-LOST.

"I don't fear you," said Bod. "Remember? And I need to take something away from here."

NOTHING EVER LEAVES, came the reply from the coiled thing in the darkness. THE KNIFE, THE BROOCH, THE GOBLET. THE SLEER GUARDS THEM IN THE DARKNESS. WE WAIT.

"Pardon me for asking," said Bod, "but was this your grave?"

MASTER SETS US HERE ON THE PLAIN TO GUARD, BURIES OUR SKULLS BENEATH THIS STONE, LEAVES US HERE KNOWING WHAT WE HAVE TO DO. WE GUARD THE TREASURES UNTIL MASTER COMES BACK.

"I expect that he's forgotten all about you," pointed out Bod. "I'm sure he's been dead himself for ages."

WE ARE THE SLEER. WE GUARD.

Bod wondered just how long ago you had to go back before the deepest tomb inside the hill was on a plain, and he knew it must have been an extremely long time ago. He could feel the Sleer winding its waves of fear around him, like the tendrils of some carnivorous plant. He was beginning to feel cold, and slow, as if he had been bitten in the heart by some arctic viper and it was starting to pump its icy venom through his body.

He took a step forward, so he was standing against the stone slab, and he reached down and closed his fingers around the coldness of the brooch.

HISH! whispered the Sleer. WE GUARD THAT FOR THE MASTER.

"He won't mind," said Bod. He took a step backward, walking toward the stone steps, avoiding the desiccated remains of people and animals on the floor.

The Sleer writhed angrily, twining around the tiny chamber like ghost-smoke. Then it slowed. IT COMES BACK, said the Sleer, in its tangled triple voice. ALWAYS COMES BACK.

Bod went up the stone steps inside the hill as fast as he could. At one point he imagined that there was something coming after him, but when he broke out of the top, into the Frobisher mausoleum, and he could breathe the cool dawn air, nothing moved or followed.

Bod sat in the open air on the top of the hill and held the brooch. He thought it was all black, at first, but then the sun rose, and he could see that the stone in the center of the black metal was a swirling red. It was the size of a robin's egg, and Bod stared into the stone wondering if there were things moving in its heart, his eyes and soul deep in the crimson world. If Bod had been smaller he would have wanted to put it into his mouth.

116

The stone was held in place by a black metal clasp, by something that looked like claws, with something else crawling around it. The something else looked almost snake-like, but it had too many heads. Bod wondered if that was what the Sleer looked like, in the daylight.

He wandered down the hill, taking all the shortcuts he knew, through the ivy tangle that covered the Bartleby family vault (and inside, the sound of the Bartlebys grumbling and readying for sleep) and on and over and through the railings and into the Potter's Field.

He called "Liza! Liza!" and looked around.

"Good morrow, young lummox," said Liza's voice. Bod could not see her, but there was an extra shadow beneath the hawthorn tree, and, as he approached it, the shadow resolved itself into something pearlescent and translucent in the early-morning light. Something girl-like. Something grey-eyed. "I should be decently sleeping," she said. "What kind of carrying on is this?"

"Your headstone," he said. "I wanted to know what you want on it."

"My name," she said. "It must have my name on it, with a big E, for Elizabeth, like the old queen that died when I was born, and a big Haitch, for Hempstock. More than that I care not, for I did never master my letters."

"What about dates?" asked Bod.

"Willyum the Conker ten sixty-six," she sang, in the whisper of the dawn-wind in the hawthorn tree. "A big E if you please. And a big Haitch."

"Did you have a job?" asked Bod. "I mean, when you weren't being a witch?"

"I done laundry," said the dead girl, and then the morning sunlight flooded the wasteland, and Bod was alone.

It was nine in the morning, when all the world is sleeping. Bod was determined to stay awake. He was, after all, on a mission. He was eight years old, and the world beyond the graveyard held no terrors for him.

Clothes. He would need clothes. His usual dress, of a grey winding sheet, was, he knew, quite wrong. It was good in the graveyard, the same color as stone and as shadows. But if he was going to dare the world beyond the graveyard walls, he would need to blend in there.

There were some clothes in the crypt beneath the ruined church, but Bod did not want to go down to the crypt, not even in daylight. While Bod was prepared to justify himself to Master and Mistress Owens, he was not about to explain himself to Silas; the very thought of those dark eyes angry, or worse still, disappointed, filled him with shame.

There was a gardener's hut at the far end of the graveyard, a small green building that smelled like motor oil, and in which the old mower sat and rusted, unused, along with an assortment of ancient garden tools. The hut had been abandoned when the last gardener had retired, before Bod was born, and the task of keeping the graveyard had been shared between the council (who sent in a man to cut the grass and clean the paths, once a month from April to

September) and the local volunteers in the Friends of the Graveyard.

A huge padlock on the door protected the contents of the hut, but Bod had long ago discovered the loose wooden board in the back. Sometimes he would go to the gardener's hut and sit, and think, when he wanted to be by himself.

As long as he had been going to the hut there had been a brown workingman's jacket hanging on the back of the door, forgotten or abandoned years before, along with a green-stained pair of gardening jeans. The jeans were much too big for him, but he rolled up the cuffs until his feet showed, then he made a belt out of brown garden-twine, and tied it around his waist. There were boots in one corner, and he tried putting them on, but they were so big and encrusted with mud and concrete that he could barely shuffle in them, and if he took a step, the boots remained on the floor of the shed. He pushed the jacket out through the space in the loose board, squeezed himself out, then put it on. If he rolled up the sleeves, he decided, it worked quite well. It had big pockets, and he thrust his hands into them, and felt quite the dandy.

Bod walked down to the main gate of the graveyard, and looked out through the bars. A bus rattled past, in the street; there were cars there and noise and shops. Behind him, a cool green shade, overgrown with trees and ivy: home.

His heart pounding, Bod walked out into the world.

Abanazer Bolger had seen some odd types in his time; if you owned a shop like Abanazer's, you'd see them too. The shop, in the warren of streets in the Old Town—a little bit antiques shop, a little bit junk shop, a little bit pawnbroker's (and not even Abanazer himself was entirely certain which bit was which) brought odd types and strange people, some of them wanting to buy, some of them needing to sell. Abanazer Bolger traded over the counter, buying and selling, and he did a better trade behind the counter and in the back room, accepting objects that may not have been acquired entirely honestly, and then quietly shifting them on. His business was an iceberg. Only the dusty little shop was visible on the surface. The rest of it was underneath, and that was just how Abanazer Bolger wanted it.

Abanazer Bolger had thick spectacles and a permanent expression of mild distaste, as if he had just realized that the milk in his tea had been on the turn, and he could not get the sour taste of it out of his mouth. The expression served him well when people tried to sell him things. "Honestly," he would tell them, sour-faced, "it's not really worth anything at all. I'll give you what I can, though, as it has sentimental value." You were lucky to get anything like what you thought you wanted from Abanazer Bolger.

A business like Abanazer Bolger's brought in strange people, but the boy who came in that morning was one of the strangest Abanazer could remember in a lifetime of cheating strange people out of their valuables. He looked to be about seven years old, and dressed in his grand-father's clothes. He smelled like a shed. His hair was long and shaggy, and he seemed extremely grave. His hands were deep in the pockets of a dusty brown jacket, but even with the hands out of sight, Abanazer could see that some-thing was clutched extremely tightly—protectively—in the boy's right hand.

"Excuse me," said the boy.

"Aye-aye, Sonny-Jim," said Abanazer Bolger warily. *Kids*, he thought. *Either they've nicked something, or they're trying to sell their toys*. Either way, he usually said no. Buy stolen property from a kid, and next thing you knew you'd have an enraged adult accusing you of having given little Johnnie or Matilda a tenner for their wedding ring. More trouble than they was worth, kids.

"I need something for a friend of mine," said the boy. "And I thought maybe you could buy something I've got."

"I don't buy stuff from kids," said Abanazer Bolger flatly.

Bod took his hand out of his pocket and put the brooch down on the grimy countertop. Bolger glanced down at it, then he looked at it. He removed his spectacles. He took an eyepiece from the countertop and he screwed it into his eye. He turned on a little light on the counter and exam-ined the brooch through the eyeglass. "Snakestone?" he said, to himself, not to the boy. Then he took the eyepiece out, replaced his glasses, and fixed the boy with a sour and suspicious look.

"Where did you get this?" Abanazer Bolger asked.

121

Bod said, "Do you want to buy it?"

"You stole it. You've nicked this from a museum or somewhere, didn't you?"

"No," said Bod flatly. "Are you going to buy it, or shall I go and find somebody who will?"

Abanazer Bolger's sour mood changed then. Suddenly he was all affability. He smiled broadly. "I'm sorry," he said. "It's just you don't see many pieces like this. Not in a shop like this. Not outside of a museum. But I would certainly like it. Tell you what. Why don't we sit down over tea and biscuits—I've got a packet of chocolate chip cookies in the back room—and decide how much something like this is worth? Eh?"

Bod was relieved that the man was finally being friendly. "I need enough to buy a stone," he said. "A headstone for a friend of mine. Well, she's not really my friend. Just someone I know. I think she helped make my leg better, you see."

Abanazer Bolger, paying little attention to the boy's prattle, led him behind the counter, and opened the door to the storeroom, a windowless little space, every inch of which was crammed high with teetering cardboard boxes, each filled with junk. There was a safe in there, in the corner, a big old one. There was a box filled with violins, an accumulation of stuffed dead animals, chairs without seats, books and prints.

There was a small desk beside the door, and Abanazer

122

Bolger pulled up the only chair, and sat down, letting Bod stand. Abanazer rummaged in a drawer, in which Bod could see a half-empty bottle of whisky, and pulled out an almost-finished packet of chocolate chip cookies, and he offered one to the boy; he turned on the desk light, looked at the brooch again, the swirls of red and orange in the stone, and he examined the black metal band that encircled it, suppressing a little shiver at the expression on the heads of the snake-things. "This is old," he said. "It's"—*priceless*, he thought—"probably not really worth much, but you never know." Bod's face fell. Abanazer Bolger tried to look reassuring. "I just need to know that it's not stolen, though, before I can give you a penny. Did you take it from your mum's dresser? Nick it from a museum? You can tell me. I'll not get you into trouble. I just need to know."

Bod shook his head. He munched on his cookie.

"Then where did you get it?"

Bod said nothing.

Abanazer Bolger did not want to put down the brooch, but he pushed it across the desk to the boy. "If you can't tell me," he said, "you'd better take it back. There has to be trust on both sides, after all. Nice doing business with you. Sorry it couldn't go any further."

Bod looked worried. Then he said, "I found it in an old grave. But I can't say where." He stopped, because naked greed and excitement had replaced the friendliness on Abanazer Bolger's face.

123

"And there's more like this there?"

Bod said, "If you don't want to buy it, I'll find someone else. Thank you for the biscuit."

Bolger said, "You're in a hurry, eh? Mum and dad waiting for you, I expect?"

The boy shook his head, then wished he had nodded.

"Nobody waiting. Good." Abanazer Bolger closed his hands around the brooch. "Now, you tell me exactly where you found this. Eh?"

"I don't remember," said Bod.

"Too late for that," said Abanazer Bolger. "Suppose you have a little think for a bit about where it came from. Then, when you've thought, we'll have a little chat, and you'll tell me."

He got up and walked out of the room, closing the door behind him. He locked it with a large metal key.

He opened his hand and looked at the brooch and smiled, hungrily.

There was a *ding* from the bell above the shop door, to let him know someone had entered, and he looked up, guiltily, but there was no one there. The door was slightly ajar though, and Bolger pushed it shut, and then for good measure he turned around the sign in the window, so it said CLOSED. He pushed the bolt shut. Didn't want any busybodies turning up today.

The autumn day had turned from sunny to grey, and a light patter of rain ran down the grubby shop window.

Abanazer Bolger picked up the telephone from the

counter and pushed at the buttons with fingers that barely shook.

"Paydirt, Tom," he said. "Get over here, soon as you can."

Bod realized that he was trapped when he heard the lock turn in the door. He pulled on the door, but it held fast. He felt stupid for having been lured inside, foolish for not trusting his first impulses, to get as far away from the sour-faced man as possible. He had broken all the rules of the graveyard, and everything had gone wrong. What would Silas say? Or the Owenses? He could feel himself beginning to panic, and he suppressed it, pushing the worry back down inside him. It would all be good. He knew that. Of course, he needed to get out. . . .

He examined the room he was trapped in. It was little more than a storeroom with a desk in it. The only entrance was the door.

He opened the desk drawer, finding nothing but small pots of paint (used for brightening up antiques) and a paint-brush. He wondered if he would be able to throw paint in the man's face, and blind him for long enough to escape. He opened the top of a pot of paint and dipped in his finger.

"What're you doin'?" asked a voice close to his ear.

"Nothing," said Bod, screwing the top on the paintpot, and dropping it into one of the jacket's enormous pockets.

Liza Hempstock looked at him, unimpressed. "Why are you in here?" she asked. "And who's old bag-of-lard out there?"

"It's his shop. I was trying to sell him something."

"Why?"

"None of your beeswax."

She sniffed. "Well," she said, "you should get on back to the graveyard."

"I can't. He's locked me in."

"'Course you can. Just slip through the wall—"

He shook his head. "I can't. I can only do it at home because they gave me the Freedom of the Graveyard when I was a baby." He looked up at her, under the electric light. It was hard to see her properly, but Bod had spent his life talking to dead people. "Anyway, what are you doing here? What are you doing out from the graveyard? It's daytime. And you're not like Silas. You're meant to stay in the graveyard."

She said, "There's rules for those in graveyards, but not for those as was buried in unhallowed ground. Nobody tells *me* what to do, or where to go." She glared at the door. "I don't like that man," she said. "I'm going to see what he's doing."

A flicker, and Bod was alone in the room once more. He heard a rumble of distant thunder.

In the cluttered darkness of Bolger's Antiquities, Abanazer Bolger looked up suspiciously, certain that someone was watching him, then realized he was being foolish. "The boy's locked in the room," he told himself. "The front door's locked." He was polishing the metal clasp surrounding the snakestone, as gently and as carefully as an

126

archaeologist on a dig, taking off the black and revealing the glittering silver beneath it.

He was beginning to regret calling Tom Hustings over, although Hustings was big and good for scaring people. He was also beginning to regret that he was going to have to sell the brooch, when he was done. It was special. The more it glittered, under the tiny light on his counter, the more he wanted it to be his, and only his.

There was more where this came from, though. The boy would tell him. The boy would lead him to it.

The boy . . .

An idea struck him. He put down the brooch, reluctantly, and opened a drawer behind the counter, taking out a metal biscuit tin filled with envelopes and cards and slips of paper.

He reached in, and took out a card, only slightly larger than a business card. It was black-edged. There was no name or address printed on it, though. Only one word, handwritten in the center in an ink that had faded to brown: *Jack*.

On the back of the card, in pencil, Abanazer Bolger had written instructions to himself, in his tiny, precise handwriting, as a reminder, although he would not have been likely to forget the use of the card, how to use it to summon the man Jack. No, not summon. *Invite*. You did not summon people like him.

A knocking on the outer door of the shop.

Bolger tossed the card down onto the counter, and

walked over to the door, peering out into the wet afternoon.

"Hurry up," called Tom Hustings, "it's miserable out here. Dismal. I'm getting soaked."

Bolger unlocked the door and Tom Hustings pushed his way in, his raincoat and hair dripping. "What's so important that you can't talk about it over the phone, then?"

"Our fortune," said Abanazer Bolger, with his sour face. "That's what."

Hustings took off his raincoat and hung it on the back of the shopdoor. "What is it? Something good fell off the back of a lorry?"

"Treasure," said Abanazer Bolger. "Two kinds." He took his friend over to the counter, showed him the brooch, under the little light.

"It's old, isn't it?"

"From pagan times," said Abanazer. "Before. From Druid times. Before the Romans came. It's called a snakestone. Seen 'em in museums. I've never seen metalwork like that, or one so fine. Must have belonged to a king. The lad who found it says it come from a grave—think of a barrow filled with stuff like this."

"Might be worth doing it legit," said Hustings, thoughtfully. "Declare it as treasure trove. They have to pay us market value for it, and we could make them name it after us. The Hustings–Bolger Bequest."

"Bolger–Hustings," said Abanazer, automatically. Then he said, "There's a few people I know of, people with real

128

money, would pay more than market value, if they could hold it as you are"—for Tom Hustings was fingering the brooch, gently, like a man stroking a kitten—"and there'd be no questions asked." He reached out his hand and, reluctantly, Tom Hustings passed him the brooch.

"You said two kinds of treasure," said Hustings. "What's t'other?"

Abanazer Bolger picked up the black-edged card, held it out for his friend's inspection. "Do you know what this is?"

His friend shook his head.

Abanazer put the card down on the counter. "There's a party is looking for another party."

"So?"

"The way I heard it," said Abanazer Bolger, "the other party is a boy."

"There's boys everywhere," said Tom Hustings. "Running all around. Getting into trouble. I can't abide them. So, there's a party looking for a particular boy?"

"This lad looks to be the right sort of age. He's dressed—well, you'll see how he's dressed. And he found this. It could be him."

"And if it is him?"

Abanazer Bolger picked up the card again, by the edge, and waved it back and forth, slowly, as if running the edge along an imaginary flame. "Here comes a candle to light you to bed . . ." he began.

". . . and here comes a chopper to chop off your head," concluded Tom Hustings, thoughtfully. "But look you. If we call the man Jack, we lose the boy. And if we lose the boy, we lose the treasure."

And the two men went back and forth on it, weighing the merits and disadvantages of reporting the boy or of collecting the treasure, which had grown in their minds to a huge underground cavern filled with precious things, and as they debated Abanazer pulled a bottle of sloe gin from beneath the counter and poured them both a generous tot, "to assist the cerebrations."

Liza was soon bored with their discussion, which went back and forth and around like a whirligig, getting nowhere, and so she went back into the storeroom, to find Bod standing in the middle of the room with his eyes tightly closed and his fists clenched and his face all screwed up as if he had a toothache, almost purple from holding his breath.

"What you a-doin' of now?" she asked, unimpressed.

He opened his eyes and relaxed. "Trying to Fade," he said.

Liza sniffed. "Try again," she said.

He did, holding his breath even longer this time.

"Stop that," she told him. "Or you'll pop."

Bod took a deep breath and then sighed. "It doesn't work," he said. "Maybe I could hit him with a rock, and just run for it." There wasn't a rock, so he picked up a colored glass paperweight, hefted it in his hand, wondering if he could throw it hard enough to stop Abanazer Bolger in his tracks.

130

"There's two of them out there now," said Liza. "And if the one don't get you, t'other one will. They say they want to get you to show them where you got the brooch, and then dig up the grave and take the treasure." She did not tell him about the other discussions they were having, nor about the black-edged card. She shook her head. "Why did you do something as stupid as this anyway? You know the rules about leaving the graveyard. Just asking for trouble, it was."

Bod felt very insignificant, and very foolish. "I wanted to get you a headstone," he admitted, in a small voice. "And I thought it would cost more money. So I was going to sell him the brooch, to buy you one."

She didn't say anything.

"Are you angry?"

She shook her head. "It's the first nice thing anyone's done for me in five hundred years," she said, with a hint of a goblin smile. "Why would I be angry?" Then she said, "What do you do, when you try to Fade?"

"What Mr. Pennyworth told me. *'I am an empty doorway, I am a vacant alley, I am nothing. Eyes will not see me, glances slip over me.'* But it never works."

"It's because you're alive," said Liza, with a sniff. "There's stuff as works for us, the dead, who have to fight to be noticed at the best of times, that won't never work for you people."

She hugged herself tightly, moving her body back and forth, as if she was debating something. Then she said, "It's because of me you got into this. . . . Come here, Nobody Owens."

He took a step towards her, in that tiny room, and she put her cold hand on his forehead. It felt like a wet silk scarf against his skin.

"Now," she said. "Perhaps I can do a good turn for you."

And with that, she began to mutter to herself, mumbling words that Bod could not make out. Then she said, clear and loud,

> *"Be hole, be dust, be dream, be wind*
> *Be night, be dark, be wish, be mind,*
> *Now slip, now slide, now move unseen,*
> *Above, beneath, betwixt, between."*

Something huge touched him, brushed him from head to feet, and he shivered. His hair prickled, and his skin was all gooseflesh. Something had changed. "What did you do?" he asked.

"Just gived you a helping hand," she said. "I may be dead, but I'm a dead witch, remember. And we don't forget."

"But—"

"Hush up," she said. "They're coming back."

The key rattled in the storeroom lock. "Now then, chummy," said a voice Bod had not heard clearly before, "I'm sure we're all going to be great friends," and with that Tom Hustings pushed open the door. Then he stood in the doorway looking around, looking puzzled. He was a big,

big man, with foxy-red hair and a bottle-red nose. "Here. Abanazer? I thought you said he was in here?"

"I did," said Bolger, from behind him.

"Well, I can't see hide nor hair of him."

Bolger's face appeared behind the ruddy man's and he peered into the room. "Hiding," he said, staring straight at where Bod was standing. "No use hiding," he announced, loudly. "I can see you there. Come on out."

The two men walked into the little room, and Bod stood stock still between them and thought of Mr. Pennyworth's lessons. He did not react, he did not move. He let the men's glances slide from him without seeing him.

"You're going to wish you'd come out when I called," said Bolger, and he shut the door. "Right," he said to Tom Hustings. "You block the door, so he can't get past." And with that he walked around the room, peering behind things, and bending, awkwardly, to look beneath the desk. He walked straight past Bod and opened the cupboard. "Now I see you!" he shouted. "Come out!"

Liza giggled.

"What was that?" asked Tom Hustings, spinning round.

"I didn't hear nothing," said Abanazer Bolger.

Liza giggled again. Then she put her lips together and blew, making a noise that began as a whistling, and then sounded like a distant wind. The electric lights in the little room flickered and buzzed, then they went out.

"Bloody fuses," said Abanazer Bolger. "Come on. This is a waste of time."

The key clicked in the lock, and Liza and Bod were left alone in the room.

"He's got away," said Abanazer Bolger. Bod could hear him now, through the door. "Room like that. There wasn't anywhere he could have been hiding. We'd've seen him if he was."

"The man Jack won't like that."

"Who's going to tell him?"

A pause.

"Here. Tom Hustings. Where's the brooch gone?"

"Mm? That? Here. I was keeping it safe."

"Keeping it safe? In your pocket? Funny place to be keeping it safe, if you ask me. More like you were planning to make off with it—like you was planing to keep my brooch for your own."

"Your brooch, Abanazer? *Your* brooch? Our brooch, you mean."

"Ours, indeed. I don't remember you being here, when I got it from that boy."

"That boy that you couldn't even keep safe for the man Jack, you mean? Can you imagine what he'll do, when he finds *you* had the boy he was looking for, and *you* let him go?"

"Probably not the same boy. Lots of boys in the world, what're the odds it was the one he was looking for? Out the back door as soon as my back was turned, I'll bet."

And then Abanazer Bolger said, in a high, wheedling voice,

"Don't you worry about the man Jack, Tom Hustings. I'm sure that it was a different boy. My old mind playing tricks. And we're almost out of sloe gin—how would you fancy a good Scotch? I've whisky in the back room. You just wait here a moment."

The storeroom door was unlocked, and Abanazer entered, holding a walking stick and a flashlight, looking even more sour of face than before.

"If you're still in here," he said, in a sour mutter, "don't even think of making a run for it. I've called the police on you, that's what I've done." A rummage in a drawer produced the half-filled bottle of whisky, and then a tiny black bottle. Abanazer poured several drops from the little bottle into the larger, then he pocketed the tiny bottle. "My brooch, and mine alone," he muttered, and followed it with a barked, "Just coming, Tom!"

He glared around the dark room, staring past Bod, then he left the storeroom, carrying the whisky in front of him. He locked the door behind him.

"Here you go," came Abanazer Bolger's voice through the door. "Give us your glass then, Tom. Nice drop of Scotch, put hairs on your chest. Say when."

Silence. "Cheap muck. Aren't you drinking?"

"That sloe gin's gone to my innards. Give it a minute for my stomach to settle . . ." Then, "Here—Tom! What have you done with my brooch?"

"*Your* brooch is it now? Whoa—what did you . . . you put something in my drink, you little grub!"

"What if I did? I could read on your face what you was planning, Tom Hustings. Thief."

And then there was shouting, and several crashes, and loud bangs, as if heavy items of furniture were being overturned . . .

. . . then silence.

Liza said, "Quickly now. Let's get you out of here."

"But the door's locked." He looked at her. "Is there something you can do?"

"Me? I don't have any magics will get you out of a locked room, boy."

Bod crouched, and peered out through the keyhole. It was blocked; the key sat in the keyhole. Bod thought, then he smiled, momentarily, and it lit his face like the flash of a lightbulb. He pulled a crumpled sheet of newspaper from a packing case, flattened it out as best he could, then pushed it underneath the door, leaving only a corner on his side of the doorway.

"What are you playing at?" asked Liza, impatiently.

"I need something like a pencil. Only thinner . . ." he said. "Here we go." And he took a thin paintbrush from the top of the desk, and pushed the brushless end into the lock, jiggled it and pushed some more.

There was a muffled clunk as the key was pushed out, as it dropped from the lock onto the newspaper. Bod pulled the paper back under the door, now with the key sitting on it.

Liza laughed, delighted. "That's wit, young man," she said. "That's wisdom."

Bod put the key in the lock, turned it, and pushed open the storeroom door.

There were two men on the floor, in the middle of the crowded antiques shop. Furniture had indeed fallen; the place was a chaos of wrecked clocks and chairs, and in the midst of it the bulk of Tom Hustings lay, fallen on the smaller figure of Abanazer Bolger. Neither of them was moving.

"Are they dead?" asked Bod.

"No such luck," said Liza.

On the floor beside the men was a brooch of glittering silver; a crimson-orange-banded stone, held in place with claws and with snake-heads, and the expression on the snake-heads was one of triumph and avarice and satisfaction.

Bod dropped the brooch into his pocket, where it sat beside the heavy glass paperweight, the paintbrush, and the little pot of paint.

"Take this too," said Liza.

Bod looked at the black-edged card with the word *Jack* handwritten on one side. It disturbed him. There was something familiar about it, something that stirred old memories, something dangerous. "I don't want it."

"You can't leave it here with them," said Liza. "They were going to use it to hurt you."

"I don't want it," said Bod. "It's bad. Burn it."

"No!" Liza gasped. "Don't do that. You mustn't do that."

"Then I'll give it to Silas," said Bod. And he put the little card into an envelope so he had to touch it as little as possible, and put the envelope into the inside pocket of his old gardening jacket, beside his heart.

Two hundred miles away, the man Jack woke from his sleep, and sniffed the air. He walked downstairs.

"What is it?" asked his grandmother, stirring the contents of a big iron pot on the stove. "What's got into you now?"

"I don't know," he said. "Something's happening. Something . . . interesting." And then he licked his lips. "Smells tasty," he said. "Very tasty."

Lightning illuminated the cobbled street.

Bod hurried through the rain through the Old Town, always heading up the hill toward the graveyard. The grey day had become an early night while he was inside the storeroom, and it came as no surprise to him when a familiar shadow swirled beneath the street lamps. Bod hesitated, and a flutter of night-black velvet resolved itself into a man-shape.

Silas stood in front of him, arms folded. He strode forward, impatiently.

"Well?" he said.

Bod said, "I'm sorry, Silas."

"I'm disappointed in you, Bod," Silas said, and he shook his head. "I've been looking for you since I woke. You have the smell of trouble all around you. And you know you're not allowed to go out here, into the living world."

"I know. I'm sorry." There was rain on the boy's face, running down like tears.

"First of all, we need to get you back to safety." Silas reached down, and enfolded the living child inside his cloak, and Bod felt the ground fall away beneath him.

"Silas," he said.

Silas did not answer.

"I was a bit scared," he said. "But I knew you'd come and get me if it got too bad. And Liza was there. She helped a lot."

"Liza?" Silas's voice was sharp.

"The witch. From the Potter's Field."

"And you say she helped you?"

"Yes. She especially helped me with my Fading. I think I can do it now."

Silas grunted. "You can tell me all about it when we're home." And Bod was quiet until they landed beside the chapel. They went inside, into the empty hall, as the rain redoubled, splashing up from the puddles that covered the ground.

Bod produced the envelope containing the black-edged card. "Um," he said. "I thought you should have this. Well, Liza did, really."

Silas looked at it. Then he opened it, removed the card, stared at it, turned it over, and read Abanazer Bolger's penciled note to himself, in tiny handwriting, explaining the precise manner of use of the card.

"Tell me everything," he said.

Bod told him everything he could remember about the day. And at the end, Silas shook his head, slowly, thoughtfully.

"Am I in trouble?" asked Bod.

"Nobody Owens," said Silas. "You are indeed in trouble. However, I believe I shall leave it to your parents to administer whatever discipline and reproach they believe to be needed. In the meantime, I need to dispose of this."

The black-edged card vanished inside the velvet cloak, and then, in the manner of his kind, Silas was gone.

Bod pulled the jacket up over his head, and clambered up the slippery paths to the top of the hill, to the Frobisher mausoleum. He pulled aside Ephraim Pettyfer's coffin, and he went down, and down, and still further down.

He replaced the brooch beside the goblet and the knife.

"Here you go," he said. "All polished up. Looking pretty."

IT COMES BACK, said the Sleer, with satisfaction in its smoke-tendril voice. IT ALWAYS COMES BACK.

It had been a long night.

Bod was walking, sleepily and a little gingerly, past the small tomb of the wonderfully named Miss Liberty Roach (*What she spent is lost, what she gave remains with her always. Reader be Charitable*), past the final resting place of Harrison Westwood, Baker of this Parish, and his wives, Marion and Joan, to the Potter's Field. Mr. and Mrs.

Owens had died several hundred years before it had been decided that beating children was wrong and Mr. Owens had, regretfully, that night, done what he saw as his duty, and Bod's bottom stung like anything. Still, the look of worry on Mrs. Owens's face had hurt Bod worse than any beating could have done.

He reached the iron railings that bounded the Potter's Field, and slipped between them.

"Hullo?" he called. There was no answer. Not even an extra shadow in the hawthorn tree. "I hope I didn't get you into trouble, too," he said.

Nothing.

He had replaced the jeans in the gardener's hut—he was more comfortable in just his grey winding sheet—but he had kept the jacket. He liked having the pockets.

When he had gone to the shed to return the jeans, he had taken a small hand-scythe from the wall where it hung, and with it he attacked the nettle-patch in the Potter's Field, sending the nettles flying, slashing and gutting them till there was nothing but stinging stubble on the ground.

From his pocket he took the large glass paperweight, its insides a multitude of bright colors, along with the paint pot, and the paintbrush.

He dipped the brush into the paint and carefully painted, in brown paint, on the surface of the paperweight, the letters . . .

and beneath them he wrote . . .

we don't forget

Bedtime, soon, and it would not be wise for him to be late to bed for some time to come.

He put the paperweight down on the ground that had once been a nettle-patch, placed it in the place that he estimated her head would have been, and pausing only to look at his handiwork for a moment, he went through the railings and made his way, rather less gingerly, back up the hill.

"Not bad," said a pert voice from the Potter's Field, behind him. "Not bad at all."

But when he turned to look, there was no one there.

CHAPTER FIVE

Danse Macabre

SOMETHING WAS GOING ON, Bod was certain of it. It was there in the crisp winter air, in the stars, in the wind, in the darkness. It was there in the rhythms of the long nights and the fleeting days.

Mistress Owens pushed him out of the Owenses' little tomb. "Get along with you," she said. "I've got business to attend to."

Bod looked at his mother. "But it's cold out there," he said.

"I should hope so," she said, "it being winter. That's as it should be. Now," she said, more to herself than to Bod, "shoes. And look at this dress—it needs hemming. And cobwebs—there are cobwebs all over, for heaven's sakes. You get along," this to Bod once more. "I've plenty to be getting on with, and I don't need you underfoot."

And then she sang to herself, a little couplet Bod had never heard before.

"Rich man, poor man, come away.
Come to dance the Macabray."

"What's that?" asked Bod, but it was the wrong thing to have said, for Mistress Owens looked dark as a thundercloud, and Bod hurried out of the tomb before she could express her displeasure more forcefully.

It was cold in the graveyard, cold and dark, and the stars were already out. Bod passed Mother Slaughter in the ivy-covered Egyptian Walk, squinting at the greenery.

"Your eyes are younger than mine, young man," she said. "Can you see blossom?"

"Blossom? In winter?"

"Don't you look at me with that face on, young man," she said. "Things blossom in their time. They bud and bloom, blossom and fade. Everything in its time." She huddled deeper into her cloak and bonnet and she said,

Time to work and time to play,
Time to dance the Macabray. Eh, boy?"

"I don't know," said Bod. "What's the Macabray?"

But Mother Slaughter had pushed into the ivy and was gone from sight.

"How odd," said Bod, aloud. He sought warmth and company in the bustling Bartleby mausoleum, but the Bartleby family—seven generations of them—had no time for him that night. They were cleaning and tidying, all of them, from the oldest (d. 1831) to the youngest (d. 1690).

Fortinbras Bartleby, ten years old when he had died

(of *consumption*, he had told Bod, who had mistakenly believed for several years that Fortinbras had been eaten by lions or bears, and was extremely disappointed to learn it was merely a disease), now apologized to Bod.

"We cannot stop to play, Master Bod. For soon enough, *tomorrow night* comes. And how often can a man say that?"

"Every night," said Bod. "Tomorrow night *always* comes."

"Not *this* one," said Fortinbras. "Not once in a blue moon, or a month of Sundays."

"It's not Guy Fawkes Night," said Bod, "or Hallowe'en. It's not Christmas or New Year's Day."

Fortinbras smiled, a huge smile that filled his pie-shaped, freckly face with joy.

"None of *them*," he said. "*This* one's special."

"What's it called?" asked Bod. "What happens tomorrow?"

"It's the best day," said Fortinbras, and Bod was certain he would have continued but his grandmother, Louisa Bartleby (who was only twenty) called him over to her, and said something sharply in his ear.

"Nothing," said Fortinbras. Then to Bod, "Sorry. I have to work now." And he took a rag and began to buff the side of his dusty coffin with it. "La, la, la, *oomp*," he sang. "La la la, *oomp*." And with each "oomp," he would do a wild, whole-body flourish with his rag.

"Aren't you going to sing that song?"

"What song?"

"The one everybody's singing?"

147

"No time for that," said Fortinbras. "It's *tomorrow*, tomorrow, after all."

"No time," said Louisa, who had died in childbirth, giving birth to twins. "Be about your business."

And in her sweet, clear voice, she sang,

"One and all will hear and stay
Come and dance the Macabray."

Bod walked down to the crumbling little church. He slipped between the stones, and into the crypt, where he sat and waited for Silas to return. He was cold, true, but the cold did not bother Bod, not really: the graveyard embraced him, and the dead do not mind the cold.

His guardian returned in the small hours of the morning; he had a large plastic bag with him.

"What's in there?"

"Clothes. For you. Try them on." Silas produced a grey sweater the color of Bod's winding sheet, a pair of jeans, underwear, and shoes—pale green sneakers.

"What are they for?"

"You mean, apart from wearing? Well, firstly, I think you're old enough—what are you, ten years old now?— and normal, living people clothes are wise. You'll have to wear them one day, so why not pick up the habit right now? And they could also be camouflage."

"What's camouflage?"

"When something looks enough like something else that people watching don't know what it is they're looking at."

"Oh. I see. I think." Bod put the clothes on. The shoelaces

gave him a little trouble and Silas had to teach him how to tie them. It seemed remarkably complicated to Bod, and he had to tie and re-tie his laces several times before he had done it to Silas's satisfaction. Only then did Bod dare to ask his question.

"Silas. What's a Macabray?"

Silas's eyebrows raised and his head tipped to one side. "Where did you hear about that?"

"Everyone in the graveyard is talking about it. I think it's something that happens tomorrow night. What's a Macabray?"

"It's a dance, " said Silas.

"*All must dance the Macabray,*" said Bod, remembering. "Have you danced it? What kind of dance is it?"

His guardian looked at him with eyes like black pools and said, "I do not know. I know many things, Bod, for I have been walking this earth at night for a very long time, but I do not know what it is like to dance the Macabray. You must be alive or you must be dead to dance it—and I am neither."

Bod shivered. He wanted to embrace his guardian, to hold him and tell him that he would never desert him, but the action was unthinkable. He could no more hug Silas than he could hold a moonbeam, not because his guardian was insubstantial, but because it would be wrong. There were people you could hug, and then there was Silas.

His guardian inspected Bod thoughtfully, a boy in his new clothes. "You'll do," he said. "Now you look like

149

you've lived outside the graveyard all your life."

Bod smiled proudly. Then the smile stopped and he looked grave once again. He said, "But you'll always be here, Silas, won't you? And I won't ever have to leave, if I don't want to?"

"Everything in its season," said Silas, and he said no more that night.

Bod woke early the next day, when the sun was a silver coin high in the grey winter sky. It was too easy to sleep through the hours of daylight, to spend all his winter in one long night and never see the sun, and so each night before he slept he would promise himself that he would wake in daylight, and leave the Owenses' cozy tomb.

There was a strange scent in the air, sharp and floral. Bod followed it up the hill to the Egyptian Walk, where the winter ivy hung in green tumbles, an evergreen tangle that hid the mock-Egyptian walls and statues and hieroglyphs.

The perfume was heaviest there, and for a moment Bod wondered if snow might have fallen, for there were white clusters on the greenery. Bod examined a cluster more closely. It was made of small five-petaled flowers, and he had just put his head in to sniff the perfume when he heard footsteps coming up the path.

Bod Faded into the ivy, and watched. Three men and a woman, all alive, came up the path and into the Egyptian Walk. The woman had an ornate chain around her neck.

"Is this it?" she asked.

"Yes, Mrs. Caraway," said one of the men—chubby and white-haired and short of breath. Like each of the men, he carried a large, empty wicker basket.

She seemed both vague and puzzled. "Well, if you say so," she said. "But I cannot say that I understand it." She looked up at the flowers. "What do I do now?"

The smallest of the men reached into his wicker basket and brought out a tarnished pair of silver scissors. "The scissors, Lady Mayoress, " he said.

She took the scissors from him and began to cut the clumps of blossom, and she and the three men started to fill the baskets with the flowers.

"This is," said Mrs. Caraway, the Lady Mayoress, after a little while, "perfectly ridiculous."

"It *is*," said the fat man, "a *tradition*."

"Perfectly ridiculous," said Mrs. Caraway, but she continued to cut the white blossoms and drop them into the wicker baskets. When they had filled the first basket, she asked, "Isn't that enough?"

"We need to fill all four baskets," said the smaller man, "and then distribute a flower to everyone in the Old Town."

"And what kind of tradition is that?" said Mrs. Caraway. "I asked the Lord Mayor before me, and he said he'd never heard of it." Then she said, "Do you get a feeling someone's watching us?"

"What?" said the third man, who had not spoken until now. He had a beard and a turban and two wicker baskets.

"Ghosts, you mean? I do not believe in ghosts."

"Not ghosts," said Mrs. Caraway. "Just a feeling like someone's looking."

Bod fought the urge to push further back into the ivy.

"It's not surprising that the previous Lord Mayor did not know about this tradition," said the chubby man, whose basket was almost full. "It's the first time the winter blossoms have bloomed in eighty years."

The man with the beard and the turban, who did not believe in ghosts, was looking around him nervously.

"Everyone in the Old Town gets a flower," said the small man. "Man, woman, and child." Then he said, slowly, as if he were trying to remember something he had learned a very long time ago, *"One to leave and one to stay and all to dance the Macabray."*

Mrs. Caraway sniffed. "Stuff and nonsense," she said, and kept on snipping the blossoms.

Dusk fell early in the afternoon, and it was night by half past four. Bod wandered the paths of the graveyard, looking for someone to talk to, but there was no one about. He walked down to the Potter's Field to see if Liza Hempstock was about, but found no one there. He went back to the Owenses' tomb, but found it also deserted: neither his father nor Mistress Owens was anywhere to be seen.

Panic started then, a low-level panic. It was the first time in his ten years that Bod could remember feeling abandoned in the place he had always thought of as his home: he ran down the hill to the old chapel, where he waited for Silas.

Silas did not come.

"Perhaps I missed him," thought Bod, but he did not believe this. He walked up the hill to the very top, and looked out. The stars hung in the chilly sky, while the patterned lights of the city spread below him, streetlights and car headlights and things in motion. He walked slowly down from the hill until he reached the graveyard's main gates, and he stopped there.

He could hear music.

Bod had listened to all kinds of music: the sweet chimes of the ice-cream van, the songs that played on workmen's radios, the tunes that Claretty Jake played the dead on his dusty fiddle, but he had never heard anything like this before: a series of deep swells, like the music at the beginning of something, a prelude perhaps, or an overture.

He slipped through the locked gates, walked down the hill, and into the Old Town.

He passed the Lady Mayoress, standing on a corner, and as he watched, she reached out and pinned a little white flower to the lapel of a passing businessman.

"I don't make personal charitable donations," said the man. "I leave that to the office."

"It's not for charity," said Mrs. Caraway. "It's a local tradition."

"Ah," he said, and he pushed his chest out, displaying the little white flower to the world, and walked off, proud as Punch.

A young woman pushing a baby buggy was the next to go past.

"Wossit for?" she asked suspiciously, as the Mayoress approached.

"One for you, one for the little one," said the Mayoress.

She pinned the flower to the young woman's winter coat. She stuck the flower for the baby to its coat with tape.

"But wossit *for*?" asked the young woman.

"It's an Old Town thing," said the Lady Mayoress, vaguely. "Some sort of tradition."

Bod walked on. Everywhere he went he saw people wearing the white flowers. On the other street corners, he passed the men who had been with the Lady Mayoress, each man with a basket, handing out the white flowers. Not everyone took a flower, but most people did.

The music was still playing: somewhere, at the edge of perception, solemn and strange. Bod cocked his head to one side, trying to locate where it was coming from, without success. It was in the air and all around. It was playing in the flapping of flags and awnings, in the rumble of distant traffic, the click of heels on the dry paving stones . . .

And there was an oddness, thought Bod, as he watched the people heading home. They were walking in time to the music.

The man with the beard and the turban was almost out of flowers. Bod walked over to him.

"Excuse me," said Bod.

The man started. "I did not see you," he said, accusingly.

"Sorry," said Bod. "Can I have a flower as well?"

The man with the turban looked at Bod with suspicion. "Do you live around here?" he asked.

"Oh yes," said Bod.

The man passed Bod a white flower. Bod took it, then said, "Ow," as something stabbed into the base of his thumb.

"You pin it to your coat," said the man. "Watch out for the pin."

A bead of crimson was coming up on Bod's thumb. He sucked at it while the man pinned the flower to Bod's sweater. "I've never seen you around here," he told Bod.

"I live here, all right," said Bod. "What are the flowers for?"

"It was a tradition in the Old Town," said the man, "before the city grew up around it. When the winter flowers bloom in the graveyard on the hill they are cut and given out to everybody, man or woman, young or old, rich or poor."

The music was louder now. Bod wondered if he could hear it better because he was wearing the flower—he could make out a beat, like distant drums, and a skirling, hesitant melody that made him want to pick up his heels and march in time to the sound.

Bod had never walked anywhere as a sightseer before. He had forgotten the prohibitions on leaving the graveyard, forgotten that tonight in the graveyard on the hill the dead were no longer in their places; all that he thought of was the Old Town, and he trotted through it down to the municipal gardens in front of the Old Town Hall (which was now a museum and tourist information center, the town hall itself having moved into much more imposing, if newer and duller, offices halfway across the city).

There were already people around, wandering the municipal gardens—now in midwinter, little more than a large grassy field with, here and there, some steps, a shrub, a statue.

Bod listened to the music, entranced. There were people trickling into the square, in ones and twos, in families or alone. He had never seen so many living people at one time. There must have been hundreds of them, all of them breathing, each of them as alive as he was, each with a white flower.

Is this what living people do? thought Bod, but he knew that it was not: that *this*, whatever it was, was special.

The young woman he had seen earlier pushing a baby buggy stood beside him, holding her baby, swaying her head to the music.

"How long does the music go on for?" Bod asked her, but she said nothing, just swayed and smiled. Bod did not think she smiled much normally. And only when he was certain that she had not heard him, that he had Faded, or was simply not someone she cared enough about to listen to, she said, "Blimmen 'eck. It's like Christmases." She said it like a woman in a dream, as if she was seeing herself from the outside. In the same not-really-there tone of voice, she said, "Puts me in mind of me Gran's sister, Aunt Clara. The night before Christmas we'd go to her, after me Gran passed away, and she'd play music on her old piano, and she'd sing, sometimes, and we'd eat chocolates and nuts and I can't remember any of the songs she sung. But that music, it's like all of them songs playing at once."

The baby seemed asleep with its head on her shoulder, but even the baby was swaying its hands gently in time to the music.

And then the music stopped and there was silence in the square, a muffled silence, like the silence of falling snow, all noise swallowed by the night and the bodies in the square, no one stamping or shuffling, scarcely even breathing.

A clock began to strike somewhere close at hand: the chimes of midnight, and they came.

They walked down the hill in a slow procession, all stepping gravely, all in time, filling the road, five abreast. Bod knew them or knew most of them. In the first row, he recognized Mother Slaughter and Josiah Worthington, and the old earl who had been wounded in the Crusades and came home to die, and Doctor Trefusis, all of them looking solemn and important.

There were gasps from the people in the square. Someone began to cry, saying, "Lord have mercy, it's a judgment on us, that's what it is!" Most of the people simply stared, as unsurprised as they would have been if this had happened in a dream.

The dead walked on, row on row, until they reached the square.

Josiah Worthington walked up the steps until he reached Mrs. Caraway, the Lady Mayoress. He extended his arm and said, loud enough that the whole square could hear him, "Gracious lady, this I pray: Join me in the Macabray."

Mrs. Caraway hesitated. She glanced up at the man beside her for guidance: he wore a robe and pajamas and slippers, and he had a white flower pinned to the lapel of his robe. He smiled and nodded to Mrs. Caraway. "Of course," Mr. Caraway said.

She reached out a hand. As her fingers touched Josiah Worthington's, the music began once more. If the music Bod had heard until then was a prelude, it was a prelude no longer. This was the music they had all come to hear, a melody that plucked at their feet and fingers.

They took hands, the living with the dead, and they began to dance. Bod saw Mother Slaughter dancing with the man in the turban, while the businessman was dancing with Louisa Bartleby. Mistress Owens smiled at Bod as she took the hand of the old newspaper seller, and Mr. Owens reached out and took the hand of a small girl, without condescension, and she took his hand as if she had been waiting to dance with him her whole life. Then Bod stopped looking because someone's hand closed around his, and the dance began.

Liza Hempstock grinned at him. "This is fine," she said,

as they began to tread the steps of the dance together.

Then she sang, to the tune of the dance,

"Step and turn, and walk and stay,
Now we dance the Macabray."

The music filled Bod's head and chest with a fierce joy, and his feet moved as if they knew the steps already, had known them forever.

He danced with Liza Hempstock, and then, when that measure ended, he found his hand taken by Fortinbras Bartleby, and he danced with Fortinbras, stepping past lines of dancers, lines that parted as they came through.

Bod saw Abanazer Bolger dancing with Miss Borrows, his old former teacher. He saw the living dancing with the dead. And the one-on-one dances became long lines of people stepping together in unison, walking and kicking (*La-la-la-oomp*! *La-la-la-oomp!*) a line dance that had been ancient a thousand years before.

Now he was in the line beside Liza Hempstock. He said, "Where does the music come from?"

She shrugged.

"Who's making all this happen?"

"It always happens," she told him. "The living may not remember, but we always do . . ." And she broke off, excited. *"Look!"*

Bod had never seen a real horse before, only in the pages of picture books, but the white horse that clopped down the street towards them was nothing like the horses he had imagined. It was bigger, by far, with a long, serious face. There was a woman riding on the horse's bare back, wearing a long grey dress that hung and gleamed beneath the December moon like cobwebs in the dew.

She reached the square, and the horse stopped, and the woman in grey slipped off it easily and stood on the earth, facing them all, the living and the dead of them.

She curtseyed.

And, as one, they bowed or curtseyed in return, and the dance began anew.

"Now the Lady on the Grey
Leads us in the Macabray,"

sang Liza Hempstock, before the whirl of the dance took her off and away from Bod. They stomped to the music, and stepped and spun and kicked, and the lady danced with them, stepping and spinning and kicking with enthusiasm. Even the white horse swayed its head and stepped and shifted to the music.

The dance sped up, and the dancers with it. Bod was breathless, but he could not imagine the dance ever stopping: the Macabray, the dance of the living and the dead, the dance with Death. Bod was smiling, and everyone was smiling.

He caught sight of the lady in the grey dress from time to time, as he spun and stomped his way across the municipal gardens.

Everyone, thought Bod, *everyone is dancing!* He thought it, and as soon as he thought it he realized that he was mistaken. In the shadows by the Old Town Hall, a man was standing, dressed all in black. He was not dancing. He was watching them.

Bod wondered if it was longing that he saw on Silas's face, or sorrow, or something else, but his guardian's face was unreadable.

He called out, "Silas!" hoping to make his guardian come to them, to join the dance, to have the fun they were having, but when he heard his name, Silas stepped back into the shadows and was lost to sight.

"Last dance!" someone called, and the music skirled up into something stately and slow and final.

Each of the dancers took a partner, the living with the dead, each to each. Bod reached out his hand and found himself touching fingers with, and gazing into the grey eyes of, the lady in the cobweb dress.

She smiled at him.

"Hello, Bod," she said.

"Hello," he said, as he danced with her. "I don't know your name."

"Names aren't really important," she said.

"I love your horse. He's so big! I never knew horses could be that big."

"He is gentle enough to bear the mightiest of you away on his broad back, and strong enough for the smallest of you as well."

"Can I ride him?" asked Bod.

"One day," she told him, and her cobweb skirts shimmered. "One day. Everybody does."

"Promise?"

"I promise."

And with that, the dance was done. Bod bowed low to his dancing partner, and then, and only then, did he feel exhausted, feel as if he had been dancing for hour after hour. He could feel all his muscles aching and protesting. He was out of breath.

A clock somewhere began to strike the hour, and Bod counted along with it. Twelve chimes. He wondered if they had been dancing for twelve hours or twenty-four or for no time at all.

He straightened up, and looked around him. The dead had gone, and the Lady on the Grey. Only the living remained, and they were beginning to make their way home—leaving the town square sleepily, stiffly, like people who had awakened from a deep sleep, walking without truly waking.

The town square was covered with tiny white flowers. It looked as if there had been a wedding.

Bod woke the next afternoon in the Owenses' tomb feeling like he knew a huge secret, that he had done something important, and was burning to talk about it.

When Mistress Owens got up, Bod said, "That was amazing last night!"

Mistress Owens said, "Oh yes?"

"We danced," said Bod. "All of us. Down in the Old Town."

"Did we indeed?" said Mistress Owens, with a snort. "Dancing is it? And you know you aren't allowed down into the town."

Bod knew better than even to try to talk to his mother when she was in this kind of mood. He slipped out of the tomb into the gathering dusk.

He walked up the hill, to the black obelisk, and Josiah Worthington's stone, where there was a natural amphitheater, and he could look out at the Old Town and at the lights of the city around it.

Josiah Worthington was standing beside him.

Bod said, "You began the dance. With the Mayor. You danced with her."

Josiah Worthington looked at him and said nothing.

"You *did*," said Bod.

Josiah Worthington said, "The dead and the living do not mingle, boy. We are no longer part of their world; they are no part of ours. If it happened that we danced the *danse macabre* with them, the dance of death, then we would not speak of it, and we certainly would not to speak of it to the living."

"But *I'm* one of you."

"Not yet, boy. Not for a lifetime."

And Bod realized why he had danced as one of the living, and not as one of the crew that had walked down the hill, and he said only, "I see . . . I think."

He went down the hill at a run, a ten-year-old boy in a hurry, going so fast he almost tripped over Digby Poole

(1785–1860, *As I Am So Shall You Be*), righting himself by effort of will, and charged down to the old chapel, scared he would miss Silas, that his guardian would already be gone by the time Bod got there.

Bod sat down on the bench.

There was a movement beside him, although he heard nothing move, and his guardian said, "Good evening, Bod."

"You were there last night," said Bod. "Don't try and say you weren't there or something because I know you were."

"Yes," said Silas.

"I danced with her. With the lady on the white horse."

"Did you?"

"You saw it! You watched us! The living and the dead! We were dancing. Why won't anyone *talk* about it?"

"Because there are mysteries. Because there are things that people are forbidden to speak about. Because there are things they do not remember."

"But you're speaking about it right now. We're talking about the Macabray."

"I have not danced it," said Silas.

"You saw it, though."

Silas said only, "I don't know what I saw."

"I danced with the lady, Silas!" exclaimed Bod. His guardian looked almost heartbroken then, and Bod found himself scared, like a child who has woken a sleeping panther.

But all Silas said was, "This conversation is at an end."

Bod might have said something—there were a hundred

164

things he wanted to say, unwise though it might have been to say them—when something distracted his attention: a rustling noise, soft and gentle, and a cold feather-touch as something brushed his face.

All thoughts of dancing were forgotten then, and his fear was replaced with delight and with awe.

It was the third time in his life that he had seen it.

"Look, Silas, it's snowing!" he said, joy filling his chest and his head, leaving no room for anything else. "It's really snow!"

INTERLUDE

The Convocation

A SMALL SIGN IN THE hotel lobby announced that the Washington Room was taken that night by a private function, although there was no information as to what kind of function this might be. Truthfully, if you were to look at the inhabitants of the Washington Room that night, you would have no clearer idea of what was happening, although a rapid glance would tell you that there were no women in there. They were all men, that much was clear, and they sat at round dinner tables, and they were finishing their dessert.

There were about a hundred of them, all in sober black suits, but the suits were all they had in common. They had white hair or dark hair or fair hair or red hair or no hair at all. They had friendly faces or unfriendly, helpful or sullen, open or secretive, brutish or sensitive. The majority of them were pink-skinned, but there were black-skinned men and brown-skinned. They were European, African, Indian, Chinese, South American, Filipino, American. They

all spoke English when they talked to each other, or to the waiters, but the accents were as diverse as the gentlemen. They came from all across Europe and from all over the world.

The men in black suits sat around their tables while up on a platform one of their number, a wide, cheery man dressed in a morning suit, as if he had just come from a wedding, was announcing Good Deeds Done. Children from poor places had been taken on exotic holidays. A bus had been bought to take people who needed it on excursions.

The man Jack sat at the front center table, beside a dapper man with silver-white hair. They were waiting for coffee.

"Time's a-ticking," said the silver-haired man, "and we're none of us getting any younger."

The man Jack said, "I've been thinking. That business in San Francisco four years ago—"

"Was unfortunate, but like the flowers that bloom in the spring, tra-la, absolutely nothing to do with the case. You failed, Jack. You were meant to take care of them all. That included the baby. Especially the baby. *Nearly* only counts in horseshoes and hand-grenades."

A waiter in a white jacket poured coffee for each of the men at the table: a small man with a pencil-thin black mustache, a tall blond man good-looking enough to be a film star or a model, and a dark-skinned man with a huge head who glared out at the world like an angry bull. These

168

men were making a point of not listening to Jack's conversation, and instead were paying attention to the speaker, even clapping from time to time. The silver-haired man added several heaped spoonfuls of sugar to his coffee, stirred it briskly.

"Ten years," he said. "Time and tide wait for no man. The babe will soon be grown. And then what?"

"I still have time, Mister Dandy," the man Jack began, but the silver-haired man cut him off, stabbing a large pink finger in his direction.

"You *had* time. Now, you just have a deadline. Now, you've got to get smart. We can't cut you any slack, not any more. Sick of waiting, we are, every man Jack of us."

The man Jack nodded, curtly. "I have leads to follow," he said.

The silver-haired man slurped his black coffee. "Really?"

"Really. And I repeat, I think it's connected with the trouble we had in San Francisco."

"You've discussed this with the secretary?" Mr. Dandy indicated the man at the podium, who was, at that moment, telling them about hospital equipment bought in the previous year from their generosity. ("Not one, not two, but *three* kidney machines," he was saying. The men in the room applauded themselves and their generosity politely.)

The man Jack nodded. "I've mentioned it."

"And?"

"He's not interested. He just wants results. He wants me to finish the business I started."

169

"We all do, sunshine," said the silver-haired man. "The boy's still alive. And time is no longer our friend."

The other men at the table, who had pretended not to be listening, grunted and nodded their agreement.

"Like I say," Mr. Dandy said, without emotion. "Time's a-ticking."

CHAPTER SIX

Nobody Owens' School Days

RAIN IN THE GRAVEYARD, and the world puddled into blurred reflections. Bod sat, concealed from anyone, living or dead, who might come looking for him, under the arch that separated the Egyptian Walk and the northwestern wilderness beyond it from the rest of the graveyard, and he read his book.

"Damm'ee!" came a shout from down the path. "Damm'ee, sir, and blast your eyes! When I catch you—and find you I shall—I shall make you rue the day you were born!"

Bod sighed and he lowered the book, and leaned out enough to see Thackeray Porringer (1720–1734, *son of the above*) come stamping up the slippery path. Thackeray was a big boy—he had been fourteen when he died, following his initiation as an apprentice to a master house painter: he had been given eight copper pennies and told not to come back without a half-a-gallon of red and white striped paint for painting barber's poles. Thackeray had spent five hours

174

being sent all over the town one slushy January morning, being laughed at in each establishment he visited and then sent on to the next; when he realized he had been made a fool of, he had taken an angry case of apoplexy, which carried him off within the week, and he died glaring furiously at the other apprentices and even at Mr. Horrobin, the master painter, who had undergone so much worse back when *he* was a 'prentice that he could scarcely see what all the fuss was about.

So Thackeray Porringer had died in a fury, clutching his copy of *Robinson Crusoe* which was, apart from a silver sixpence with the edges clipped and the clothes he had formerly been standing up in, all that he owned, and, at his mother's request, he was buried with his book. Death had not improved Thackeray Porringer's temper, and now he was shouting, "I know you're here somewhere! Come out and take your punishment, you, you thief!"

Bod closed the book. "I'm not a thief, Thackeray. I'm only borrowing it. I promise I'll give the book back when I've finished it."

Thackeray looked up, saw Bod nestled behind the statue of Osiris. "I told you not to!"

Bod sighed. "But there are so few books here. It's just up to a good bit anyway. He's found a footprint. It's not his. That means someone else is on the island!"

"It's my book," said Thackeray Porringer, obstinately. "Give it back."

Bod was ready to argue or simply to negotiate, but he

saw the hurt look on Thackeray's face, and he relented. Bod clambered down the side of the arch, jumped the last few feet. He held out the book. "Here." Thackeray took it gracelessly, and glared.

"I could read it to you," offered Bod. "I could do that."

"You could go and boil your fat head," said Thackeray, and he swung a punch at Bod's ear. It connected, and it stung, although judging from the look on Thackeray Porringer's face, Bod realized it must have hurt his fist as much as it hurt Bod.

The bigger boy stomped off down the path, and Bod watched him go, ear hurting, eyes stinging. Then he walked though the rain back down the treacherous ivy-covered path. At one point he slipped and scraped his knee, tearing his jeans.

There was a willow-grove beside the wall, and Bod almost ran into Miss Euphemia Horsfall and Tom Sands, who had been stepping out together for many years. Tom had been buried so long ago that his stone was just a weathered rock, and he had lived and died during the Hundred Years War with France, while Miss Euphemia (1861–1883, *She Sleeps, Aye, Yet She Sleeps with Angels*) had been buried in Victorian times, after the graveyard had been expanded and extended and became, for some fifty years, a successful commercial enterprise, and she had a whole tomb to herself behind a black door in the Willow Walk. But the couple seemed to have no troubles with the difference in their historical periods.

"You should slow down, young Bod," said Tom. "You'll do yourself an injury."

"You already did," said Miss Euphemia. "Oh dear, Bod. I have no doubt that your mother will have words with you about that. It's not as if we can easily repair those pantaloons."

"Um. Sorry," said Bod.

"And your guardian was looking for you," added Tom.

Bod looked up at the grey sky. "But it's still daylight," he said.

"He's up betimes," said Tom, a word which, Bod knew, meant *early*, "and said to tell you he wanted you. If we saw you."

Bod nodded.

"There's ripe hazel-nuts in the thicket just beyond the Littlejohns' monument," said Tom with a smile, as if softening a blow.

"Thank you," said Bod. He ran on, pell-mell, through the rain and down the winding path into the lower slopes of the graveyard, running until he reached the old chapel.

The chapel door was open and Silas, who had love for neither the rain nor for the remnants of the daylight, was standing inside, in the shadows.

"I heard you were looking for me," said Bod.

"Yes," said Silas. Then, "It appears you've torn your trousers."

"I was running," said Bod. "Um. I got into a bit of a fight with Thackeray Porringer. I wanted to read *Robinson*

Crusoe. It's a book about a man on a boat—that's a thing that goes in the sea, which is water like an enormous puddle—and how the ship is wrecked on an island, which is a place on the sea where you can stand, and—"

Silas said, "It has been eleven years, Bod. Eleven years that you have been with us."

"Right," said Bod. "If you say so."

Silas looked down at his charge. The boy was lean, and his mouse-colored hair had darkened slightly with age.

Inside the old chapel, it was all shadows.

"I think," said Silas, "it is time to talk about where you came from."

Bod breathed in deeply. He said, "It doesn't have to be now. Not if you don't want to." He said it as easily as he could, but his heart was thudding in his chest.

Silence. Only the patter of the rain and the wash of the water from the drainpipes. A silence that stretched until Bod thought that he would break.

Silas said, "You know you're different. That you are alive. That we took you in—*they* took you in here—and that I agreed to be your guardian."

Bod said nothing.

Silas continued, in his voice like velvet, "You had parents. An older sister. They were killed. I believe that you were to have been killed as well, and that you were not was due to chance, and the intervention of the Owenses."

"And you," said Bod, who had had that night described to him over the years by many people, some of whom had

178

even been there. It had been a big night in the graveyard.

Silas said, "Out there, the man who killed your family is, I believe, still looking for you, still intends to kill you."

Bod shrugged. "So?" he said. "It's only death. I mean, all of my best friends are dead."

"Yes." Silas hesitated. "They are. And they are, for the most part, done with the world. You are not. You're *alive*, Bod. That means you have infinite potential. You can do anything, make anything, dream anything. If you change the world, the world will change. Potential. Once you're dead, it's gone. Over. You've made what you've made, dreamed your dream, written your name. You may be buried here, you may even walk. But that potential is finished."

Bod thought about this. It seemed almost true, although he could think of exceptions—his parents adopting him, for example. But the dead and the living were different, he knew that, even if his sympathies were with the dead.

"What about you?" he asked Silas.

"What about me?"

"Well, you aren't alive. And you go around and do things."

"I," said Silas, "am precisely what I am, and nothing more. I am, as you say, not alive. But if I am ended, I shall simply cease to be. My kind *are*, or we are *not*. If you see what I mean."

"Not really."

Silas sighed. The rain was done and the cloudy gloaming had become true twilight. "Bod," he said, "there are many

179

reasons why it is important that we keep you safe."

Bod said, "The person who hurt my family. The one who wants to kill me. You are certain that he's still out there?" It was something he had been thinking about for a while now, and he knew what he wanted.

"Yes. He's still out there."

"Then," said Bod, and said the unsayable, "I want to go to school."

Silas was imperturbable. The world could have ended, and he would not have turned a hair. But now his mouth opened and his brow furrowed, and he said only,

"What?"

"I've learned a lot in this graveyard," said Bod. "I can Fade and I can Haunt. I can open a ghoul-gate and I know the constellations. But there's a world out there, with the sea in it, and islands, and shipwrecks and pigs. I mean, it's filled with things I don't know. And the teachers here have taught me lots of things, but I need more. If I'm going to survive out there, one day."

Silas seemed unimpressed. "Out of the question. Here we can keep you safe. How could we keep you safe, out there? Outside, anything could happen."

"Yes," agreed Bod. "That's the potential thing you were talking about." He fell silent. Then, "Someone killed my mother and my father and my sister."

"Yes. Someone did."

"A man?"

"A man."

"Which means," said Bod, "you're asking the wrong question."

Silas raised an eyebrow. "How so?"

"Well," said Bod. "If I go outside in the world, the question isn't 'who will keep me safe from him?'"

"No?"

"No. It's 'who will keep him safe from me?'"

Twigs scratched against the high windows, as if they needed to be let in. Silas flicked an imaginary speck of dust from his sleeve with a fingernail as sharp as a blade. He said, "We will need to find you a school."

No one noticed the boy, not at first. No one even noticed that they hadn't noticed him. He sat halfway back in class. He didn't answer much, not unless he was directly asked a question, and even then his answers were short and forgettable, colorless: he faded, in mind and in memory.

"Do you think they're religious, his family?" asked Mr. Kirby, in the teachers' staff room. He was marking essays.

"Whose family?" asked Mrs. McKinnon.

"Owens in Eight B," said Mr. Kirby.

"The tall spotty lad?"

"I don't think so. Sort of medium height."

Mrs. McKinnon shrugged. "What about him?"

"Handwrites everything," said Mr. Kirby. "Lovely handwriting. What they used to call copperplate."

"And that makes him religious because . . . ?"

"He says they don't have a computer."

"And?"

"He doesn't have a phone."

"I don't see why that makes him religious," said Mrs. McKinnon, who had taken up crocheting when they had banned smoking in the staff room, and was sitting and crocheting a baby blanket for no one in particular.

Mr. Kirby shrugged. "He's a smart lad," he said. "There's just stuff he doesn't know. And in History he'll throw in little made-up details, stuff not in the books . . ."

"What kind of stuff?"

Mr. Kirby finished marking Bod's essay and put it down on the pile. Without something immediately in front of him the whole matter seemed vague and unimportant. "Stuff," he said, and forgot about it. Just as he forgot to enter Bod's name on the roll. Just as Bod's name was not to be found on the school databases.

The boy was a model pupil, forgettable and easily forgotten, and he spent much of his spare time in the back of the English class where there were shelves of old paperbacks, and in the school library, a large room filled with books and old armchairs, where he read stories as enthusiastically as some children ate.

Even the other kids forgot about him. Not when he was sitting in front of them: they remembered him then. But when that Owens kid was out of sight he was out of mind. They didn't think about him. They didn't need to. If someone asked all the kids in Eight B to close their eyes and list the twenty-five boys and girls in the class, that

Owens kid wouldn't have been on the list. His presence was almost ghostly.

It was different if he was there, of course.

Nick Farthing was twelve, but he could pass—and did sometimes—for sixteen: a large boy with a crooked smile, and little imagination. He was practical, in a basic sort of way, an efficient shoplifter, and occasional thug who did not care about being liked as long as the other kids, all smaller, did what he said. Anyway, he had a friend. Her name was Maureen Quilling, but everyone called her Mo, and she was thin and had pale skin and pale yellow hair, watery blue eyes, and a sharp, inquisitive nose. Nick liked to shoplift, but Mo told him what to steal. Nick could hit and hurt and intimidate, but Mo pointed him at the people who needed to be intimidated. They were, as she told him sometimes, a perfect team.

They were sitting in the corner of the library splitting their take of the year sevens' pocket money. They had eight or nine of the eleven-year-olds trained to hand over their pocket money every week.

"The Singh kid hasn't coughed up yet," said Mo. "You'll have to find him."

"Yeah," said Nick, "he'll pay."

"What was it he nicked? A CD?"

Nick nodded.

"Just point out the error of his ways," said Mo, who wanted to sound like the hard cases from the television.

"Easy," said Nick. "We're a good team."

"Like Batman and Robin," said Mo.

"More like Doctor Jekyll and Mister Hyde," said somebody, who had been reading, unnoticed, in a window seat, and he got up and walked out of the room.

Paul Singh was sitting on a windowsill by the changing rooms, his hands deep in his pockets, thinking dark thoughts. He took one hand out of his pocket, opened it, looked at the handful of pound coins, shook his head, closed his hand around the coins once more.

"Is that what Nick and Mo are waiting for?" somebody asked, and Paul jumped, scattering money all over the floor.

The other boy helped him pick the coins up, handed them over. He was an older boy, and Paul thought he had seen him around before, but he could not be certain. Paul said, "Are you with them? Nick and Mo?"

The other boy shook his head. "Nope. I think that they are fairly repulsive." He hesitated. Then he said, "Actually, I came to give you a bit of advice."

"Yeah?"

"Don't pay them."

"Easy for you to say."

"Because they aren't blackmailing me?"

The boy looked at Paul and Paul looked away, ashamed.

"They hit you or threatened you until you shoplifted a CD for them. Then they told you that unless you handed over your pocket money to them, they'd tell on you. What did they do, film you doing it?"

Paul nodded.

"Just say no," said the boy. "Don't do it."

"They'll kill me. And they said . . ."

"Tell them that you think the police and school authorities could be a lot more interested in a couple of kids who are getting younger kids to steal for them and then forcing them to hand over their pocket money than they ever would be in one kid forced to steal a CD against his will. That if they touch you again, you'll make the call to the police. And that you've written it all up, and if anything happens to you, anything at all, if you get a black eye or anything, your friends will automatically send it to the school authorities and the police."

Paul said, "But. I can't."

"Then you'll pay them your pocket money for the rest of your time in this school. And you'll stay scared of them."

Paul thought. "Why don't I just tell the police anyway?" he asked.

"Can if you like."

"I'll try it your way first," Paul said. He smiled. It wasn't a big smile, but it was a smile, right enough, his first in three weeks.

So Paul Singh explained to Nick Farthing just how and why he wouldn't be paying him any longer, and walked away while Nick Farthing just stood and didn't say anything, clenching and unclenching his fists. And the next day another five eleven-year-olds found Nick Farthing in the playground, and told him they wanted their money

185

back, all the pocket money they'd handed over in the previous month, or *they'd* be going to the police, and now Nick Farthing was an extremely unhappy young man.

Mo said, "It was *him. He* started it. If it wasn't for him . . . they'd never have thought of it on their own. He's the one we have to teach a lesson. Then they'll all behave."

"Who?" said Nick.

"The one who's always reading. The one from the library. Bob Owens. Him."

Nick nodded slowly. Then he said, "Which one is he?"

"I'll point him out to you," said Mo.

Bod was used to being ignored, to existing in the shadows. When glances naturally slip from you, you become very aware of eyes upon you, of glances in your direction, of attention. And if you barely exist in people's minds as another living person then being pointed to, being followed around . . . these things draw attention to themselves.

They followed him out of the school and up the road, past the corner newsagent, and across the railway bridge. He took his time, making certain that the two who were following him, a burly boy and a fair, sharp-faced girl, did not lose him, then he walked into the tiny churchyard at the end of the road, a miniature graveyard behind the local church and he waited beside the tomb of Roderick Persson and his wife Amabella, and also his second wife, Portunia, *(They Sleep to Wake Again)*.

"You're that kid," said a girl's voice. "Bob Owens. Well,

186

you're in really big trouble, Bob Owens."

"It's Bod, actually," said Bod, and he looked at them. "With a D. And you're Jekyll and Hyde."

"It was you," said the girl. "You got to the seventh formers."

"So we're going to teach you a lesson," said Nick Farthing, and he smiled without humor.

"I quite like lessons," said Bod. "If you paid more attention to yours, you wouldn't have to blackmail younger kids for pocket money."

Nick's brow crinkled. Then he said, "You're dead, Owens."

Bod shook his head, and he gestured around him. "I'm not actually," he said. "*They* are."

"Who are?" said Mo.

"The people in this place," said Bod. "Look. I brought you here to give you a choice—"

"You didn't bring us here," said Nick.

"You're here," said Bod. "I wanted you here. I came here. You followed me. Same thing."

Mo looked around nervously. "You've got friends here?" she asked.

Bod said, "You're missing the point, I'm afraid. You two need to stop this. Stop behaving like other people don't matter. Stop hurting people."

Mo grinned a sharp grin. "For heaven's sake," she said to Nick. "Hit him."

"I gave you a chance," said Bod. Nick swung a vicious fist

187

at Bod, who was no longer there, and Nick's fist slammed into the side of the gravestone.

"Where did he go?" said Mo. Nick was swearing and shaking his hand. She looked around the shadowy cemetery, puzzled. "He was here. You know he was."

Nick had little imagination, and he was not about to start thinking now. "Maybe he ran away," he said.

"He didn't run," said Mo. "He just wasn't there anymore." Mo had an imagination. The ideas were hers. It was twilight in a spooky churchyard, and the hairs on the back of her neck were prickling. "Something is really, really wrong," said Mo. Then she said, in a higher-pitched panicky voice, "We have to get out of here."

"I'm going to find that kid," said Nick Farthing. "I'm going to beat the stuffing out of him." Mo felt something unsettled in the pit of her stomach. The shadows seemed to move around them.

"Nick," said Mo, "I'm scared."

Fear is contagious. You can catch it. Sometimes all it takes is for someone to say that they're scared for the fear to become real. Mo was terrified, and now Nick was too.

Nick didn't say anything. He just ran, and Mo ran close on his heels. The streetlights were coming on as they ran back towards the world, turning the twilight into night, making the shadows into dark places in which anything could be happening.

They ran until they reached Nick's house, and they went inside and turned on all the lights, and Mo called her mother and demanded, half crying, to be picked up and driven the short distance to her own house, because she wasn't walking home that night.

Bod had watched them run with satisfaction.

"That was good, dear," said someone behind him, a tall woman in white. "A nice Fade, first. Then the Fear."

"Thank you," said Bod. "I hadn't even tried the Fear out on living people. I mean, I knew the theory, but. Well."

"It worked a treat," she said, cheerfully. "I'm Amabella Persson."

"Bod. Nobody Owens."

"The *live* boy? From the big graveyard on the hill? Really?"

"Um." Bod hadn't realized that anyone knew who he was beyond his own graveyard. Amabella was knocking on the side of the tomb. "Roddy? Portunia? Come and see who's here!"

There were three of them there, then, and Amabella was introducing Bod and he was shaking hands and saying, "Charmed, I am sure," because he could greet people politely over nine hundred years of changing manners.

"Master Owens here was frightening some children who doubtless deserved it," Amabella was explaining.

"Good show," said Roderick Persson. "Bounders guilty of reprehensible behavior, eh?"

"They were bullies," said Bod. "Making kids hand over their pocket money. Stuff like that."

"A Frightening is certainly a good beginning," said

Portunia Persson, who was a stout woman, much older than Amabella. "And what have you planned if it does not work?"

"I hadn't really thought—" Bod began, but Amabella interrupted.

"I should suggest that Dreamwalking might be the most efficient remedy. You *can* Dreamwalk, can you not?"

"I'm not sure," said Bod. "Mister Pennyworth showed me how, but I haven't really—well, there's things I only really know in theory, and—"

Portunia Persson said, "Dreamwalking is all very well, but might I suggest a good Visitation? That's the only language that these people understand."

"Oh," said Amabella. "A Visitation? Portunia my dear, I don't really think so—"

"No, you don't. Luckily, *one* of us thinks."

"I have to be getting home," said Bod, hastily. "They'll be worrying about me."

"Of course," said the Persson family, and "Lovely to meet you," and "A very good evening to you, young man." Amabella Persson and Portunia Persson glared at each other. Roderick Persson said, "If you'll forgive me asking, but your guardian. He is well?"

"Silas? Yes, he's fine."

"Give him our regards. I'm afraid a small churchyard like this, well, we're never going to meet an actual member of the Honour Guard. Still. It's good to know that they're there."

"Good night," said Bod, who had no idea what the man was talking about, but filed it away for later. "I'll tell him."

He picked up his bag of schoolbooks, and he walked home, taking comfort in the shadows.

Going to school with the living did not excuse Bod from his lessons with the dead. The nights were long, and sometimes Bod would apologize and crawl to bed exhausted before midnight. Mostly, he just kept going.

Mr. Pennyworth had little to complain of these days. Bod studied hard, and asked questions. Tonight Bod asked about Hauntings, getting more and more specific, which exasperated Mr. Pennyworth, who had never gone in for that sort of thing himself.

"How exactly do I make a cold spot in the air?" he asked, and "I think I've got Fear down, but how do I take it up all the way to Terror?" and Mr. Pennyworth sighed and hurrumphed and did his best to explain, and it was gone four in the morning before they were done.

Bod was tired at school the next day. The first class was History—a subject Bod mostly enjoyed, although he often had to resist the urge to say that it hadn't happened like that, not according to people who had been there anyway—but this morning Bod was fighting to stay awake.

He was doing all he could do to concentrate on the lesson, so he was not paying attention to much else going on around him. He was thinking about King Charles the First, and about his parents, of Mr. and Mrs. Owens and of the other family, the one he could not remember, when there was a knock on the door. The class and Mr. Kirby all looked to see who was there (it was a year seven, who had been sent to borrow a textbook). And as they turned, Bod felt something stab in the back of his hand. He did not cry out. He just looked up.

Nick Farthing grinned down at him, a sharpened pencil in his fist. "I'm not afraid of you," whispered Nick Farthing. Bod looked at the back of his hand. A small drop of blood welled up where the point of the pencil had punctured it.

Mo Quilling passed Bod in the corridor that afternoon, her eyes so wide he could see the whites all around them.

"You're weird," she said. "You don't have any friends."

"I didn't come here for friends," said Bod truthfully. "I came here to learn."

Mo's nose twitched. "Do you know how weird *that* is?" She asked. "Nobody comes to school to *learn*. I mean, you come because you have to."

Bod shrugged.

"I'm not afraid of you," she said. "Whatever trick you did yesterday. You didn't scare me."

"Okay," said Bod, and he walked on down the corridor.

He wondered if he had made a mistake, getting involved. He had made a mis-step in judgment, that was for certain. Mo and Nick had begun to talk about him, probably the year sevens had as well. Other kids were looking at him, pointing him out to each other. He was becoming a presence, rather than an absence, and that made him uncomfortable. Silas had warned him to keep a low profile, told him to go through school partly Faded, but everything was changing.

He talked to his guardian that evening, told him the whole story. He was not expecting Silas's reaction.

"I cannot believe," said Silas, "that you could have been so . . . so stupid. Everything I told you about remaining just this side of invisibility. And now you've become the talk of the school?"

"Well, what did you want me to do?"

"Not this," said Silas. "It's not like the olden times. They can keep track of you, Bod. They can find you." Silas's unmoving exterior was like the hard crust of rock over molten lava. Bod knew how angry Silas was only because he knew Silas. He seemed to be fighting his anger, controlling it.

Bod swallowed.

"What should I do?" he said, simply.

"Don't go back," said Silas. "This school business was an experiment. Let us simply acknowledge that it was not a successful one."

Bod said nothing. Then he said, "It's not just the learning stuff. It's the other stuff. Do you know how nice it is to be in a room filled with people and for all of them to be breathing?"

"It's not something in which I've ever taken pleasure," said Silas. "So. You don't go back to school tomorrow."

"I'm *not* running away. Not from Mo or Nick or school.

193

I'd leave here first."

"You will do as you are told, boy," said Silas, a knot of velvet anger in the darkness.

"Or what?" said Bod, his cheeks burning. "What would you do to keep me here? *Kill* me?" And he turned on his heel and began to walk down the path that led to the gates and out of the graveyard.

Silas began to call the boy back, then he stopped, and stood there in the night alone.

At the best of times his face was unreadable. Now his face was a book written in a language long forgotten, in an alphabet unimagined. Silas wrapped the shadows around him like a blanket, and stared after the way the boy had gone, and did not move to follow.

Nick Farthing was in his bed, asleep and dreaming of pirates on the sunny blue sea, when it all went wrong. One moment he was the captain of his own pirate ship—a happy place, crewed by obedient eleven-year-olds, except for the girls, who were all a year or two older than Nick and who looked especially pretty in their pirate costumes—and the next he was alone on the deck, and a huge, dark ship the size of an oil tanker, with ragged black sails and a skull for a figurehead, was crashing through the storm towards him.

And then, in the way of dreams, he was standing on the black deck of the new ship, and someone was looking down at him.

"You're not afraid of me," said the man standing over him.

Nick looked up. He *was* scared, in his dream, scared of this dead-faced man in pirate costume, his hand on the hilt of a cutlass.

"Do you think you're a pirate, Nick?" asked his captor, and suddenly something about him seemed familiar to Nick.

"You're that kid," he said. "Bob Owens."

"I," said his captor, "am Nobody. And you need to change. Turn over a new leaf. Reform. All that. Or things will get very bad for you."

"Bad how?"

"Bad in your head," said the Pirate King, who was now only the boy from his class and they were in the school hall, not the deck of the pirate ship, although the storm had not abated and the floor of the hall pitched and rolled like a ship at sea.

"This is a dream," Nick said.

"Of course it's a dream," said the other boy. "I would have to be some kind of monster to do this in real life."

"What can you do to me in a dream?" asked Nick. He smiled. "I'm not afraid of you. You've still got my pencil in the back of your hand." He pointed to the back of Bod's hand, at the black mark the graphite point had made.

"I was hoping it wouldn't have to be like this," said the other boy. He tipped his head on one side as if he was listening to something. "They're hungry," he said.

"What are?" asked Nick.

"The things in the cellar. Or belowdecks. Depends whether this is a school or a ship, doesn't it?"

Nick felt himself beginning to panic. "It isn't . . . spiders . . . is it?" he said.

"It might be," said the other boy. "You'll find out, won't you?"

Nick shook his head.

"No," he said. "*Please* no."

"Well," said the other boy. "It's all up to you, isn't it? Change your ways or visit the cellar."

The noise got louder—a scuttling sort of a scuffling noise, and while Nick Farthing had no idea what it was, he was utterly, completely certain that whatever it would turn out to be would be the most scary terrible thing he had ever—would ever—encounter . . .

He woke up screaming.

Bod heard the scream, a shout of terror, and felt the satisfaction of a job well done.

He was standing on the pavement outside Nick Farthing's house, his face damp from the thick night mist. He was exhilarated and exhausted: he had felt barely in control of the Dreamwalk, had been all too aware that there was nothing else in the dream but Nick and himself, and that all Nick had been scared of was a noise.

But Bod was satisfied. The other boy would hesitate before tormenting smaller kids.

And now?

Bod put his hands in his pockets and began to walk, not certain where he was going. He would leave the school, he thought, just as he had left the graveyard. He would go somewhere no one knew him, and he would sit in a library all day and read books and listen to people breathing. He wondered if there were still deserted islands in the world, like the one on which Robinson Crusoe had been shipwrecked. He could go and live on one of those.

Bod did not look up. If he had, he would have seen a pair of watery blue eyes watching him intently from a bedroom window.

He stepped into an alley, feeling more comfortable out of the light.

"Are you running away, then?" said a girl's voice.

Bod said nothing.

"That's the difference between the living and the dead, ennit?" said the voice. It was Liza Hempstock talking, Bod knew, although the witch-girl was nowhere to be seen. "The dead dun't disappoint you. They've had their life, done what they've done. We dun't change. The living, they always disappoint you, dun't they? You meet a boy who's all brave and noble, and he grows up to run away."

"That's not fair!" said Bod.

"The Nobody Owens I knew wouldn't've run off from the graveyard without saying so much as a fare-thee-well to those who cared for him. You'll break Mistress Owens's heart."

Bod had not thought of that. He said, "I had a fight with Silas."

"So?"

"He wants me to come back to the graveyard. To stop school. He thinks it's too dangerous."

"Why? Between your talents and my bespellment, they'll barely notice you."

"I was getting involved. There were these kids bullying other kids. I wanted them to stop. I drew attention to myself . . ."

Liza could be seen now, a misty shape in the alleyway keeping pace with Bod.

"He's out here, somewhere, and he wants you dead," she said. "Him as killed your family. Us in the graveyard, we wants you to stay alive. We wants you to surprise us and disappoint us and impress us and amaze us. Come home, Bod."

"I think . . . I said things to Silas. He'll be angry."

"If he didn't care about you, you couldn't upset him," was all she said.

The fallen autumn leaves were slick beneath Bod's feet, and the mists blurred the edges of the world. Nothing was as clean-cut as he had thought it, a few minutes before.

"I did a Dreamwalk," he said.

"How did it go?"

"Good," he said. "Well, all right."

"You should tell Mr. Pennyworth. He'll be pleased."

"You're right," he said. "I should."

He reached the end of the alley, and instead of turning right, as he had planned, and off into the world, he turned left, onto the High Street, the road that would take him back to Dunstan Road and the graveyard on the hill.

"What?" said Liza Hempstock. "What you doin'?"

"Going home," said Bod. "Like you said."

There were shop-lights now. Bod could smell the hot grease from the chip shop on the corner. The paving stones glistened.

"That's good," said Liza Hempstock, now only a voice once more. Then the voice said, "Run! Or Fade! Something's wrong!"

Bod was about to tell her that there was nothing wrong, that she was being foolish, when a large car with a light flashing on the top came veering across the road and pulled up in front of him.

Two men got out from it. "Excuse me, young man," said one of the men. "Police. Might I ask what you're doing out so late?"

"I didn't know there was a law against it," said Bod.

The largest of the policemen opened the rear door of the car. "Is this the young man you saw, Miss?" he said.

Mo Quilling got out of the car, and looked at Bod, and smiled. "That's him," she said. "He was in our back garden breaking things. And then he ran away." She looked Bod in the eye. "I saw you from my bedroom," she said. "I think he's the one who's been breaking windows."

"What's your name?" asked the smaller policeman. He

had a ginger mustache.

"Nobody," said Bod. Then, "Ow," because the ginger policeman had taken Bod's ear between finger and thumb, and had given it a hard squeeze. "Don't give me that," said the policeman. "Just answer the questions politely. Right?"

Bod said nothing.

"Where exactly do you live?" asked the policeman.

Bod said nothing. He tried to Fade, but Fading—even when boosted by a witch—relies on people's attention sliding away from you, and everybody's attention—not to mention a large pair of official hands—was on him then.

Bod said, "You can't arrest me for not telling you my name or address."

"No," said the policeman. "I can't. But I can take you down to the station until you give us the name of a parent, guardian, responsible adult, into whose care we can release you."

He put Bod into the back of the car, where Mo Quilling sat, with the smile on her face of a cat who has eaten all the canaries. "I saw you from my front window," she said, quietly. "So I called the police."

"I wasn't doing anything," said Bod. "I wasn't even in your garden. And why are they bringing you out to find me?"

"Quiet back there!" said the large policeman. Everyone was quiet until the car pulled up in front of a house that had to be Mo's. The large policeman opened the door for her, and she got out.

"We'll call you tomorrow, let your mom and dad know

what we found," said the large policeman.

"Thanks, Uncle Tam," said Mo, and she smiled. "Just doing my duty."

They drove back through the town in silence, Bod trying to Fade as best he could, with no success. He felt sick and miserable. In one evening, he had had his first real argument with Silas, had attempted to run away from home, had failed to run away, and now failed to return home. He could not tell the police where he lived, or his name. He would spend the rest of his life in a police cell, or in a prison for kids. *Did they have prison for kids?* he didn't know.

"Excuse me? Do they have prisons for kids?" he asked the men in the front seat.

"Getting worried, now, are you?" said Mo's uncle Tam. "I don't blame you. You kids. Running wild. Some of you need locking up, I'll tell you."

Bod wasn't sure if that was a yes or a no. He glanced out of the car window. Something huge was flying through the air, above the car and to one side, something darker and bigger than the biggest bird. Something man-size that flickered and fluttered as it moved, like the strobing flight of a bat.

The ginger policeman said, "When we get to the station, best if you just give us your name, tell us who to call to come and get you, we can tell them we gave you a bollocking, they can take you home. See? You cooperate, we have an easy night, less paperwork for everyone. We're your friends."

"You're too easy on him. A night in the cells isn't that hard," said the large policeman to his friend. Then he looked back at Bod, and said, "Unless it's a busy night, and we have to put you in with some of the drunks. *They* can be nasty."

Bod thought, *He's lying!* and *They're doing this on purpose, the friendly one and the tough one . . .*

Then the police car turned a corner, and there was a *thump!* Something big rode up onto the hood of the car and was knocked off into the dark. A screech of brakes as the car stopped, and the ginger policeman began to swear under his breath.

"He just ran out into the road!" he said. "You saw it!"

"I'm not sure what I saw," said the larger policeman. "You hit something, though."

They got out of the car, shone lights around. The ginger policeman said, "He was wearing black! You can't see it."

"He's over here," shouted the large policeman. The two men hurried over to the body on the ground, holding flashlights.

Bod tried the door handles on the backseat. They did not work. And there was a metal grille between the back and the front. Even if he Faded, he was still stuck in the backseat of a police car.

He leaned over as far as he could, craning to try and see what had happened, what was on the road.

The ginger policeman was crouched beside a body, looking at it. The other, the large one, was standing above it, shining a light down into its face.

Bod looked at the face of the fallen body—then he began to bang on the window, frantically, desperately.

The large policeman came over to the car.

"What?" he said, irritably.

"You hit my—my dad," said Bod.

"You're kidding."

"It looks like him," said Bod. "Can I look properly?"

The large policeman's shoulders slumped. "Oy! Simon, the kid says it's his dad."

"You've got to be bloody kidding me."

"I think he's serious." The large policeman opened the door, and Bod got out.

Silas was sprawled on his back, on the ground, where the car had knocked him. He was deathly still.

Bod's eyes prickled.

He said, "Dad?" Then he said, "You killed him." He wasn't lying, he told himself—not really.

"I've called an ambulance," said Simon, the ginger-mustached policeman.

"It was an accident," said the other.

Bod crouched by Silas, and he squeezed Silas's cold hand in his. If they had already called an ambulance there was not much time. He said, "So that's your careers over, then."

"It was an accident—you saw!"

"He just stepped out—"

"What I saw," said Bod, "is that you agreed to do a favor for your niece, and frighten a kid she's been fighting with

203

at school. So you arrested me without a warrant for being out late, and then when my dad runs out into the road to try and stop you or to find out what was going on, you intentionally ran him over."

"It was an accident!" repeated Simon.

"You've been fighting with Mo at school?" said Mo's uncle Tam, but he didn't sound convincing.

"We're both in Eight B at the Old Town School," said Bod. "And you killed my dad."

Far off, he could hear the sound of sirens.

"Simon," said the large man, "we have to talk about this."

They walked over to the other side of the car, leaving Bod alone in the shadows with the fallen Silas. Bod could hear the two policemen talking heatedly—"Your bloody niece!" was used, and so was "If *you'd* kept your eyes on the road!" Simon jabbed his finger into Tam's chest . . .

Bod whispered, "They aren't looking. Now." And he Faded.

There was a swirl of deeper darkness, and the body on the ground was now standing beside him.

Silas said, "I'll take you home. Put your arms around my neck."

Bod did, holding tightly to his guardian, and they plunged through the night, heading for the graveyard.

"I'm sorry," said Bod.

"I'm sorry too," said Silas.

"Did it hurt?" asked Bod. "Letting the car hit you like that?"

"Yes," said Silas. "You should thank your little witch-friend. She came and found me, told me you were in trouble, and what kind of trouble you were in."

They landed in the graveyard. Bod looked at his home as if it was the first time he had ever seen it. He said, "What happened tonight was stupid, wasn't it? I mean, I put things at risk."

"More things than you know, young Nobody Owens. Yes."

"You were right," said Bod. "I won't go back. Not to that school, and not like that."

Maureen Quilling had had the worst week of her life: Nick Farthing was no longer speaking to her; her uncle Tam had shouted at her about the Owens kid thing, then told her not to mention anything about that evening ever to anyone, as he could lose his job, and he wouldn't want to be in her shoes if that happened; her parents were furious with her; she felt betrayed by the world; even the year sevens weren't scared of her any longer. It was rotten. She wanted to see that Owens kid, who she blamed for everything that had happened to her so far, writhing in miserable agony. If he thought being *arrested* was bad . . . and then she would concoct elaborate revenge schemes in her head, complex and vicious. They were the only thing that made her feel better, and even they didn't really help.

If there was one job that gave Mo the creeps, it was cleaning up the science labs—putting away the Bunsen burners, making sure that all test tubes, petri dishes, unused filter papers and the like were returned to their places. She only had to do it, on a strict rotation system, once every two months, but it stood to reason that here, in the worst week of her life, she would be in the science lab.

At least Mrs. Hawkins, who taught general sciences, was there, collecting papers, gathering things up at the end of the day. Having her there, having anybody there, was comforting.

"You're doing a good job, Maureen," said Mrs. Hawkins.

A white snake in a jar of preservative stared blindly down at them. Mo said, "Thanks."

"Aren't there meant to be two of you?" asked Mrs. Hawkins.

"I was supposed to be doing it with the Owens kid," said Mo. "But he hasn't been to school in days now."

The teacher frowned. "Which one was he?" she asked, absently. "I don't have him down on my list."

"Bob Owens. Brownish hair, a bit too long. Didn't talk much. He was the one who named all the bones of the skeleton in the quiz. Remember?"

"Not really," admitted Mrs. Hawkins.

"You must remember! Nobody remembers him! Not even Mr. Kirby!"

Mrs. Hawkins pushed the rest of the sheets of paper into her bag and said, "Well, I appreciate you doing it on your own, dear. Don't forget to wipe down the working surfaces, before you go." And she went, closing the door behind her.

The science labs were old. There were long, dark wooden tables, with gas jets and taps and sinks built in to them, and there were dark wooden shelves upon which were displayed a selection of things in large bottles. The things that floated in the bottles were dead, had been dead for a long time. There was even a yellowed human skeleton in one corner of the room: Mo did not know if it was real or not, but right now it was creeping her out.

Every noise she made echoed, in that long room. She turned all of the overhead lights on, even the light on the whiteboard, just to make the place less scary. The room began to feel cold. She wished she could turn up the heat. She walked over to one of the large metal radiators and touched it. It was burning hot. But still, she was shivering.

The room was empty and unsettling in its emptiness, and Mo felt as if she were not alone, as if she was being watched.

Well, of course I'm being watched, she thought. *A hundred dead things in jars are all looking at me, not to mention the skeleton*. She glanced up at the shelves.

That was when the dead things in the jars began to move. A snake with unseeing milky eyes uncoiled in its alcohol-filled jar. A faceless, spiny sea creature twisted and revolved in its liquid home. A kitten, dead for decades, showed its teeth and clawed the glass.

Mo closed her eyes. *This isn't happening*, she told herself. *I'm imagining it*. "I'm not frightened," she said, aloud.

"That's good," said someone, standing in the shadows,

by the rear door. "It seriously sucks to be frightened."

She said, "None of the teachers even remember you."

"But you remember me," said the boy, the architect of all her misfortunes.

She picked up a glass beaker and threw it at him, but her aim went wide and it smashed against a wall.

"How's Nick?" asked Bod, as if nothing had happened.

"You know how he is," she said. "He won't even talk to me. Just shuts up in class, goes home and does his homework. Probably building model railways."

"Good," he said.

"And you," she said. "You haven't been at school for a week. You're in such trouble, Bob Owens. The police came in the other day. They were looking for you."

"That reminds me . . . How's your uncle Tam?" said Bod.

Mo said nothing.

"In some ways," said Bod, "you've won. I'm leaving school. And in other ways, you haven't. Have you ever been haunted, Maureen Quilling? Ever looked in the mirror wondering if the eyes looking back at you were yours? Ever sat in an empty room, and realized you were not alone? It's not pleasant."

"You're going to haunt me?" Her voice trembled.

Bod said nothing at all. He just stared at her. In the far corner of the room, something crashed: her bag had slipped off the chair onto the floor and when she looked back, she was alone in the room. Or, at least, there was nobody that she could see in there with her.

Her way home was going to be very long and very dark.

The boy and his guardian stood at the top of the hill, looking out at the lights of the town.

"Does it still hurt?" asked the boy.

"A little," said his guardian. "But I heal fast. I'll soon be as good as ever."

"Could it have killed you? Stepping out in front of that car?"

His guardian shook his head. "There are ways to kill people like me," he said. "But they don't involve cars. I am very old and very tough."

Bod said, "I *was* wrong, wasn't I? The whole idea was to do it without anybody noticing. And then I had to get involved with the kids in the school, and the next thing you know, there's police and all sorts of stuff. Because I was selfish."

Silas raised an eyebrow. "You weren't selfish. You need to be among your own kind. Quite understandable. It's just harder out there in the world of the living, and we cannot protect you out there as easily. I wanted to keep you perfectly safe," said Silas. "But there is only one perfectly safe place for your kind and you will not reach it until all your adventures are over and none of them matter any longer."

Bod rubbed his hand over the stone of Thomas R. Stout (1817–1851. *Deeply regretted by all who knew him*), feeling the moss crumble beneath his fingers.

"He's still out there," said Bod. "The man who killed my first family. I still need to learn about people. Are you going to stop me leaving the graveyard?"

"No. That was a mistake and one that we have both learned from."

"Then what?"

"We should do our best to satisfy your interest in stories and books and the world. There are libraries. There are other ways. And there are many situations in which there might be other, living people around you, like the theater or the cinema."

"What's that? Is it like football? I enjoyed watching them play football at school."

"Football. Hmm. That's usually a little early in the day for me," said Silas. "But Miss Lupescu could take you to see a football match the next time she's here."

"I'd like that," said Bod.

They began to walk down the hill. Silas said, "We have both left too many tracks and traces in the last few weeks. They are still looking for you, you know."

"You said that before," said Bod. "How do you know? And who *are* they? And what do they want?"

But Silas only shook his head, and would be drawn no further, and with that, for the time being, Bod had to be satisfied.

CHAPTER SEVEN

Every Man Jack

SILAS HAD BEEN PREOCCUPIED for the previous several months. He had begun to leave the graveyard for days, sometimes weeks, at a time. Over Christmas, Miss Lupescu had come out for three weeks in his place, and Bod had shared her meals in her little flat in the Old Town. She had even taken him to a football match, as Silas had promised that she would, but she had gone back to the place she called "The Old Country" after squeezing Bod's cheeks and calling him *Nimeni*, which had become her pet name for him.

Now Silas was gone, and Miss Lupescu also. Mr. and Mrs. Owens were sitting in Josiah Worthington's tomb talking to Josiah Worthington. None of them was happy.

Josiah Worthington said, "You mean to say that he did not tell either of you where he was going or how the child was to be cared for?"

When the Owenses shook their heads, Josiah Worthington said, "Well, where *is* he?"

Neither Owens was able to answer. Master Owens said, "He's never been gone for so long before. And he promised, when the child came to us, promised he would be here, or someone else would be here to help us care for him. He *promised*."

Mrs. Owens said, "I worry that something must have happened to him." She seemed close to tears, and then her tears turned to anger, and she said, "This is too bad of him! Is there no way to find him, to call him back?"

"None that I know," said Josiah Worthington. "But I believe that he's left money in the crypt, for food for the boy."

"Money!" said Mrs. Owens. "What use is *money?*"

"Bod will be needing money if he's to go out there to buy food," began Mr. Owens, but Mrs. Owens turned on him.

"You're all as bad as each other!" she said.

She left the Worthington tomb, then, and she went looking for her son, whom she found, as she expected to, at the top of the hill, staring out over the town.

"Penny for your thoughts," said Mrs. Owens.

"You don't have a penny," said Bod. He was fourteen, now, and taller than his mother.

"I've got two in the coffin," said Mrs. Owens. "Probably a bit green by now, but I've still got them right enough."

"I was thinking about the world," said Bod. "How do we even know that the person who killed my family is still

215

alive? That he's out there?"

"Silas says he is," said Mrs. Owens.

"But Silas doesn't tell us anything else."

Mrs. Owens said, "He means only the best for you. You know that."

"Thanks," said Bod, unimpressed. "So where is he?"

Mrs. Owens made no reply.

Bod said, "You saw the man who killed my family, didn't you? On the day you adopted me."

Mrs. Owens nodded.

"What was he like?"

"Mostly, I had eyes for you. Let me see . . . he had dark hair, very dark. And I was frightened of him. He had a sharp face. Hungry and angry all at once, he was. Silas saw him off."

"Why didn't Silas just kill him?" said Bod, fiercely. "He should have just killed him then."

Mrs. Owens touched the back of Bod's hand with her cold fingers. She said, "He's not a monster, Bod."

"If Silas had killed him back then, I would be safe now. I could go anywhere."

"Silas knows more than you do about all this, more than any of us do. And Silas knows about life and death," said Mrs. Owens. "It's not that easy."

Bod said, "What was his name? The man who killed them."

"He didn't say it. Not then."

Bod put his head on one side, and stared at her with eyes

as grey as thunderclouds. "But you know it, don't you?"

Mrs. Owens said, "There's nothing you can do, Bod."

"There is. I can learn. I can learn *everything* I need to know, all I can. I learned about ghoul-gates. I learned to Dreamwalk. Miss Lupescu taught me how to watch the stars. Silas taught me silence. I can Haunt. I can Fade. I know every inch of this graveyard."

Mrs. Owens reached out a hand, touched her son's shoulder. "One day," she said . . . and then she hesitated. One day, she would not be able to touch him. One day, he would leave them. One day. And then she said, "Silas told me the man who killed your family was called Jack."

Bod said nothing. Then he nodded. "Mother?"

"What is it, son?"

"When will Silas come back?"

The midnight wind was cold and it came from the north.

Mrs. Owens was no longer angry. She feared for her son. She said only, "I wish I knew, my darling boy, I wish I knew."

Scarlett Amber Perkins was fifteen, and, at that moment, sitting on the upper deck of the elderly bus, she was a mass of angry hate. She hated her parents for splitting up. She hated her mother for moving away from Scotland, hated her father because he didn't seem to care that she had gone. She hated this town for being so different—nothing like Glasgow, where she had grown up—and she hated it because every now and again she would turn a corner and

217

see something and the world would all become achingly, horribly familiar.

She had lost it with her mother that morning. "At least in Glasgow I had friends!" Scarlett had said, and she wasn't quite shouting and she wasn't quite sobbing. "I'll never see them again!" All her mother had said in reply was, "At least you're somewhere you've been before. I mean, we lived here when you were little."

"I don't remember," said Scarlett. "And it's not like I still know anyone. Do you want me to find my old friends from when I was five? Is *that* what you want?"

And her mother said, "Well, I'm not stopping you."

Scarlett had gone through the whole of the school day angry, and she was angry now. She hated her school and she hated the world, and right now she particularly hated the town bus service.

Every day, when school was over, the 97 bus to the City Center would take her from her school gates all the way to the end of the street where her mother had rented a small flat. She had waited at the bus-stop on that gusty April day for almost half an hour and no 97 buses had appeared, so when she saw a 121 bus with *City Center* as its destination she had climbed aboard. But where her bus always turned right, this one turned left, into the Old Town, past the municipal gardens in the Old Town square, past the statue of Josiah Worthington, Bart., and then crept up a winding hill lined with high houses, as Scarlett's heart sank and her anger was replaced with misery.

She walked downstairs, edged forward, eyed the sign telling her not to speak to the driver when the vehicle was in motion, and said, "Excuse me. I wanted to go to Acacia Avenue."

The driver, a large woman, her skin even darker than Scarlett's said, "You should have got the 97, then."

"But this goes to the City Center."

"Eventually. But even when you get there, you'll still need to get back." The woman sighed. "Best thing you can do, get off here, walk back down the hill, there's a bus-stop in front of the town hall. From there, you can catch the number 4 or the 58, both of them will take you most of the way to Acacia Avenue. You could get off by the sports center and walk up from there. You got all that?"

"The 4 or the 58."

"I'll let you off here." It was a request stop on the side of the hill, just past a large pair of open iron gates, and it looked uninviting and dismal. Scarlett stood in the open doorway of the bus until the bus driver said, "Go on. Hop it." She stepped down onto the pavement and the bus belched black smoke and roared away.

The wind rattled the trees on the other side of the wall.

Scarlett began to walk back down the hill—*this* was why she needed a mobile phone, she thought. If she was so much as five minutes late, her mother would *freak*, but she still wouldn't buy Scarlett a phone of her own. Oh well. She would have to endure another shouting match. It wouldn't be the first and it wouldn't be the last.

By now she was level with the open gates. She glanced inside and . . .

"That's odd," she said, aloud.

There's an expression, *déja vu*, that means that you feel like you've been somewhere before, that you've somehow already dreamed it or experienced it in your mind. Scarlett had experienced it—the knowledge that a teacher was just about to tell them that she'd been to Inverness on holiday, or that someone had dropped a spoon in just that way before. This was different. This wasn't a feeling that she had been here before. This was the real thing.

Scarlett walked through the open gates into the graveyard.

A magpie flew up as she walked in, a flash of black and white and iridescent green, and settled in the branches of a yew tree, watching her. *Around that corner*, she thought, *is a church, with a bench in front of it*, and she turned a corner to see a church—much smaller than the one in her head, a sinister blocky little Gothic building of grey stone, with a jutting spire. In front of it was a weathered wooden bench. She walked over, sat down on the bench, and swung her legs as if she was still a little girl.

"Hullo. Um, hullo?" said a voice from behind her. "Awful cheek of me, I know, but would you help me hold down this, er, just really need another pair of hands, if it's not too much trouble."

Scarlett looked around, and saw a man in a fawn-colored raincoat squatting in front of a gravestone. He was holding a large sheet of paper which was blowing about in the wind. She hurried over to him.

"You hold on to it here," said the man. "One hand here, one hand there, that's it. Frightful imposition, I know. Ridiculously grateful."

He had a biscuit tin next to him, and from the tin he pulled what looked like a crayon the size of a small candle. He began rubbing it back and forth across the stone with easy, practiced movements.

"There we go," he said, cheerfully. "And here she comes . . . oops. A wiggly bit, down at the bottom here, I think it's meant to be ivy—the Victorians loved putting ivy on things, deeply symbolic you know . . . and there we are. You can let go now."

He stood up, ran one hand through his grey hair. "Ow. Needed to stand. Legs got a bit pins-and-needlesy," he said. "So. What do you reckon to that?"

The actual headstone was covered in green and yellow lichen, and so worn and faded as to almost be undecipherable, but the rubbing was clear. "Majella Godspeed, Spinster of this Parish, 1791–1870, *Lost to All But Memory*," Scarlett read aloud.

"And probably now lost even to that," said the man. His hair was thinning, and he smiled hesitantly and blinked at her through small, round glasses which made him look a little like a friendly owl.

A large raindrop splashed down on the paper, and the man hurriedly rolled it up and grabbed his tin box of crayons. Another handful of raindrops, and Scarlett picked up the portfolio the man pointed to, propped up beside a nearby gravestone, and followed him into the tiny porch of the church, where the rain could not touch them.

"Thank you so much," said the man. "I don't think it's really going to rain much. Weather forecast for this afternoon said mostly sunny."

As if in reply, the wind gusted coldly and the rain began to beat down in earnest.

"I know what you're thinking," the gravestone-rubbing man said to Scarlett.

"You do?" she said. She had been thinking, *My mum will kill me*.

"You're thinking, is this a church or a funeral chapel? And the answer is, as far as I can ascertain, that on this site there was indeed a small church, and the original graveyard would have been its churchyard. That's as long ago as eight, perhaps nine hundred A.D. Rebuilt and extended several times in there. But there was a fire here in the 1820s and by that time it was already much too small for the area. People around here were using St. Dunstan's in the village square as their parish church, so when they came to rebuild here, they made it a funeral chapel, keeping many of the original features—the stained glass windows in the far wall are said to be original . . ."

"Actually," said Scarlett, "I was thinking that my mum is going to kill me. I got the wrong bus and I am already so late home . . ."

"Good Lord, you poor thing," said the man. "Look, I only live just down the road. You wait here—" And with that he thrust his portfolio, his tin of crayons, and his rolled-up sheet of paper into her hands and he set off at a trot down to the gates, his shoulders hunched against the driving rain. A couple of minutes later, Scarlett saw the lights of a car and heard the sound of a car horn.

Scarlett ran down to the gates, where she could see the car, an elderly green Mini. The man she had been talking to was sitting in the driver's seat. He wound down his window.

"Come on," he said. "Where exactly am I taking you?"

Scarlett stood there, the rain running down her neck. "I don't take rides from strangers," she said.

"Quite right too," said the man. "But one good turn deserves, and, um, all that. Here, put the stuff in the back before it gets soaked." He pulled open the passenger door, and Scarlett leaned inside and put his graverubbing equipment down on the backseat as best she could. "Tell you what," he said. "Why don't you phone your mother—you can use my phone—and tell her my car's number plate? You can do it from inside the car. You're getting soaked out there."

Scarlett hesitated. Rain was beginning to plaster her hair down. It was cold.

The man reached over and handed her his mobile phone. Scarlett looked at it. She realized she was more afraid of calling her mother than she was of getting into the car. Then she said, "I could call the police too, couldn't I?"

"You certainly can, yes. Or you can walk home. Or you can just call your mother and ask her to come and pick you up."

Scarlett got into the passenger seat and closed the door. She kept hold of the man's phone.

"Where do you live?" the man asked.

"You really don't have to. I mean, you could just take me to the bus stop . . ."

"I'll take you home. Address?"

"102a Acacia Avenue. It's off the main road, a wee bit past the big sports center . . ."

"You *are* out of your way, aren't you? Right. Let's get you home." He took off the handbrake, swung the car around, and drove down the hill.

"Been living here long?" he said.

"Not really. We moved here just after Christmas. We lived here when I was five, though."

"Is that a brogue I detect in your accent?"

"We've been living in Scotland for ten years. There, I sounded like everyone else, and then I came down here, and now I stick out like a sore thumb." She had wanted it to sound like a joke, but it was true, and she could hear it as she said it. Not funny, just bitter.

The man drove to Acacia Avenue, parked in front of the house, then insisted on coming up to the front door with her. When the door was opened he said, "Frightfully sorry. I took the liberty of bringing your daughter back to you. Obviously, you taught her well, shouldn't accept rides from strangers. But, well, it was raining, she took the wrong bus, wound up on the other side of town. Bit of a mess all around really. Say you can find it in your heart to forgive. Forgive her. And, um, me."

Scarlett expected her mother to shout at both of them, and was surprised and relieved when her mother only said, Well, you couldn't be too careful these days, and was Mr. Um a teacher, and would he like a cup of tea?

Mr. Um said his name was Frost, but she should call him Jay, and Mrs. Perkins smiled and said he should call her Noona, and she'd put the kettle on.

Over tea, Scarlett told her mother the story of her wrong bus adventure, and how she had found herself at the graveyard, and how she met Mr. Frost by the little church . . .

Mrs. Perkins dropped her teacup.

They were sitting around the table in the kitchen, so the cup didn't fall very far, and it didn't break, just spilled tea. Mrs. Perkins apologized awkwardly, and went and got a cloth from the sink to mop it up.

Then she said, "The graveyard on the hill, in the Old Town? That one?"

"I live over that way," said Mr. Frost. "Been doing a lot of grave-rubbings. And you know it's technically a nature reserve?"

Mrs. Perkins said, "I know," thin-lipped. Then she said, "Thank you so much for giving Scarlett a ride home, Mr.

Frost." Each word might have been an ice cube. Then, "I think you should leave now."

"I say, that's a bit much," said Frost, amiably. "Didn't mean to hurt your feelings. Was it something I said? The rubbings, they're for a local history project, it's not as if I'm, you know, digging up bones or anything."

For a heartbeat, Scarlett thought that her mother was going to strike Mr. Frost, who just looked worried. But Mrs. Perkins shook her head and said, "Sorry, family history. Not your fault." As if she was making a conscious effort, she said, brightly, "You know, Scarlett actually used to play in that graveyard when she was little. This is, oh, ten years ago. She had an imaginary friend, too. A little boy called Nobody."

A smile twitched at the corner of Mr. Frost's lips. "A ghostie?"

"No, I don't think so. He just lived there. She even pointed out the tomb he lived in. So I suppose he *was* a ghost. Do you remember, love?"

Scarlett shook her head. "I must have been a funny kid," she said.

"I'm sure that you were nothing of the, um," said Mr. Frost. "You are raising a fine girl here, Noona. Well, lovely cup of tea. Always a joy to make new friends. I'll be toddling off now. Got to make myself a little dinner, then I've got a meeting of the Local History Society."

"You're making your own dinner?" said Mrs. Perkins.

"Yes, making it. Well, defrosting it really. I'm also a

226

master of the boil-in-the-bag. Eating for one. Living on my own. Bit of a crusty old bachelor. Actually, in the papers, that always means gay, doesn't it? Not gay, just never met the right woman." And for a moment, he looked rather sad.

Mrs. Perkins, who hated to cook, announced that she always cooked too much food at the weekend, and as she ushered Mr. Frost out into the hall, Scarlett heard him agree that he would love to come round for dinner on Saturday night.

When Mrs. Perkins came back from the front hall, all she said to Scarlett was, "I hope you've done your homework."

Scarlett was thinking about the afternoon's events as she lay in bed that night listening to the sound of the cars grinding their way along the main road. She *had* been there, in that graveyard, when she was little. That was why everything had seemed so familiar.

In her mind she imagined and she remembered, and somewhere in there she fell asleep, but in sleep she still walked the paths of the graveyard. It was night, but she could see everything as clearly as if it were day. She was on the side of a hill. There was a boy of about her own age standing with his back to her, looking at the lights of the city.

Scarlett said, "Boy? What're you doing?"

He looked around, seemed to have trouble focusing. "Who said that?" and then, "Oh, I can see you, sort of. Are you Dreamwalking?"

"I think I'm dreaming," she agreed.

227

"Not quite what I meant," said the boy. "Hullo. I'm Bod."

"I'm Scarlett," she said.

He looked at her again, as if he were seeing her for the first time. "Of course, you are! I knew you looked familiar. You were in the graveyard today with that man, the one with the paper."

"Mr. Frost," she said. "He's really nice. He gave me a lift home." Then she said, "Did you see us?"

"Yeah. I keep an eye on most things that happen in the graveyard."

"What kind of a name is Bod?" she asked.

"It's short for Nobody."

"Of course!" said Scarlett. "That's what this dream is about. You're my imaginary friend, from when I was little, all grown up."

He nodded.

He was taller than she was. He wore grey, although she could not have described his clothes. His hair was too long, and she thought it had been some time since he had received a haircut.

He said, "You were really brave. We went deep into the hill and we saw the Indigo Man. And we met the Sleer."

Something happened, then, in her head. A rushing and a tumbling, a whirl of darkness and a crash of images . . .

"I *remember*," said Scarlett. But she said it to the empty darkness of her bedroom, and heard nothing in reply but the low trundle of a distant lorry, making its way through the night.

* * *

Bod had stores of food, the kind that lasted, cached in the crypt, and more in some of the chillier tombs and vaults and mausoleums. Silas had made sure of that. He had enough food to keep him going for a couple of months. Unless Silas or Miss Lupescu was there, he simply would not leave the graveyard.

He missed the world beyond the graveyard gates, but he knew it was not safe out there. Not yet. The graveyard, though, was his world and his domain, and he was proud of it and loved it as only a fourteen-year-old boy can love anything.

And yet . . .

In the graveyard, no one ever changed. The little children Bod had played with when he was small were still little children; Fortinbras Bartleby, who had once been his best friend, was now four or five years younger than Bod was, and they had less to talk about each time they saw each other; Thackeray Porringer was Bod's height and age, and seemed to be in much better temper with him; he would walk with Bod in the evenings, and tell stories of unfortunate things that had happened to his friends. Normally the stories would end in the friends being hanged until they were dead for no offense of theirs and by mistake, although sometimes they were simply transported to the American Colonies and they didn't have to be hanged unless they came back.

Liza Hempstock, who had been Bod's friend for the last

six years, was different in another way; she was less likely to be there for him when Bod went down to the nettle-patch to see her, and on the rare occasions when she was, she would be short-tempered, argumentative, and often downright rude.

Bod talked to Mr. Owens about this, and, after a few moments' reflection, his father said, "It's just women, I reckon. She liked you as a boy, probably isn't sure who you are now you're a young man. I used to play with one little girl down by the duck-pond every day until she turned about your age, and then she threw an apple at my head and did not say another word to me until I was seventeen."

Mrs. Owens sniffed. "It was a pear I threw," she said, tartly, "and I was talking to you again soon enough, for we danced a measure at your cousin Ned's wedding, and that was but two days after your sixteenth birthday."

Mr. Owens said, "Of course you are right, my dear." He winked at Bod, to tell him that it was none of it serious. And then he mouthed "Seventeen," to show that, really, it was.

Bod had allowed himself no friends among the living. That way, he had realized back during his short-lived schooldays, lay only trouble. Still, he had remembered Scarlett, had missed her for years after she went away, had long ago faced the fact he would never see her again. And now she had been here in his graveyard, and he had not known her . . .

He was wandering deeper into the tangle of ivy and trees

that made the graveyard's northwest quadrant so danger-ous. Signs advised visitors to keep out, but the signs were not needed. It was uninviting and creepy once you were past the ivy-tangle that marked the end of the Egyptian Walk and the black doors in the mock-Egyptian walls that led to people's final resting places. In the northwest, nature had been reclaiming the graveyard for almost a hundred years, and the stones were tipped over, graves were forgot-ten or simply lost beneath the green ivy and the leaf-fall of fifty years. Paths were lost and impassable.

Bod walked with care. He knew the area well, and he knew how dangerous it could be.

When Bod was nine he had been exploring in just this part of the world when the soil had given way beneath him, tumbling him into a hole almost twenty feet down. The grave had been dug deep, to accommodate many coffins, but there was no headstone and only one coffin, down at the bottom, containing a rather excitable medical gentleman named Carstairs who seemed thrilled by Bod's arrival and insisted on examining Bod's wrist (which Bod had twisted in the tumble, grabbing onto a root) before he could be persuaded to go and fetch help.

Bod was making his way through the northwest quad-rant, a sludge of fallen leaves, a tangle of ivy, where the foxes made their homes and fallen angels stared up blindly, because he had an urge to talk to the Poet.

Nehemiah Trot was the Poet's name, and his grave-stone, beneath the greenery, read:

Here lies the mortal remains of

NEHEMIAH TROT

POET

1741–1774

SWANS SING BEFORE THEY DIE

Bod said, "Master Trot? Might I ask you for advice?"

Nehemiah Trot beamed, wanly. "Of course, brave boy. The advice of poets is the cordiality of kings! How may I smear unction on your, no, not unction, how may I give balm to your pain?"

"I'm not actually in pain. I just—well, there's a girl I used to know, and I wasn't sure if I should find her and talk to her or if I should just forget about it."

Nehemiah Trot drew himself up to his full height, which was less than Bod's, raised both hands to his chest excitedly, and said, "Oh! You must go to her and implore her. You must call her your Terpsichore, your Echo, your Clytemnestra. You must write poems for her, mighty odes—I shall help you write them—and thus—and only thus—shall you win your true love's heart."

"I don't actually need to win her heart. She's not my true love," said Bod. "Just someone I'd like to talk to."

"Of all the organs," said Nehemiah Trot, "the tongue is the most remarkable. For we use it both to taste our sweet wine and bitter poison, thus also do we utter words both sweet and sour with the same tongue. Go to her! Talk to her!"

"I shouldn't."

"You should, sir! You must! I shall write about it, when the battle's lost and won."

"But if I Unfade for one person, it makes it easier for other people to see me . . ."

Nehemiah Trot said, "Ah, list to me, young Leander, young Hero, young Alexander. If you dare nothing, then when the day is over, nothing is all you will have gained."

"Good point." Bod was pleased with himself, and glad he had thought of asking the Poet for advice. *Really*, he thought, *if you couldn't trust a poet to offer sensible advice, who could you trust?* Which reminded him . . .

"Mister Trot?" said Bod. "Tell me about revenge."

"Dish best served cold," said Nehemiah Trot. "Do not take revenge in the heat of the moment. Instead, wait until the hour is propitious. There was a Grub Street hack named O'Leary—an Irishman, I should add—who had the nerve, the confounded cheek to write of my first slim volume of poems, *A Nosegay of Beauty Assembled for Gentlemen of Quality*, that it was inferior doggerel of no worth whatsoever, and that the paper it was written on would have been better used as—no, I cannot say. Let us simply agree that it was a most vulgar statement."

"But you got your revenge on him?" asked Bod, curious.

"On him and on his entire pestilent breed! Oh, I had my revenge, Master Owens, and it was a terrible one. I wrote, and had published, a letter, which I nailed to the doors of the public houses in London where such low scribbling folk were wont to frequent. And I explained that, given the fragility of the genius poetical, I would henceforth write not for them, but only for myself and posterity, and that I should, as long as I lived, publish no more poems—for them! Thus I left instructions that upon my death my poems were to be buried with me, unpublished, and that only when posterity realized my genius, realized that hundreds of my verses had been lost—lost!—only then was my coffin to be disinterred, only then could my poems be removed from my cold dead hand, to finally be published to the approbation and delight of all. It is a terrible thing to be ahead of your time."

"And after you died, they dug you up, and they printed the poems?"

"Not yet, no. But there is still plenty of time. Posterity is vast."

"So . . . that was your revenge?"

"Indeed. And a mightily powerful and cunning one at that!"

"Ye-es," said Bod, unconvinced.

"Best. Served. Cold," said Nehemiah Trot, proudly.

Bod left the northwest of the graveyard, returned through the Egyptian Walk to the more orderly paths and untangled ways, and as the dusk fell, he wandered back towards the old chapel—not because he hoped Silas had returned from his travels, but because he had spent his life visiting the chapel at dusk, and it felt good to have a rhythm. And anyway, he was hungry.

Bod slipped through the crypt door, down into the

crypt. He moved a cardboard box filled with curled and damp parish papers and took out a carton of orange juice, an apple, a box of bread sticks, and a block of cheese, and he ate while pondering how and whether he would seek out Scarlett—he would Dreamwalk, perhaps, since that was how she had come to him . . .

He headed outside, was on his way to sit on the grey wooden bench, when he saw something and he hesitated. There was someone already there, sitting on his bench. She was reading a magazine.

Bod Faded even more, became a part of the graveyard, no more important than a shadow or a twig.

But she looked up. She looked straight at him, and she said, "Bod? Is that you?"

He said nothing. Then he said, "Why can you see me?"

"I almost couldn't. At first I thought you were a shadow or something. But you look like you did in my dream. You sort of came into focus."

He walked over to the bench. He said, "Can you actually read that? Isn't it too dark for you?"

Scarlett closed the magazine. She said, "It's odd. You'd think it would be too dark, but I could read it fine, no problem."

"Are you . . ." He trailed off, uncertain of what he had wanted to ask her. "Are you here on your own?"

She nodded. "I helped Mr. Frost do some grave-rubbings, after school. And then I told him I wanted to sit and think here, for a bit. When I'm done here, I promised

235

to go and have a cup of tea with him and he'll run me home. He didn't even ask why. Just said he loves sitting in graveyards too, and that he thinks they can be the most peaceful places in the world." Then she said, "Can I hug you?"

"Do you want to?" said Bod.

"Yes."

"Well. then." He thought for a moment. "I don't mind if you do."

"My hands won't go through you or anything? You're really there?"

"You won't go through me," he told her, and she threw her arms around him and squeezed him so tightly he could hardly breathe. He said, "That hurts."

Scarlett let go. "Sorry."

"No. It was nice. I mean. You just squeezed more than I was expecting."

"I just wanted to know if you were real. All these years I thought you were just something in my head. And then I sort of forgot about you. But I *didn't* make you up, and you're back, you're in my head, and you're in the world too."

Bod smiled. He said, "You used to wear a sort of a coat, it was orange, and whenever I saw that particular color orange, I'd think of you. I don't suppose you still have the coat."

"No," she said. "Not for a long time. It would be a wee bit too small for me now."

"Yes," said Bod. "Of course."

"I should go home," said Scarlett. "I thought I could come up on the weekend, though." And then, seeing the expression on Bod's face, she said, "Today's Wednesday."

"I'd like that."

She turned to go. Then she said, "How will I find you, next time?"

Bod said, "I'll find you. Don't worry. Just be on your own and I'll find you."

She nodded, and was gone.

Bod walked back into the graveyard and up the hill, until he reached the Frobisher mausoleum. He did not enter it. He climbed up the side of the building, using the thick ivy root as a foothold, and he pulled himself up onto the stone roof, where he sat and thought looking out at the world of moving things beyond the graveyard, and he remembered the way that Scarlett had held him and how safe he had felt, if only for a moment, and how fine it would be to walk safely in the lands beyond the graveyard, and how good it was to be master of his own small world.

Scarlett said that she didn't want a cup of tea, thank you. Or a chocolate biscuit. Mr. Frost was concerned.

"Honestly," he told her, "you look like you've seen a ghost. Well, a graveyard, not a bad place to see one, if you were going to, um, I had an aunt once who claimed her parrot was haunted. She was a scarlet macaw. The parrot. The aunt was an architect. Never knew the details."

"I'm fine," said Scarlett. "It was just a long day."

"I'll give you a lift home then. Any idea what this says? Been puzzling over it for half an hour." He indicated a grave-rubbing on the little table, held flat by a jam jar in each corner. "Is that name Gladstone, do you think? Could be a relative of the prime minister. But I can't make out anything else."

"'Fraid not," said Scarlett. "But I'll take another look when I come out on Saturday."

"Is your mother likely to put in an appearance?"

"She said she'd drop me off here in the morning. Then she has to go and get groceries for our dinner. She's cooking a roast chicken."

"Do you think," asked Mr. Frost, hopefully, "there are likely to be roast potatoes?"

"I expect so, yes."

Mr. Frost looked delighted. Then he said, "I wouldn't want to put her out of her way, I mean."

"She's loving it," said Scarlett, truthfully. "Thank you for giving me a lift home."

"More than welcome," said Mr. Frost. They walked together down the steps in Mr. Frost's high narrow house, to the little entrance hall at the bottom of the stairs.

In Krakow, on Wawel Hill, there are caves called the Dragon's Den, named after a long dead dragon. These are the caves that the tourists know about. There are caves beneath those caves that the tourists do not know and do not ever get to visit. They go down a long way, and they are inhabited.

Silas went first, followed by the grey hugeness of Miss Lupescu, padding quietly on four feet just behind him. Behind them was Kandar, a bandage-wrapped Assyrian mummy with powerful eagle-wings and eyes like rubies, who was carrying a small pig.

There had originally been four of them, but they had lost Haroun in a cave far above, when the Ifrit, as naturally overconfident as are all of its race, had stepped into a space bounded by three polished bronze mirrors and had been swallowed up in a blaze of bronze light. In moments the Ifrit could only be seen in the mirrors, and no longer in reality. In the mirrors his fiery eyes were wide open, and his mouth was moving as if he was shouting at them to leave and beware, and then he faded and was lost to them.

Silas, who had no problems with mirrors, had covered one of them with his coat, rendering the trap useless.

"So," said Silas. "Now there are only three of us."

"And a pig," said Kandar.

"Why?" asked Miss Lupescu, with a wolf-tongue, through wolf teeth. "Why the pig?"

"It's lucky," said Kandar.

Miss Lupescu growled, unconvinced.

"Did Haroun have a pig?" asked Kandar, simply.

"Hush," said Silas. "They are coming. From the sound of it, there are many of them."

239

"Let them come," whispered Kandar.

Miss Lupescu's hackles were rising. She said nothing, but she was ready for them, and it was only by an effort of will that she did not throw back her head and howl.

"It's beautiful up this way," said Scarlett.

"Yes," said Bod.

"So, your family were all killed?" said Scarlett. "Does anyone know who did it?"

"No. Not that I know. My guardian only says that the man who did it is still alive, and that he'll tell me the rest of what he knows one day."

"One day?"

"When I'm ready."

"What's he scared of? That you'd strap on your gun and ride out to wreak vengeance on the man who killed your family?"

Bod looked at her seriously. "Well, obviously," he said. "Not a gun, though. But yes. Something like that."

"You're joking."

Bod said nothing. His lips were tight-pressed together. He shook his head. Then he said, "I'm not joking."

It was a bright and sunny Saturday morning. They were just past the entrance to the Egyptian Walk, out of the direct sunlight, under the pines and the sprawling monkey puzzle tree.

"Your guardian. Is he a dead person too?"

Bod said, "I don't talk about him."

Scarlett looked hurt. "Not even to me?"

"Not even to you."

"Well," she said. "Be like that."

Bod said, "Look, I'm sorry, I didn't mean—" just as Scarlett said, "I promised Mr. Frost I wouldn't be too long. I'd better be getting back."

"Right," said Bod, worried he had offended her, unsure what he should say to make anything better.

He watched Scarlett head off on the winding path back to the chapel. A familiar female voice said, with derision, "Look at her! Miss high and mighty!" but there was no one to be seen.

Bod, feeling awkward, walked back to the Egyptian Walk. Miss Lillibet and Miss Violet had let him store a cardboard box filled with old paperback books in their vault, and he wanted to find something to read.

Scarlett helped Mr. Frost with his grave-rubbings until midday, when they stopped for lunch. He offered to buy her fish and chips as a thank-you, and they walked down to the fish and chip shop at the bottom of the road, and as they walked back up the hill they ate their steaming fish and chips, drenched in vinegar and glittering with salt, out of paper bags.

Scarlett said, "If you wanted to find out about a murder, where would you look? I already tried the Internet."

"Um. Depends. What kind of murder are we talking about?"

"Something local, I think. About thirteen or fourteen years ago. A family was killed around here."

"Crikey," said Mr. Frost. "This really happened?"

"Oh yes. Are you all right?"

"Not really. Bit too, well, bit of a wimp, really. Things like that, I mean, local true crime, you don't like to think about it. Things like that, happening here. Not something I'd expect a girl of your age to be interested in."

"It's not actually for me," admitted Scarlett. "It's for a friend."

Mr. Frost finished off the last of his fried cod. "The library, I suppose. If it's not on the Internet, it'll be in their newspaper files. What set you off after this?"

"Oh." Scarlett wanted to lie as little as possible. She said, "A boy I know. He was asking about it."

"Definitely the library," said Mr. Frost. "Murder. Brr. Gives me the shivers."

"Me too," said Scarlett. "A bit." Then, hopefully, "Could you maybe, possibly, drop me off at the library, this afternoon?"

Mr. Frost bit a large chip in half, chewed it, and looked at the rest of the chip, disappointed. "They get cold so fast, don't they, chips. One minute, you're burning your mouth on them, the next you're wondering how they cool off so quickly."

"I'm sorry," said Scarlett. "I shouldn't be asking for rides everywhere—"

"Not at all," said Mr. Frost. "Just wondering how best to

organize this afternoon, and whether or not your mother likes chocolates. Bottle of wine or chocolates? Not really sure. Both maybe?"

"I can make my own way home from the library," said Scarlett. "And she loves chocolates. So do I."

"Chocolates it is, then," said Mr. Frost, relieved. They had reached the middle of the row of high, terraced houses on the hill, and the little green Mini parked outside. "Get in. I'll run you over to the library."

The library was a square building, all brick and stone, dating back to the beginning of the last century. Scarlett looked around, and then went up to the desk.

The woman said, "Yes?"

Scarlett said, "I wanted to see some old newspaper clippings."

"Is it for school?" said the woman.

"It's local history," said Scarlett, nodding, proud that she hadn't actually lied.

"We've got the local paper on microfiche," said the woman. She was large, and had silver hoops in her ears. Scarlett could feel her heart pounding in her chest; she was certain she looked guilty or suspicious, but the woman led her into a room with boxes that looked like computer screens, and showed her how to use them, to project a page of the newspaper at a time onto the screen. "One day we'll have it all digitized," said the woman. "Now, what dates are you after?"

"About thirteen or fourteen years ago," said Scarlett. "I can't be more specific than that. I'll know it when I see it."

The woman gave Scarlett a small box with five years' worth of newspapers on microfilm in it. "Go wild," she said.

Scarlett assumed that the murder of a family would have been front page news but instead, when she eventually found it, it was almost buried on page five. It had happened in October, thirteen years earlier. There was no color in the article, no description, just an understated list of events: *Architect Ronald Dorian, 36, his wife, Carlotta, 34, a publisher, and their daughter, Misty, 7, were found dead at 33 Dunstan Road. Foul play is suspected. A police spokesman said that it was too early to comment at this stage in their investigations, but that significant leads are being followed.*

There was no mention of how the family died, and nothing said about a missing baby. In the weeks that followed, there was no follow-up, and the police did not ever comment, not that Scarlett could see.

But that was it. She was certain: 33 Dunstan Road. She knew the house. She had been in there.

She returned the box of microfilm to the front desk, thanked the librarian, and walked home in the April sunshine. Her mother was in the kitchen cooking—not entirely successfully, judging from the smell of burnt-bottom-of-the-saucepan that filled most of the flat. Scarlett retreated to her bedroom and opened the windows wide to let the burnt smell out, then she sat on her bed and made a phone call.

"Hello? Mr. Frost?"

"Scarlett. Everything still all right for this evening? How's your mother?"

"Oh, it's all under control," said Scarlett, which was what her mother had said when she had asked. "Um, Mr. Frost, how long have you lived at your house?"

"How long? About, well, four months now."

"How did you find it?"

"Estate agents' window. It was empty and I could afford it. Well, more or less. Well, I wanted something within walking distance of the graveyard, and this was perfect."

"Mister Frost." Scarlett wondered how to say it, and then just said it. "About thirteen years ago, three people were murdered in your house. The Dorian family."

There was a silence at the other end of the phone.

"Mister Frost? Are you there?"

"Um. Still here, Scarlett. Sorry. Not the sort of thing you expect to hear. It's an old house, I mean, you expect things to happen a long time ago. But not . . . well, what happened?"

Scarlett wondered how much she could tell him. She said, "There was a little piece on it in an old newspaper, it only gave the address and nothing else. I don't know how they died or anything."

"Well. Good lord." Mr. Frost sounded more intrigued by the news than Scarlett could have expected. "This, young Scarlett, is where we local historians come into our own. Leave it with me. I'll find out everything I can and report back."

"Thank you," said Scarlett, relieved.

"Um. I assume this phone call is because if Noona thought there were murders going on in my home, even thirteen-year-old ones, you'd never be allowed to see me or the graveyard again. So, um, suppose I won't mention it unless you do."

"Thank you, Mr. Frost!"

"See you at seven. With chocolates."

Dinner was remarkably pleasant. The burnt smell had gone from the kitchen. The chicken was good, the salad was better, the roast potatoes were too crispy, but a delighted Mr. Frost had proclaimed that this was precisely the way he liked them, and had taken a second helping.

The flowers were popular, the chocolates, which they had for dessert, were perfect, and Mr. Frost sat and talked then watched television with them until about 10 P.M., when he said that he needed to get home.

"Time, tide, and historical research wait for no man," he said. He shook Noona's hand with enthusiasm, winked at Scarlett conspiratorially, and was out the door.

Scarlett tried to find Bod in her dreams that night; she thought of him as she went to sleep, imagined herself walking the graveyard looking for him, but when she did dream it was of wandering around Glasgow city center with her friends from her old school. They were hunting for a specific street, but all they found was a succession of dead ends, one after another.

* * *

Deep beneath the hill in Krakow, in the deepest vault beneath the caves they call the Dragon's Den, Miss Lupescu stumbled and fell.

Silas crouched beside her and cradled Miss Lupescu's head in his hands. There was blood on her face, and some of it was hers.

"You must leave me," she said. "Save the boy." She was halfway now, halfway between grey wolf and woman, but her face was a woman's face.

"No," said Silas. "I won't leave you."

Behind him, Kandar cradled its piglet like a child might hold a doll. The mummy's left wing was shattered, and it would never fly again, but its bearded face was implacable.

"They will come back, Silas," Miss Lupescu whispered. "Too soon, the sun will rise."

"Then," said Silas, "we must deal with them before they are ready to attack. Can you stand?"

"*Da*. I am one of the Hounds of God," said Miss Lupescu. "I will stand." She lowered her face into the shadows, flexed her fingers. When she raised her head again, it was a wolf's head. She put her front paws down on the rock, and, laboriously, pushed herself up into a standing position: a grey wolf bigger than a bear, her coat and muzzle flecked with blood.

She threw back her head and howled a howl of fury and of challenge. Her lips curled back from her teeth and she lowered her head once more. "Now," growled Miss Lupescu. "We end this."

Late on Sunday afternoon the telephone rang. Scarlett was sitting downstairs, laboriously copying faces from the manga she had been reading onto scrap paper. Her mother picked up the phone.

"Funny, we were just talking about you," said her mother, although they hadn't been. "It was wonderful," her mother continued. "I had the best time. Honestly, it was no trouble. The chocolates? They were perfect. Just perfect. I told Scarlett to tell you, any time you want a good dinner, you just let me know." And then, "Scarlett? Yes, she's here. I'll put her on. *Scarlett?*"

"I'm just here, Mum," said Scarlett. "You don't have to shout." She took the phone. "Mister Frost?"

"Scarlett?" He sounded excited. "The. Um. The thing we were talking about. The thing that happened in my house. You can tell this friend of yours that I found out—um, listen, when you said 'a friend of yours' did you mean it in the sense of 'we're actually talking about you,' or is there a real person, if it's not a personal question—"

"I've got a real friend who wants to know," said Scarlett, amused.

Her mother shot her a puzzled look.

"Tell your friend that I did some digging—not literally, more like rummaging, well, a fair amount of actual looking around—and I think I might have unearthed some very real information. Stumbled over something hidden. Well, not something I think we should spread around . . . I, um.

I found things out."

"Like what?" asked Scarlett.

"Look . . . don't think I'm mad. But, well, as far as I can tell, three people were killed. One of them—the baby, I think—wasn't. It wasn't a family of three, it was a family of four. Only three of them died. Tell him to come and see me, your friend. I'll fill him in."

"I'll tell him," said Scarlett. She put down the phone, her heart beating like a snare.

Bod walked down the narrow stone stairs for the first time in six years. His footsteps echoed in the chamber inside the hill.

He reached the bottom of the steps and waited for the Sleer to manifest. And he waited, and waited, but nothing appeared, nothing whispered, nothing moved.

He looked around the chamber, untroubled by the deep darkness, seeing it as the dead see. He walked over to the altar stone set in the floor, where the cup and the brooch and the stone knife sat.

He reached down and touched the edge of the knife. It was sharper than he had expected, and it nicked the skin of his finger.

IT IS THE TREASURE OF THE SLEER, whispered a triple voice, but it sounded smaller than he remembered, more hesitant.

Bod said, "You're the oldest thing here. I came to talk to you. I want advice."

A pause. NOTHING COMES TO THE SLEER FOR ADVICE. THE SLEER GUARDS. THE SLEER WAITS.

"I know. But Silas isn't here. And I don't know who else to talk to."

Nothing was said. Just a silence in reply, that echoed of dust and loneliness.

"I don't know what to do," Bod said, honestly. "I think I can find out about who killed my family. Who wanted to kill me. It means leaving the graveyard, though."

The Sleer said nothing. Smoke-tendrils twined slowly around the inside of the chamber.

"I'm not frightened of dying," said Bod. "It's just, so many people I care for have spent so much time keeping me safe, teaching me, protecting me."

Again, silence.

Then he said, "I have to do this on my own."

YES.

"That's all, then. Sorry I bothered you."

It whispered into Bod's head, then, in a voice that was a sleek insinuating glide, THE SLEER WAS SET TO GUARD THE TREASURE UNTIL OUR MASTER RETURNED. ARE YOU OUR MASTER?

"No," said Bod.

And then, with a hopeful whine, WILL YOU BE OUR MASTER?

"I'm afraid not."

IF YOU WERE OUR MASTER, WE COULD HOLD YOU IN OUR COILS FOREVER. IF YOU WERE OUR MASTER, WE WOULD KEEP

YOU SAFE AND PROTECT YOU UNTIL THE END OF TIME AND
NEVER LET YOU ENDURE THE DANGERS OF THE WORLD.

"I am not your master."

NO.

Bod felt the Sleer writhing through his mind. It said,
THEN FIND YOUR NAME. And his mind was empty, and the
room was empty, and Bod was alone.

Bod walked back up the stairs carefully yet quickly. He
had come to a decision and needed to act fast, while the
decision still burned in his mind.

Scarlett was waiting for him on the bench by the chapel.
"Well?" she said.

"I'll do it. Come on," he said, and side by side they
walked the path down to the graveyard gates.

Number 33 was a tall house, spindly-thin, in the middle
of a terraced row. It was red-brick and unmemorable.
Bod looked at it uncertainly, wondering why it did not
seem familiar, or special. It was only a house, like any
other. There was a small concreted space in front of it
that wasn't a garden, a green Mini parked on the street.
The front door had once been painted a bright blue, but
had been dimmed by time and the sun.

"Well?" said Scarlett.

Bod knocked on the door. There was nothing, then
a clatter of feet on the stairs from inside, and the door
opened to reveal an entryway and stairs. Framed in the
doorway was a bespectacled man with receding grey hair,

who blinked at them, then stuck out his hand at Bod, and smiled nervously, and said, "You must be Miss Perkins's mysterious friend. Good to meet you."

"This is Bod," said Scarlett.

"Bob?"

"Bod. With a *D*," she said. "Bod, this is Mr. Frost."

Bod and Frost shook hands. "Kettle's on," said Mr. Frost. "What say we swap information over a cuppa?"

They followed him up the steps to a kitchen, where he poured three mugs of tea, then led them into a small sitting room. "The house just keeps going up," he said. "The toilet's on the next floor up, and my office, then bedrooms above that. Keeps you fit, all the stairs."

They sat on a large, extremely purple sofa ("It was already here when I came"), and they sipped their tea.

Scarlett had worried that Mr. Frost would ask Bod lots of questions, but he didn't. He just seemed excited, as if he had identified the lost gravestone of someone famous and desperately wanted to tell the world. He kept moving impatiently in his chair, as if he had something enormous to impart to them and not blurting it out immediately was a physical strain.

Scarlett said, "So what did you find out?"

Mr. Frost said, "Well, you were right. I mean, this was the house where those people were killed. And it . . . I think the crime was . . . well, not exactly hushed up, but forgotten about, let go . . . by the authorities."

"I don't understand," said Scarlett. "Murders don't get swept under the carpet."

"This one was," said Frost. He drained his tea. "There are people out there who have influence. It's the only explanation for that, and for what happened to the youngest child . . ."

"And what was that?" asked Bod.

"He lived," said Frost. "I'm sure of it. But there wasn't a manhunt. A missing toddler normally would be national news. But they, um, they must have squashed it somehow."

"Who *are* they?" asked Bod.

"The same people who had the family killed."

"Do you know any more than that?"

"Yes. Well, a little . . ." Frost trailed off. "I'm sorry. I'm. Look. Given what I found. It's all too incredible."

Scarlett was starting to feel frustrated. "What was? What did you find?"

Frost looked shamefaced. "You're right. I'm sorry. Getting into keeping secrets. Not a good idea. Historians don't bury things. We dig them up. Show people. Yes." He stopped, hesitated, then he said, "I found a letter. Upstairs. It was hidden under a loose floorboard." He turned to Bod. "Young man, would I be correct in assuming your, well, your interest in this business, this dreadful business, is personal?"

Bod nodded.

"I won't ask any more," said Mr. Frost, and he stood up.

"Come on," he said to Bod. "Not you, though," to Scarlett, "not yet. I'll show *him*. And if he says it's all right, I'll show you as well. Deal?"

"Deal," said Scarlett.

"We won't be long," said Mr. Frost. "Come on, lad."

Bod stood up, darted a concerned look at Scarlett. "It's okay," she said, and smiled at him as reassuringly as she could. "I'll wait here for you."

She watched their shadows as they walked out of the room and up the stairs. She felt nervous, but expectant. She wondered what Bod would learn, and was happy that he would learn it first. It was his story, after all. It was his right.

Out on the stairs, Mr. Frost led the way.

Bod looked around as he walked up toward the top of the house, but nothing seemed familiar. It all seemed strange.

"All the way to the very top," said Mr. Frost. They went up another flight of stairs. He said, "I don't—well, you don't have to answer if you don't want to, but—um, you're the boy, aren't you?"

Bod said nothing.

"Here we are," said Mr. Frost. He turned the key in the door at the top of the house, pushed it open, and they went inside.

The room was small, an attic room with a sloping ceiling. Thirteen years before, it had held a crib. It barely held the man and the boy.

"Stroke of luck, really," said Mr. Frost. "Under my own nose, so to speak." He crouched down, pulled back the threadbare carpet.

"So you know why my family were murdered?" asked Bod.

Mr. Frost said, "It's all in here." He reached down to a short length of floorboard and pushed at it until he was able to lever it out. "This would have been the baby's room," said Mr. Frost. "I'll show you the . . . you know, the only thing we don't know is just who did it. Nothing at all. We don't have the tiniest clue."

"We know he has dark hair," said Bod, in the room that had once been his bedroom. "And we know that his name is Jack."

Mr. Frost put his hand down into the empty space where the floorboard had been. "It's been almost thirteen years," he said. "And hair gets thin and goes gray, in thirteen years. But yes, that's right. It's Jack."

He straightened up. The hand that had been in the hole in the floor was holding a large, sharp knife.

"Now," said the man Jack. "Now, boy. Time to finish this."

Bod stared at him. It was as if Mr. Frost had been a coat or a hat the man had been wearing, that he had now discarded. The affable exterior had gone.

The light glinted on the man's spectacles, and on the blade of the knife.

A voice called up to them from further down the stairs—Scarlett's. "Mr. Frost? There's someone knocking at the front door. Should I get it?"

The man Jack only glanced away for a moment, but Bod knew that the moment was all he had, and he Faded, as completely, as utterly as he could. The man Jack looked back to where Bod had been, then stared around the room, puzzlement and rage competing on his face. He took a step further into the room, his head swinging from side to side like an old tiger scenting prey.

"You're here somewhere," growled the man Jack. "I can smell you!"

Behind him, the little door to the attic bedroom slammed closed, and as he swung around he heard the key turn in the lock.

The man Jack raised his voice. "It buys you moments, but it won't stop me, boy," he called through the locked door. Then added, simply, "We have unfinished business, you and I."

Bod threw himself down the stairs, bouncing into the walls, almost tumbling headlong in his rush to reach Scarlett.

"Scarlett!" he said, when he saw her. "It's him! Come on!"

"It's who? What are you talking about?"

"Him! Frost. He's Jack. He tried to kill me!"

A *bang!* from above as the man Jack kicked at the door.

"But." Scarlett tried to make sense of what she was hearing, "But he's *nice*."

"No," said Bod, grabbing her hand and pulling her down the stairs, into the hallway. "No, he's not."

Scarlett pulled open the front door.

"Ah. Good evening, young lady," said the man at the door, looking down at her. "We are looking for Mr. Frost. I believe this is his neck of the woods." He had silver-white hair, and he smelled of cologne.

"Are you friends of his?" she asked.

"Oh yes," said a smaller man, standing just behind. He had a small black mustache and was the only one of the men to wear a hat.

"Certainly are," said a third, a younger man, huge and Nordic blond.

"Every man Jack of us," said the last of the men, wide and bull-like, with a massive head. His skin was brown.

"He. Mr. Frost. He had to go out," she said.

"But his car's here," said the white-haired man, as the blond one said, "Who are you, anyway?"

"He's a friend of my mum's," said Scarlett.

She could see Bod, now, on the other side of the group of men, gesturing frantically to her to leave the men and follow him.

She said, as breezily as she could, "He just popped out. Popped out for a newspaper. From the corner shop down there." And she closed the door behind her, stepped around the men and began to walk away.

"Where are you going?" asked the man with the mus-tache.

"I've got a bus to catch," she said. Scarlett walked up the hill towards the bus-stop and the graveyard, and did not, resolutely did not, look back.

Bod walked beside her. Even to Scarlett he seemed shadowy in the deepening dusk, like something that was almost not there, a shimmer of heat haze, a skittery leaf that for a moment had seemed to be a boy.

"Walk faster," said Bod. "They're all looking at you. But don't run."

"Who are they?" asked Scarlett, quietly.

"I don't know," said Bod. "But they all felt weird. Like they weren't properly people. I want to go back and listen to them."

"Of course they're people," said Scarlett, and she walked up the hill as fast as she could without actually running, no longer certain that Bod was by her side.

The four men stood at the door to number 33. "I don't like this," said the big man with the bull-neck.

"You don't like this, Mr. Tar?" said the white-haired man. "None of us like it. All wrong. Everything's going wrong."

"Krakow's gone. They aren't answering. And after Melbourne and Vancouver . . ." said the man with the mustache. "For all we know, we four are all that's left."

"Quiet, please, Mr. Ketch," said the white-haired man. "I'm thinking."

"Sorry, sir," said Mr. Ketch, and he patted his mustache with one gloved finger, looked up the hill and down again, and whistled through his teeth.

"I think . . . we should go after her," said the bull-necked man, Mr. Tar.

"I think you people should listen to me," said the white-haired man. "I said quiet. And what I meant was, *quiet*."

"Sorry, Mr. Dandy," said the blond man.

They were quiet.

In the silence, they could hear thumping sounds coming from high inside the house.

"I'm going in," said Mr. Dandy. "Mr. Tar, you're with me. Nimble and Ketch, get that girl. Bring her back."

"Dead or alive?" asked Mr. Ketch, with a smug smile.

"Alive, you moron," said Mr. Dandy. "I want to know what she knows."

"Maybe she's one of them," said Mr. Tar. "The ones who done for us in Vancouver and Melbourne and—"

"Get her," said Mr. Dandy. "Get her *now*." The blond man and the hat-and-mustache hurried up the hill.

Mr. Dandy and Mr. Tar stood outside the door to number 33.

"Force it," said Mr. Dandy.

Mr. Tar put his shoulder against the door and began to lean his weight on it. "It's reinforced," he said. "Protected."

Mr. Dandy said, "Nothing one Jack can do that another can't fix." He pulled off his glove, put his hand against the door, muttered something in a language older than English. "Now try it," he said.

Tar leaned against the door, grunted and pushed. This time the lock gave and the door swung open.

"Nicely done," said Mr. Dandy.

There was a crashing noise from far above them, up at

the top of the house.

The man Jack met them halfway down the stairs. Mr. Dandy grinned at him, without any humor but with perfect teeth. "Hello, Jack Frost," he said. "I thought you had the boy."

"I did," said the man Jack. "He got away."

"Again?" Jack Dandy's smile grew wider and chillier and even more perfect. "Once is a mistake, Jack. Twice is a disaster."

"We'll get him," said the man Jack. "This ends tonight."

"It had better," said Mr. Dandy.

"He'll be in the graveyard," said the man Jack. The three men hurried down the stairs.

The man Jack sniffed the air. He had the scent of the boy in his nostrils, a prickle at the nape of his neck. He felt like all this had happened years before. He paused, pulled on his long black coat, which had hung in the front hall, incongruous beside Mr. Frost's tweed jacket and fawn mackintosh.

The front door was open to the street, and the daylight had almost gone. This time the man Jack knew exactly which way to go. He did not pause, but simply walked out of the house, and hurried up the hill towards the graveyard.

The graveyard gates were closed when Scarlett reached them. Scarlett pulled at them desperately, but the gates were padlocked for the night. And then Bod was beside her. "Do you know where the key is?" she asked.

260

"We don't have time," said Bod. He pushed close to the metal bars. "Put your arms around me."

"You what?"

"Just put your arms around me and close your eyes."

Scarlett stared at Bod, as if daring him to try something, then she held him tightly and screwed her eyes shut. "Okay."

Bod leaned against the bars of the graveyard gates. They counted as part of the graveyard, and he hoped that his Freedom of the Graveyard might just, possibly, just this time, cover other people too. And then, like smoke, Bod slipped though the bars.

"You can open your eyes," he said.

She did.

"How did you do that?"

"This is my home," he said. "I can do things here."

The sound of shoes slapping against the pavement, and two men were on the other side of the gates, rattling them, pulling at them.

"Hul-lo," said Jack Ketch, with a twitch of his mustache, and he smiled at Scarlett through the bars like a rabbit with a secret. He had a black silk cord tied around his left forearm, and now he was tugging at it with his gloved right hand. He pulled it off his arm and into his hand, testing it, running it from hand to hand as if he was about to make a cat's cradle. "Come on out, girlie. It's all right. No one's going to hurt you."

"We just need you to answer some questions," said the

261

big blond man, Mr. Nimble. "We're on official business." (He lied. There was nothing official about the Jacks of All Trades, although there had been Jacks in governments and in police forces and in other places besides.)

"Run!" said Bod to Scarlett, pulling at her hand. She ran.

"Did you see that?" said the Jack they called Ketch.

"What?"

"I saw somebody with her. A boy."

"*The* boy?" asked the Jack called Nimble.

"How would I know? Here. Give me a hand up." The bigger man put his hands out, linked them to make a step, and Jack Ketch's black-clad foot went into it. Lifted up, he scrambled onto the top of the gates and jumped down to the drive, landing on all fours like a frog. He stood up, said, "Find another way in. I'm going after them." And he sprinted off up the winding path that led into the grave-yard.

Scarlett said, "Just tell me what we're doing." Bod was walking fast through the twilit graveyard, but he was not running, not yet.

"How do you mean?"

"I think that man wanted to kill me. Did you see how he was playing with that black cord?"

"I'm sure he does. That man Jack—your Mister Frost—*he* was going to kill me. He's got a knife."

"He's not *my* Mister Frost. Well, I suppose he is, sort of. Sorry. Where are we going?"

"First we put you somewhere safe. Then I deal with them."

All around Bod, the inhabitants of the graveyard were waking and gathering, worried and alarmed.

"Bod?" said Caius Pompeius. "What is happening?"

"Bad people," said Bod. "Can our lot keep an eye on them? Let me know where they are at all times. We have to hide Scarlett. Any ideas?"

"The chapel crypt?" said Thackeray Porringer.

"First place they'll look."

"Who are you talking to?" asked Scarlett, staring at Bod as if he had gone mad.

Caius Pompeius said, "Inside the hill?"

Bod thought. "Yes. Good call. Scarlett, do you remember the place where we found the Indigo Man?"

"Kind of. A dark place. I remember there wasn't anything to be scared of."

"I'm taking you up there."

They hurried up the path. Scarlett could tell that Bod was talking to people as he went, but could only hear his side of the conversation. It was like hearing someone talk on a phone. Which reminded her . . .

"My mum's going to go spare," she said. "I'm dead."

"No," said Bod. "You're not. Not yet. Not for a long time." Then, to someone else, "Two of them, now. Together? Okay."

They reached the Frobisher mausoleum. "The entrance is behind the bottom coffin on the left," Bod said. "If you

263

hear anyone coming and it's not me, go straight down to the very bottom . . . do you have anything to make light?"

"Yeah. A little LED thing on my keyring."

"Good."

He pulled open the door to the mausoleum. "And be careful. Don't trip or anything."

"Where are you going?" asked Scarlett.

"This is my home," said Bod. "I'm going to protect it."

Scarlett squeezed the LED keyring, and went down on her hands and knees. The space behind the coffin was tight, but she went though the hole into the hill and pulled the coffin back as best she could. In the dim LED light she could see stone steps. She stood upright, and, hand on the wall, walked down three steps, then stopped and sat, hoping that Bod knew what he was doing, and she waited.

Bod said, "Where are they now?"

His father said, "One fellow's up by the Egyptian Walk, looking for you. His friend's waiting down by the alley wall. Three others are on their way over, climbing up the alley wall on all the big bins."

"I wish Silas was here. He'd make short work of them. Or Miss Lupescu."

"You don't need them," said Mr. Owens encouragingly.

"Where's Mum?"

"Down by the alley wall."

"Tell her I've hidden Scarlett in the back of the Frobisher's place. Ask her to keep an eye on her if anything happens to me."

Bod ran through the darkened graveyard. The only way into the northwest part of the graveyard was through the Egyptian Walk. And to get there he would have to go past the little man with the black silk rope. A man who was looking for him, and who wanted him dead . . .

He was Nobody Owens, he told himself. He was a part of the graveyard. He would be fine.

He nearly missed the little man—the Jack called Ketch—as he hurried into the Egyptian Walk. The man was almost part of the shadows.

Bod breathed in, Faded as deeply as he could Fade, and moved past the man like dust blown on an evening breeze.

He walked down the green-hung length of the Egyptian Walk, and then, with an effort of will, he became as obvious as he could, and kicked at a pebble.

He saw the shadow by the arch detach itself and come after him, almost as silent as the dead.

Bod pushed through the trailing ivy that blocked the Walk and into the northwest corner of the graveyard. He would have to time this just right, he knew. Too fast and the man would lose him, yet if he moved too slowly a black silk rope would wrap itself around his neck, taking his breath with it and all his tomorrows.

He pushed noisily through the tangle of ivy, disturbing one of the graveyard's many foxes, which sprinted off into the undergrowth. It was a jungle here, of fallen headstones and headless statues, of trees and holly bushes, of slippery piles of half-rotted fallen leaves, but it was a jungle that

Bod had explored since he had been old enough to walk and to wander.

Now he was hurrying carefully, stepping from root-tangle of ivy to stone to earth, confident that this was his graveyard. He could feel the graveyard itself trying to hide him, to protect him, to make him vanish, and he fought it, worked to be seen.

He saw Nehemiah Trot, and hesitated.

"Hola, young Bod!" called the poet. "I hear that excitement is the master of the hour, that you fling yourself through these dominions like a comet across the firmament. What's the word, good Bod?"

"Stand there," said Bod. "Just where you are. Look back the way I came. Tell me when he comes close."

Bod skirted the ivy-covered Carstairs grave, and then he stood, panting as if out of breath, with his back to his pursuer.

And he waited. It was only for a few seconds, but it felt like a small forever.

("He's here, lad," said Nehemiah Trot. "About twenty paces behind you.")

The Jack called Ketch saw the boy in front of him. He pulled his black silk cord tight between his hands. It had been stretched around many necks, over the years, and had been the end of every one of the people it had embraced. It was very soft and very strong and invisible to X-rays.

Ketch's mustache moved, but nothing else. He had his

prey in his sight, and did not want to startle it. He began to advance, silent as a shadow.

The boy straightened up.

Jack Ketch darted forward, his polished black shoes almost soundless on the leaf-mold.

("He comes, lad!" called Nehemiah Trot.)

The boy turned around, and Jack Ketch made a leap towards him—

And Mr. Ketch felt the world tumbling away beneath him. He grabbed at the world with one gloved hand, but tumbled down and down into the old grave, all of twenty feet, before crash-landing on Mr. Carstairs's coffin, splintering the coffin-lid and his ankle at the same time.

"That's one," said Bod, calmly, although he felt anything but calm.

"Elegantly accomplished," said Nehemiah Trot. "I shall compose an Ode. Would you like to stay and listen?"

"No time," said Bod. "Where are the other men?"

Euphemia Horsfall said, "Three of them are on the southwestern path, heading up the hill."

Tom Sands said, "And there's another. Right now he's just walking around the chapel. He's the one who's been all around the graveyard for the last month. But there's something different about him."

Bod said, "Keep an eye on the man in with Mr. Carstairs—and please apologize to Mr. Carstairs for me . . ."

He ducked under a pine-branch and loped around the

hill, on the paths when it suited him, off the paths, jumping from monument to stone, when that was quicker.

He passed the old apple tree. "There's four of them,
still," said a tart female voice. "Four of them, and all kill-
ers. And the rest of them won't all of them fall into open
graves to oblige you."

"Hullo, Liza. I thought you were angry at me."

"I might be and I mightn't," she said, nothing more than
a voice. "But I'm not going to let them cut you up, nohow."

"Then trip them for me, trip them and confuse them
and slow them down. Can you do that?"

"While you runs away again? Nobody Owens, why don't
you just Fade, and hide in your mam's nice tomb, where
they'll never find you, and soon enough Silas will be back
to take care of them—"

"Maybe he will and maybe he won't," said Bod. "I'll
meet you by the lightning tree."

"I am still not talking to you," said Liza Hempstock's
voice, proud as a peacock and pert as a sparrow.

"Actually, you are. I mean, we're talking right now."

"Only during this emergency. After that, not a word."

Bod made for the lightning tree, an oak that had been
burned by lightning twenty years ago and now was nothing
more than a blackened limb clutching at the sky.

He had an idea. It was not fully formed. It depended
on whether he could remember Miss Lupescu's lessons,
remember everything he had seen and heard as a child.

It was harder to find the grave than he had expected,

even looking for it, but he found it—an ugly grave tipped at an odd angle, its stone topped by a headless, water-stained angel that had the appearance of a gargantuan fungus. It was only when he touched it, and felt the chill, that he knew it for certain.

He sat down on the grave, forced himself to become entirely visible.

"You've not Faded," said Liza's voice. "Anyone could find you."

"Good," said Bod. "I want them to find me."

"More know Jack Fool than Jack Fool knows," said Liza.

The moon was rising. It was huge now and low in the sky. Bod wondered if it would be overdoing it if he began to whistle.

"I can see him!"

A man ran towards him, tripping and stumbling, two other men close behind.

Bod was aware of the dead clustered around them, watching the scene, but he forced himself to ignore them. He made himself more comfortable on the ugly grave. He felt like the bait in a trap, and it was not a good feeling.

The bull-like man was the first to reach the grave, followed closely by the man with the white hair who had done all the talking, and the tall blond man.

Bod stayed where he was.

The man with the white hair said, "Ah. The elusive Dorian boy, I presume. Astonishing. There's our Jack Frost hunting the whole world over, and here you are, just

269

where he left you, thirteen years ago."

Bod said, "That man killed my family."

"Indeed he did."

"Why?"

"Does it matter? You're never going to tell anyone."

"Then it's no skin off your nose to tell me, is it?"

The white-haired man barked a laugh. "Hah! Funny boy. What *I* want to know is, how have you lived in a graveyard for thirteen years without anyone catching wise?"

"I'll answer your question if you answer mine."

The bull-necked man said, "You don't talk to Mr. Dandy like that, little snot! I split you, I will—"

The white-haired man took another step closer to the grave. "Hush, Jack Tar. All right. An answer for an answer. We—my friends and I—are members of a fraternal organization, known as the Jacks of All Trades, or the Knaves, or by other names. We go back an extremely long way. We know . . . we remember things that most people have forgotten. The Old Knowledge."

Bod said, "Magic. You know a little magic."

The man nodded agreeably. "If you want to call it that. But it is a very specific sort of magic. There's a magic you take from death. Something leaves the world, something else comes into it."

"You killed my family for—for what? For magic powers? That's ridiculous."

"No. We killed you for protection. Long time ago, one of our people—this was back in Egypt, in pyramid days—

he foresaw that one day, there would be a child born who would walk the borderland between the living and the dead. That if this child grew to adulthood it would mean the end of our order and all we stand for. We had people casting nativities before London was a village, we had your family in our sights before New Amsterdam became New York. And we sent what we thought was the best and the sharpest and the most dangerous of all the Jacks to deal with you. To do it properly, so we could take all the bad Juju and make it work for us instead, and keep everything tickety-boo for another five thousand years. Only he didn't."

Bod looked at the three men.

"So where is he? Why isn't he here?"

The blond man said, "We can take care of you. He's got a good nose on him, has our Jack Frost. He's on the trail of your little girlfriend. Can't leave any witnesses. Not to something like this."

Bod leaned forward, dug his hands into the wild weed-grass that grew on the unkempt grave.

"Come and get me," was all that he said.

The blond man grinned, the bull-necked man lunged, and—yes—even Mr. Dandy took several steps forward.

Bod pushed his fingers as deeply as he could into the grass, and he pulled his lips back from his teeth, and he said three words in a language that was already ancient before the Indigo Man was born.

"Skagh! Thegh! Khavagah!"

He opened the ghoul-gate.

The grave swung up like a trapdoor. In the deep hole below the door Bod could see stars, a darkness filled with glimmering lights.

The bull-man, Mr. Tar, at the edge of the hole, could not stop, and stumbled, surprised, into the darkness.

Mr. Nimble jumped toward Bod, his arms extended, leaping over the hole. Bod watched as the man stopped in the air at the zenith of his spring, and hung there for a moment, before he was sucked through the ghoul-gate, down and down.

Mr. Dandy stood at the edge of the ghoul-gate, on a lip of stone and looked down into the darkness beneath. Then he raised his eyes to Bod, and thin-lipped, he smiled.

"I don't know what you just did," said Mr. Dandy. "But it didn't work." He pulled his gloved hand out of his pocket, holding a gun, pointed directly at Bod. "I should have just done this thirteen years ago," said Mr. Dandy. "You can't trust other people. If it's important, you have to do it yourself."

A desert wind came up from the open ghoul-gate, hot and dry, with grit in it. Bod said, "There's a desert down there. If you look for water, you should find some. There's things to eat if you look hard, but don't antagonize the night-gaunts. Avoid Ghûlheim. The ghouls might wipe your memories and make you into one of them, or they might wait until you've rotted down, and then eat you. Either way, you can do better."

The gun barrel did not waver. Mr. Dandy said, "Why are

you telling me this?"

Bod pointed across the graveyard. "Because of them," he said, and as he said it, as Mr. Dandy glanced away, only for a moment, Bod Faded. Mr. Dandy's eyes flickered away and back, but Bod was no longer by the broken statue. From deep in the hole something called, like the lonely wail of a night bird.

Mr. Dandy looked around, his forehead a slash, his body a mass of indecision and rage. "Where are you?" he growled. "The Deuce take you! Where *are* you?"

He thought he heard a voice say, "Ghoul-gates are made to be opened and then closed again. You can't leave them open. They want to close."

The lip of the hole shuddered and shook. Mr. Dandy had been in an earthquake once, years before, in Bangladesh. It felt like that: the earth juddered, and Mr. Dandy fell, would have fallen into the darkness, but he caught hold of the fallen headstone, threw his arms about it and locked on. He did not know what was beneath him, only that he had no wish to find out.

The earth shook, and he felt the headstone begin to shift, beneath his weight.

He looked up. The boy was there, looking down at him curiously.

"I'm going to let the gate close now," he said. "I think if you keep holding onto that thing, it might close on you, and crush you, or it might just absorb you and make you into part of the gate. Don't know. But I'm giving you a chance, more than you ever gave my family."

A ragged judder. Mr. Dandy looked up into the boy's grey eyes, and he swore. Then he said, "You can't ever escape us. We're the Jacks of All Trades. We're everywhere. It's not over."

"It is for you," said Bod. "The end of your people and all you stand for. Like your man in Egypt predicted. You didn't kill me. You were everywhere. Now it's all over." Then Bod smiled. "That's what Silas is doing, isn't it? That's where he is."

Mr. Dandy's face confirmed everything that Bod had suspected.

And what Mr. Dandy might have said to that, Bod would never know, because the man let go of the headstone and tumbled slowly down into the open ghoul-gate.

Bod said, *"Wegh Khârados."*

The ghoul-gate was a grave once again, nothing more.

Something was tugging at his sleeve. Fortinbras Bartleby looked up at him. "Bod! The man by the chapel. He's going up the hill."

The man Jack followed his nose. He had left the others, not least because the stink of Jack Dandy's cologne made finding anything subtler impossible.

He could not find the boy by scent. Not here. The boy smelled like the graveyard. But the girl smelled like her mother's house, like the dab of perfume she had touched to her neck before school that morning. She smelled like a victim too, like fear-sweat, thought Jack, like his quarry. And wherever she was, the boy would be too, sooner or later.

His hand closed around the handle of his knife and he walked up the hill. He was almost at the top of the hill when it occurred to him—a hunch he knew was a truth—that Jack Dandy and the rest of them were gone. *Good*, he thought. *There's always room at the top.* The man Jack's own rise through the Order had slowed and stopped after he had failed to kill all of the Dorian family. It was as if he had no longer been trusted.

Now, soon, everything would change.

At the top of the hill the man Jack lost the girl's scent. He knew she was near.

He retraced his steps, almost casually, caught her perfume again about fifty feet away, beside a small mausoleum with a closed metal gateway. He pulled on the gate and it swung wide.

Her scent was strong now. He could smell that she was afraid. He pulled down the coffins, one by one, from their shelves, and let them clatter onto the ground, shattering the old wood, spilling their contents onto the mausoleum floor. No, she was not hiding in any of those . . .

Then where?

He examined the wall. Solid. He went down on his hands and knees, pulled the last coffin out and reached back. His hand found an opening . . .

"Scarlett," he called, trying to remember how he would

have called her name when he was Mr. Frost, but he could not even find that part of himself any longer: he was the man Jack now, and that was all he was. On his hands and knees he crawled through the hole in the wall.

When Scarlett heard the crashing noise from above she made her way, carefully, down the steps, her left hand touching the wall, her right hand holding the little LED keyring, which cast just enough light to allow her to see where she was placing her feet. She made it to the bottom of the stone steps and edged back in the open chamber, her heart thumping.

She was scared: scared of nice Mr. Frost and his scarier friends; scared of this room and its memories; even, if she were honest, a little afraid of Bod. He was no longer a quiet boy with a mystery, a link to her childhood. He was something different, something not quite human.

She thought, *I wonder what Mum's thinking right now. She'll be phoning Mr. Frost's house over and over to find out when I'm going to get back.* She thought, *If I get out of this alive, I'm going to force her to get me a phone. It's ridiculous. I'm the only person in my year who doesn't have her own phone, practically.*

She thought, *I miss my mum.*

She had not thought anyone human could move that silently through the dark, but a gloved hand closed upon her mouth, and a voice that was only barely recognizable as Mr. Frost's said, without emotion, "Do anything clever—do anything at all—and I will cut your throat. Nod if you understand me."

Scarlett nodded.

Bod saw the chaos on the floor of the Frobisher mausoleum, the fallen coffins with their contents scattered across over the aisle. There were many Frobishers and Frobyshers, and several Pettyfers, all in various states of upset and consternation.

"He is already down there," said Ephraim.

"Thank you," said Bod. He clambered through the hole into the inside of the hill, and he went down the stairs.

Bod saw as the dead see: he saw the steps, and he saw the chamber at the bottom. And when he got halfway down the steps, he saw the man Jack holding Scarlett. He had her arm twisted up behind her back, and a large, wicked, boning-knife at her neck.

The man Jack looked up in the darkness.

"Hello, boy," he said.

Bod said nothing. He concentrated on his Fade, took another step.

"You think I can't see you," said the man Jack. "And you're right. I can't. Not really. But I can smell your fear. And I can hear you move and hear you breathe. And now that I know about your clever vanishing trick, I can *feel* you. Say something now. Say it so I can hear it, or I start to cut little pieces out of the young lady. Do you understand me?"

"Yes," said Bod, his voice echoing in the chamber room. "I understand."

"Good," said Jack. "Now, come here. Let's have a little chat."

Bod began to walk down the steps. He concentrated on the Fear, on raising the level of panic in the room, of making the Terror something tangible. . . .

"Stop that," said the man Jack. "Whatever it is you're doing. Don't do it."

Bod let it go.

"You think," said Jack, "that you can do your little magics on me? Do you know what I am, boy?"

Bod said, "You're a Jack. You killed my family. And you should have killed me."

Jack raised an eyebrow. He said, "I should have killed you?"

"Oh yes. The old man said that if you let me grow to adulthood your Order would be destroyed. I did. You failed and you lost."

"My order goes back before Babylon. Nothing can harm it."

"They didn't tell you, did they?" Bod was standing five paces from the man Jack. "Those four. They were the last of the Jacks. What was it . . . Krakow and Vancouver and Melbourne. All gone."

Scarlett said, "Please, Bod. Make him let go of me."

"Don't worry," said Bod, with a calm he did not feel. He said to Jack, "There's no point in hurting her. There's

278

no point in killing me. Don't you understand? There isn't even an order of Jacks of All Trades. Not anymore."

Jack nodded thoughtfully. "If this is true," said Jack, "and if I am now a Jack-all-alone, then I have an excellent reason for killing you both."

Bod said nothing.

"Pride," said the man Jack. "Pride in my work. Pride in finishing what I began." And then he said, "What are you doing?"

Bod's hair prickled. He could feel a smoke-tendril presence twining through the room. He said, "It's not me. It's the Sleer. It guards the treasure that's buried here."

"Don't lie."

Scarlett said, "He's not lying. It's true."

Jack said, "True? Buried treasure? Don't make me—"

THE SLEER GUARDS THE TREASURE FOR THE MASTER.

"Who said that?" asked the man Jack, looking around.

"You heard it?" asked Bod, puzzled.

"I heard it," said Jack. "Yes."

Scarlett said, "I didn't hear anything."

The man Jack said, "What is this place, boy? Where are we?"

Before Bod could speak, the Sleer's voice spoke, echoing through the chamber, THIS IS THE PLACE OF THE TREASURE. THIS IS THE PLACE OF POWER. THIS IS WHERE THE SLEER GUARDS AND WAITS FOR ITS MASTER TO RETURN.

Bod said, "Jack?"

The man Jack tilted his head on one side. He said, "It's

good to hear my name in your mouth, boy. If you'd used it before, I could have found you sooner."

"Jack. What was my real name? What did my family call me?"

"Why should that matter to you now?"

Bod said, "The Sleer told me to find my name. What was it?"

Jack said, "Let me see. Was it Peter? Or Paul? Or Roderick—you look like a Roderick. Maybe you were a Stephen . . ." He was playing with the boy.

"You might as well tell me. You're going to kill me anyway," said Bod. Jack shrugged and nodded in the darkness, as if to say *obviously*.

"I want you to let the girl go," said Bod. "Let Scarlett go."

Jack peered into the darkness, then said, "That's an altar stone, isn't it?"

"I suppose so."

"And a knife? And a cup? And a brooch?"

He was smiling now, in the darkness. Bod could see it on his face: a strange, delighted smile that seemed out of place on that face, a smile of discovery and of understanding. Scarlett couldn't see anything but a blackness that sometimes erupted in flashes inside her eyeballs, but she could hear the delight in Jack's voice.

The man Jack said, "So the Brotherhood is over and the Convocation is at an end. And yet, if there are no more Jacks of All Trades but me, what does it matter? There can be a new Brotherhood, more powerful than the last."

POWER, echoed the Sleer.

"This is perfect," said the man Jack. "Look at us. We are in a place for which my people have hunted for thousands of years, with everything necessary for the ceremony waiting for us. It makes you believe in Providence, doesn't it? Or in the massed prayers of all the Jacks who have gone before us, that at our lowest ebb, we are given this."

Bod could feel the Sleer listening to Jack's words, could feel a low susurrus of excitement building in the chamber.

The man Jack said, "I am going to put out my hand, boy. Scarlett, my knife is still at your throat—do not try to run when I let go of you. Boy, you will place the cup and the knife and the brooch in my hand."

THE TREASURE OF THE SLEER, whispered the triple voice. IT ALWAYS COMES BACK. WE GUARD IT FOR THE MASTER.

Bod bent down, took the objects from the altar stone, put them in Jack's open gloved hand. Jack grinned.

"Scarlett. I am going to release you. When I take the knife away, I want you to lie, facedown, on the ground, with your hands behind your head. Move or try anything, and I will kill you painfully. Do you understand?"

She gulped. Her mouth was dry, but she took one shaky step forward. Her right arm, which had been twisted up to the small of her back, was now numb, and she felt only pins and needles in her shoulder. She lay down, her cheek resting on the packed earth.

We are dead, she thought, and it was not even tinged with emotion. It felt as if she were watching something happening to other people, a surreal drama that had turned into a game of Murder in the Dark. She heard the noise of Jack taking hold of Bod . . .

Bod's voice said, "Let her go."

The man Jack's voice: "If you do everything I say, I won't kill her. I won't even hurt her."

"I don't believe you. She can identify you."

"No." The adult voice seemed certain. "She can't." And then it said, "Ten thousand years, and the knife is still sharp . . ." The admiration in the voice was palpable. "Boy. Go and kneel on that altar stone. Hands behind your back. Now."

IT HAS BEEN SO LONG, said the Sleer, but all Scarlett heard was a slithering noise, as if of enormous coils winding around the chamber.

But the man Jack heard. "You want to know your name, boy, before I spill your blood on the stone?"

Bod felt the cold of the knife at his neck. And in that moment, Bod understood. Everything slowed. Everything came into focus. "I know my name," he said. "I'm Nobody Owens. That's who I am." And, kneeling on the cold altar stone, it all seemed very simple.

"Sleer," he said to the chamber. "Do you still want a master?"

THE SLEER GUARDS THE TREASURE UNTIL THE MASTER RETURNS.

"Well," said Bod, "haven't you finally found the master you've been looking for?"

He could sense the Sleer writhing and expanding, hear a noise like the scratching of a thousand dead twigs, as if something huge and muscular were snaking its way around the inside of the chamber. And then, for the first time, Bod saw the Sleer. Afterwards, he was never able to describe what he had seen: something huge, yes; something with the body of an enormous snake, but with the head of a what . . . ? There were three of them: three heads, three necks. The faces were dead, as if someone had constructed dolls from parts of the corpses of humans and of animals. The faces were covered in purple patterns, tattooed in swirls of indigo, turning the dead faces into strange, expressive monstrous things.

The faces of the Sleer nuzzled the air about Jack tentatively, as if they wanted to stroke or caress him.

"What's happening?" said Jack. "What is it? What does it do?"

"It's called the Sleer. It guards the place. It needs a master to tell it what to do," said Bod.

Jack hefted the flint knife in his hand. "Beautiful," he said to himself. And then, "Of course. It's been waiting for me. And yes. Obviously, I *am* its new master."

The Sleer encircled the interior of the chamber. MASTER? it said, like a dog who had waited patiently for too long. It said MASTER? again, as if testing the word to see how it tasted. And it tasted good, so it said one more time, with a sigh of delight and of longing, MASTER . . .

Jack looked down at Bod. "Thirteen years ago I missed

you, and now, now we are reunited. The end of one order. The beginning of another. Good-bye, boy." With one hand he lowered the knife to the boy's throat. The other hand held the goblet.

"Bod," said Bod. "Not Boy. Bod." He raised his voice. "Sleer," he said. "What will you do with your new master?"

The Sleer sighed. WE WILL PROTECT HIM UNTIL THE END OF TIME. THE SLEER WILL HOLD HIM IN ITS COILS FOREVER AND NEVER LET HIM ENDURE THE DANGERS OF THE WORLD.

"Then protect him," said Bod. "Now."

"I am your master. You will obey me," said the man Jack.

THE SLEER HAS WAITED SO LONG, said the triple voice of the Sleer, triumphantly. SO LONG A TIME. It began to loop its huge, lazy coils around the man Jack.

The man Jack dropped the goblet. Now he had a knife in each hand—a flint knife, and a knife with a black bone handle—and he said, "Get back! Keep away from me! Don't get any closer!" He slashed out with the knife, as the Sleer twined about him, and in a huge crushing movement, engulfed the man Jack in its coils.

Bod ran over to Scarlett, and helped her up. "I want to see," she said. "I want to see what's happening." She pulled out her LED light, and turned it on . . .

What Scarlett saw was not what Bod saw. She did not see the Sleer, and that was a mercy. She saw the man Jack, though. She saw the fear on his face, which made him look like Mr. Frost had once looked. In his terror he was once

284

more the nice man who had driven her home. He was floating in the air, five, then ten feet above the ground, slashing wildly at the air with two knives, trying to stab something she could not see, in a display that was obviously having no effect.

Mr. Frost, the man Jack, whoever he was, was forced away from them, pulled back until he was spread-eagled, arms and legs wide and flailing, against the side of the chamber wall.

It seemed to Scarlett that Mr. Frost was being forced through the wall, pulled into the rock, was being swallowed up by it. Now there was nothing visible but a face. He was shouting wildly, desperately, shouting at Bod to call the thing off, to save him, please, please . . . and then the man's face was pulled through the wall, and the voice was silenced.

Bod walked back to the altar stone. He picked up the stone knife, and the goblet, and the brooch, from the ground and he replaced them where they belonged. He left the black metal knife where it fell.

Scarlett said, "I thought you said the Sleer couldn't hurt people. I thought all it could do was frighten us."

"Yes," said Bod. "But it wanted a master to protect. It told me so."

Scarlett said, "You mean you knew. You *knew* that would happen . . ."

"Yes. I hoped it would."

He helped her up the steps and out into the chaos of the Frobisher mausoleum. "I'll need to clean this all up," said Bod, casually. Scarlett tried not to look at the things on the floor.

They stepped out into the graveyard. Scarlett said, dully, once more, "You knew that would happen."

This time Bod said nothing.

She looked at him as if unsure of what she was looking at. "So you knew. That the Sleer would take him. Was *that* why you hid me down there? Was it? What was I, then, *bait*?"

Bod said, "It wasn't like that." Then he said, "We're still alive, aren't we? And he won't trouble us any longer."

Scarlett could feel the anger and the rage welling up inside her. The fear had gone, and now all she was left with was the need to lash out, to shout. She fought the urge. "And what about those other men? Did you kill them too?"

"I didn't kill anyone."

"Then where are they?"

"One of them's at the bottom of a deep grave, with a broken ankle. The other three are, well, they're a long way away."

"You didn't kill them?"

"Of course not." Bod said, "This is my home. Why would I want them hanging around here for the rest of time?" Then, "Look, it's okay. I dealt with them."

Scarlett took a step away from him. She said, "You aren't a person. People don't behave like you. You're as bad as he was. You're a monster."

Bod felt the blood drain from his face. After everything

he had been through that night, after everything that had happened, this was somehow the hardest thing to take. "No," he said. "It wasn't like that."

Scarlett began to back away from Bod.

She took one step, two steps, and was about to flee, to turn and run madly, desperately away through the moonlit graveyard, when a tall man in black velvet put a hand on her arm, and said, "I am afraid you do Bod an injustice. But you will undoubtedly be happier if you remember none of this. So let us walk together, you and I, and discuss what has happened to you over the last few days, and what it might be wise for you to remember, and what it might be better for you to forget."

Bod said, "Silas. You *can't*. You can't make her forget me."

"It will be safest that way," said Silas, simply. "For her, if not for all of us."

"Don't—don't I get a say in this?" asked Scarlett.

Silas said nothing. Bod took a step towards Scarlett, said, "Look, it's over. I know it was hard. But. We did it. You and me. We beat them."

Her head was shaking gently, as if she was denying everything she saw, everything she was experiencing.

She looked up at Silas, and said only, "I want to go home. Please?"

Silas nodded. He walked, with the girl, down the path that would eventually lead them both out of the graveyard. Bod stared at Scarlett as she walked away, hoping that she would turn and look back, that she would smile or just look at him without fear in her eyes. But Scarlett did not turn. She simply walked away.

Bod went back into the mausoleum. He had to do something, so he began to pick up the fallen coffins, to remove the debris, and to replace the tangle of tumbled bones into the coffins, disappointed to discover that none of the many Frobishers and Frobyshers and Pettyfers gathered around to watch seemed to be quite certain whose bones belonged in which container.

A man brought Scarlett home. Later, Scarlett's mother could not remember quite what he had told her, although disappointingly, she had learned that that nice Jay Frost had unavoidably been forced to leave town.

The man talked with them, in the kitchen, about their lives and their dreams, and by the end of the conversation Scarlett's mother had somehow decided that they would be returning to Glasgow: Scarlett would be happy to be near her father, and to see her old friends again.

Silas left the girl and her mother talking in the kitchen, discussing the challenges of moving back to Scotland, with Noona promising to buy Scarlett a phone of her own. They barely remembered that Silas had ever been there, which was the way he liked it.

Silas returned to the graveyard and found Bod sitting in the amphitheater by the obelisk, his face set.

"How is she?"

"I took her memories," said Silas. "They will return to

Glasgow. She has friends there."

"How could you make her forget me?"

Silas said, "People want to forget the impossible. It makes their world safer."

Bod said, "I liked her."

"I'm sorry."

Bod tried to smile, but he could not find a smile inside himself. "The men . . . they spoke about trouble they were having in Krakow and Melbourne and Vancouver. That was you, wasn't it?"

"I was not alone," said Silas.

"Miss Lupescu?" said Bod. Then, seeing the expression on his guardian's face, "Is she all right?"

Silas shook his head, and for a moment his face was terrible for Bod to behold. "She fought bravely. She fought for you, Bod."

Bod said, "The Sleer has the man Jack. Three of the others went through the ghoul-gate. There's one injured but still alive at the bottom of the Carstairs grave."

Silas said, "He is the last of the Jacks. I will need to talk to him, then, before sunrise."

The wind that blew across the graveyard was cold, but neither the man nor the boy seemed to feel it.

Bod said, "She was scared of me."

"Yes."

"But why? I saved her life. I'm not a bad person. And I'm just like her. I'm alive too." Then he said, "How did Miss Lupescu fall?"

"Bravely," said Silas. "In battle. Protecting others."

Bod's eyes were dark. "You could have brought her back here. Buried her here. Then I could have talked to her."

Silas said, "That was not an option."

Bod felt his eyes stinging. He said, "She used to call me *Nimeni*. No one will ever call me that again."

Silas said, "Shall we go and get food for you?"

"*We?* You want me to come with you? Out of the graveyard?"

Silas said, "No one is trying to kill you. Not right now. There are a lot of things they are not going to be doing, not any longer. So, yes. What would you like to eat?"

Bod thought about saying that he wasn't hungry, but that simply was not true. He felt a little sick, and a little lightheaded, and he was starving. "Pizza?" he suggested.

They walked through the graveyard, down to the gates. As Bod walked, he saw the inhabitants of the graveyard, but they let the boy and his guardian pass among them without a word. They only watched.

Bod tried to thank them for their help, to call out his gratitude, but the dead said nothing.

The lights of the pizza restaurant were bright, brighter than Bod was comfortable with. He and Silas sat near the back, and Silas showed him how to use a menu, how to order food. (Silas ordered a glass of water and a small salad for himself, which he pushed around the bowl with his fork but never actually put to his lips.)

Bod ate his pizza with his fingers and enthusiasm. He

did not ask questions. Silas would talk in his own time, or he would not.

Silas said, "We had known of them . . . of the Jacks . . . for a long, long time, but we knew of them only from the results of their activities. We suspected there was an organization behind it, but they hid too well. And then they came after you, and they killed your family. And, slowly, I was able to follow their trail."

"Is *we* you and Miss Lupescu?" asked Bod.

"Us and others like us."

"The Honour Guard," said Bod.

"How did you hear about—?" said Silas. Then, "No matter. *Little pitchers have big ears*, as they say. Yes. The Honour Guard." Silas picked up his glass of water. He put the water glass to his lips, moistened them, then put it down on the polished black tabletop.

The surface of the tabletop was almost mirrored, and, had anyone cared to look, they might have observed that the tall man had no reflection.

Bod said, "So. Now you're done . . . done with all this. Are you going to stay?"

"I gave my word," said Silas. "I am here until you are grown."

"I'm grown," said Bod.

"No," said Silas. "Almost. Not yet."

He put a ten-pound note down on the tabletop.

"That girl," said Bod. "Scarlett. Why was she so scared of me, Silas?"

But Silas said nothing, and the question hung in the air as the man and the youth walked out of the bright pizza restaurant into the waiting darkness; and soon enough they were swallowed by the night.

CHAPTER EIGHT

Leavings and Partings

SOMETIMES HE COULD NO longer see the dead. It had begun a month or two previously, in April or in May. At first it had only happened occasionally, but now it seemed to be happening more and more.

The world was changing.

Bod wandered over to the northwestern part of the graveyard, to the tangle of ivy that hung from a yew tree and half-blocked the far exit from the Egyptian Walk. He saw a red fox and a large black cat, with a white collar and paws, who sat conversing together in the middle of the path. At Bod's approach they looked up, startled, then fled into the undergrowth, as if they had been caught conspiring.

Odd, he thought. He had known that fox since it had been a cub, and the cat had prowled through the graveyard for as long as Bod could remember. They knew him. If they were feeling friendly they even let him pet them.

Bod started to slip through the ivy but he found his way blocked. He bent down, pushed the ivy out of the way and squeezed through. He walked down the path carefully, avoiding the ruts and holes until he reached the impressive stone that marked the final resting place of Alonso Tomás Garcia Jones (1837–1905, *Traveler Lay Down Thy Staff*).

Bod had been coming down here every few days for several months: Alonso Jones had been all over the world, and he took great pleasure in telling Bod stories of his travels. He would begin by saying, "Nothing interesting has ever happened to me," then would add, gloomily, "and I have told you all my tales," and then his eyes would flash, and he would remark, "Except . . . did I ever tell you about . . . ?" And whatever the next words were: "The time I had to escape from Moscow?" or "The time I lost an Alaskan gold mine, worth a fortune?" or "The cattle stampede on the pampas?," Bod would always shake his head and look expectant and soon enough his head would be swimming with tales of derring-do and high adventure, tales of beautiful maidens kissed, of evildoers shot with pistols or fought with swords, of bags of gold, of diamonds as big as the tip of your thumb, of lost cities and of vast mountains, of steam-trains and clipper ships, of pampas, oceans, deserts, tundra.

Bod walked over to the pointed stone—tall, carved with upside-down torches, and he waited, but saw no one. He called to Alonso Jones, even knocked on the side of the stone, but there was no response. Bod leaned down, to push his head into the grave and call his friend, but instead of his head slipping though the solid matter like a shadow passing through a deeper shadow, his head met the ground

296

with a hard and painful thump. He called again, but saw nothing and no one, and, carefully, he made his way out of the tangle of greenery and of grey stones and back to the path. Three magpies perched in a hawthorn tree took wing as he passed them.

He did not see another soul until he reached the graveyard's southwestern slope, where the familiar shape of Mother Slaughter, tiny in her high bonnet and her cloak, could be seen, walking between the gravestones, head bent, looking at wildflowers.

"Here, boy!" she called. "There's nasturshalums growing wild over here. Why don't you pick some for me, and put them over by my stone."

So Bod picked the red and yellow nasturtiums, and he carried them over to Mother Slaughter's headstone, so cracked and worn and weathered that all it said now was,

LAUGH

which had puzzled the local historians for over a hundred years. He put down the flowers in front of the stone, respectfully.

Mother Slaughter smiled at him. "You're a good lad. I don't know what we'll do without you."

"Thank you," said Bod. Then, "Where is everyone? You're the first person I've seen tonight."

Mother Slaughter peered at him sharply. "What did you do to your forehead?" she asked.

"I bumped it, on Mr. Jones's grave. It was solid. I . . ."

But Mother Slaughter was pursing her lips and tilting

her head. Bright old eyes scrutinized Bod from beneath her bonnet. "I called you *boy*, didn't I? But time passes in the blink of an eye, and it's a young man you are now, isn't it? How old are you?"

"About fifteen, I think. Though I still feel the same as I always did," Bod said, but Mother Slaughter interrupted, "And I still feels like I done when I was a tiny slip of a thing, making daisy chains in the old pasture. You're always you, and that don't change, and you're always changing, and there's nothing you can do about it."

She sat down on her broken stone, and said, "I remember you the night you came here, boy. I says, 'We can't let the little fellow leave,' and your mother agrees, and all of them starts argufying and what-not until the Lady on the Grey rides up. 'People of the Graveyard,' she says, 'Listen to Mother Slaughter. Have you not got any charity in your bones?' and then all of them agreed with me." She trailed off, shook her little head, "There's not much happens here to make one day unlike the next. The seasons change. The ivy grows. Stones fall over. But you coming here . . . well, I'm glad you did, that's all."

She stood up and pulled a grubby piece of linen from her sleeve, spat on it, and reached up as high as she could and scrubbed the blood from Bod's forehead. "There, that ought to make you look presentable," she said, severely. "Seeing as I don't know when next I'll see you, anyway. Keep safe."

Feeling discomfited in a way he could not remember

having felt before, Bod made his way back to the Owenses' tomb, and was pleased to see both of his parents waiting for him beside it. As he got closer, his pleasure turned into concern: why did Mr. and Mrs. Owens stand like that, arranged on each side of the tomb like characters from a stained-glass window? He could not read their faces.

His father took a step forward and said, "Evening, Bod. I trust you are keeping well."

"Tolerably well," said Bod, which was what Mr. Owens always said to his friends when they asked him the same question.

Mr. Owens said, "Mistress Owens and I spent our lives wishing that we had a child. I do not believe that we could have ever had a better young man than you, Bod." He looked up at his son with pride.

Bod said, "Well, yes, thank you, but . . ." He turned to his mother, certain he could get her to tell him what was happening, but she was no longer there. "Where did she go?"

"Oh. Yes." Mr. Owens seemed ill at ease. "Ah, you know Betsy. There's things, times. When, well, you don't know what to say. You know?"

"No," said Bod.

"I expect Silas is waiting for you," said his father, and then he was gone.

It was past midnight. Bod began to walk toward the old chapel. The tree that grew out of the gutter on the spire had fallen in the last storm, taking a handful of the slate-black roof tiles with it.

Bod waited on the grey wooden bench, but there was no sign of Silas.

The wind gusted. It was late on a summer's night, when the twilight lasts forever, and it was warm, but still, Bod felt goose-pimples rising on his arms.

A voice by his ear said, "Say you'll miss me, you lumpkin."

"Liza?" said Bod. He had not seen or heard from the witch-girl for over a year—not since the night of the Jacks of All Trades. "Where have you been?"

"Watching," she said. "Does a lady have to tell everything she does?"

"Watching *me*?" asked Bod

Liza's voice, close to his ear, said, "Truly, life is wasted on the living, Nobody Owens. For one of us is too foolish to live, and it is not I. Say you will miss me."

"Where are you going?" asked Bod. Then, "Of course I will miss you, wherever you go . . ."

"Too stupid," whispered Liza Hempstock's voice, and he could feel the touch of her hand on his hand. "Too stupid to live." The touch of her lips against his cheek, against the corner of his lips. She kissed him gently and he was too perplexed, too utterly wrong-footed, to know what to do.

Her voice said, "I will miss you too. Always." A breath of wind ruffled his hair, if it was not the touch of her hand, and then he was, he knew, alone on the bench.

He got up.

Bod walked over to the chapel door, lifted the stone

beside the porch and pulled out the spare key, left there by a long-dead sexton. He unlocked the big wooden door without even testing to see if he could slip through it. It creaked open, protesting.

The inside of the chapel was dark, and Bod found himself squinting as he tried to see.

"Come in, Bod." It was Silas's voice.

"I can't see anything," said Bod. "It's too dark."

"Already?" said Silas. He sighed. Bod heard a velvet rustle, then a match was struck, and it flamed, and was used to light two huge candles that sat on great carved wooden candlesticks at the back of the room. In the candlelight, Bod could see his guardian standing beside a large leather chest, of the kind they call a steamer trunk—big enough that a tall man could have curled up and slept inside it. Beside it was Silas's black leather bag, which Bod had seen before, on a handful of occasions, but which he still found impressive.

The steamer trunk was lined with whiteness. Bod put a hand into the empty trunk, touched the silk lining, touched dried earth.

"Is this where you sleep?" he asked.

"When I am far from my house, yes," said Silas.

Bod was taken aback: Silas had been here as long as he could remember and before. "Isn't *this* your home?"

Silas shook his head. "My house is a long, long way from here," said Silas. "That is, if it is still habitable. There have been problems in my native land, and I am far from certain what I will find on my return."

"You're going back?" asked Bod. Things that had been immutable were changing. "You're really leaving? But. You're my guardian."

"I *was* your guardian. But you are old enough to guard yourself. I have other things to protect."

Silas closed the lid of the brown leather trunk, and began to do up the straps and the buckles.

"Can't I stay here? In the graveyard?"

"You must not," said Silas, more gently than Bod could remember him ever saying anything. "All the people here have had their lives, Bod, even if they were short ones. Now it's your turn. You need to live."

"Can I come with you?"

Silas shook his head.

"Will I see you again?"

"Perhaps." There was kindness in Silas's voice, and something more. "And whether you see me or not, I have no doubt that I will see you." He put the leather trunk against the wall, walked over to the door in the far corner. "Follow me." Bod walked behind Silas, followed him down the small spiral staircase to the crypt. "I took the liberty of packing a case for you," Silas explained, as they reached the bottom.

On top of the box of mildewed hymn books was a small leather suitcase, a miniature twin to Silas's own. "Your possessions are all in there," said Silas.

Bod said, "Tell me about the Honour Guard, Silas.

302

You're in it. Miss Lupescu was. Who else? Are there a lot of you? What do you do?"

"We don't do enough," said Silas. "And mostly, we guard the borderlands. We protect the borders of things."

"What kind of borders?"

Silas said nothing.

"You mean like stopping the man Jack and his people?"

Silas said, "We do what we have to." He sounded weary.

"But you did the right thing. I mean, stopping the Jacks. They were terrible. They were monsters."

Silas took a step closer to Bod, which made the youth tilt back his head to look up at the tall man's pale face. Silas said, "I have not always done the right thing. When I was younger . . . I did worse things than Jack. Worse than any of them. I was the monster, then, Bod, and worse than any monster."

It did not even cross Bod's mind to wonder if his guardian was lying or joking. He knew that he was being told the truth. He said, "But you aren't that any longer, are you?"

Silas said, "People can change," and then fell silent. Bod wondered if his guardian—if Silas—was remembering. Then, "It was an honor to be your guardian, young man." His hand vanished inside his cloak, reappeared holding a battered old wallet. "This is for you. Take it."

Bod took the wallet, but did not open it.

"It contains money. Enough to give you a start in the world, but nothing more."

Bod said, "I went to see Alonso Jones today but he wasn't there, or if he was I couldn't see him. I wanted him to tell me about distant places he'd visited. Islands and porpoises and glaciers and mountains. Places where people dress and eat in the strangest ways." Bod hesitated. Then, "Those places. They're still there. I mean, there's a whole world out there. Can I see it? Can I go there?"

Silas nodded. "There is a whole world out there, yes. You have a passport in the inner pocket of your suitcase. It's made out in the name of Nobody Owens. And was not easy to obtain."

Bod said, "If I change my mind can I come back here?" And then he answered his own question. "If I come back, it will be a place, but it won't be home any longer."

Silas said, "Would you like me to walk you to the front gate?"

Bod shook his head. "Best if I do it on my own. Um. Silas. If you're ever in trouble, call me. I'll come and help."

"I," said Silas, "do not get into trouble."

"No. I don't suppose you do. But still."

It was dark in the crypt, and it smelled of mildew and damp and old stones, and it seemed, for the first time, very small.

Bod said, "I want to see life. I want to hold it in my hands. I want to leave a footprint on the sand of a desert island. I want to play football with people. I want," he said, and then he paused and he thought. "I want *everything*."

"Good," said Silas. Then he put up his hand as if he were

brushing away the hair from his eyes—a most uncharacteristic gesture. He said, "If ever it transpires that I am in trouble, I shall indeed send for you."

"Even though you don't get into trouble?"

"As you say."

There was something at the edge of Silas's lips that might have been a smile, and might have been regret, and might just have been a trick of the shadows.

"Good-bye, then, Silas." Bod held out his hand, as he had when he was a small boy, and Silas took it, in a cold hand the color of old ivory, and shook it gravely.

"Good-bye, Nobody Owens."

Bod picked up the little suitcase. He opened the door to let himself out of the crypt, walked back up the gentle slope to the path without looking back.

It was well after the gates were locked. He wondered as he reached them if the gates would still let him walk through them, or if he would have to go back into the chapel to get a key, but when he got to the entrance he found the small pedestrian gate was unlocked and wide open, as if it was waiting for him, as if the graveyard itself was bidding him good-bye.

One pale, plump figure waited in front of the open gate, and she smiled up at him as he came towards her, and there were tears in her eyes in the moonlight.

"Hullo, Mother," said Bod.

Mistress Owens rubbed her eyes with a knuckle, then dabbed at them with her apron, and she shook her head.

"Do you know what you're going to do now?" she asked.

"See the world," said Bod. "Get into trouble. Get out of trouble again. Visit jungles and volcanoes and deserts and islands. And people. I want to meet an awful lot of people."

Mistress Owens made no immediate reply. She stared up at him, and then she began to sing a song that Bod remembered, a song she used to sing him when he was a tiny thing, a song that she had used to lull him to sleep when he was small.

> *"Sleep my little babby-oh*
> *Sleep until you waken*
> *When you wake you'll see the world*
> *If I'm not mistaken . . ."*

"You're not," whispered Bod. "And I shall."

> *"Kiss a lover*
> *Dance a measure,*
> *Find your name*
> *And buried treasure . . ."*

Then the last lines of the song came back to Mistress Owens, and she sang them to her son.

> *"Face your life*
> *Its pain, its pleasure,*
> *Leave no path untaken"*

"Leave no path untaken," repeated Bod. "A difficult challenge, but I can try my best."

He tried to put his arms around his mother then, as he had when he was a child, although he might as well have been trying to hold mist, for he was alone on the path.

He took a step forward, through the gate that took him out of the graveyard. He thought a voice said, "I am so proud of you, my son," but he might, perhaps, have imagined it.

The midsummer sky was already beginning to lighten in the east, and that was the way that Bod began to walk: down the hill, towards the living people, and the city, and the dawn.

There was a passport in his bag, money in his pocket. There was a smile dancing on his lips, although it was a wary smile, for the world is a bigger place than a little graveyard on a hill; and there would be dangers in it and mysteries, new friends to make, old friends to rediscover, mistakes to be made and many paths to be walked before he would, finally, return to the graveyard or ride with the Lady on the broad back of her great grey stallion.

But between now and then, there was Life; and Bod walked into it with his eyes and his heart wide open.

ACKNOWLEDGMENTS

First, foremost, and forever: I owe an enormous debt, conscious and, I have no doubt, unconscious, to Rudyard Kipling and the two volumes of his remarkable work *The Jungle Book*. I read them as a child, excited and impressed, and I've read and reread them many times since. If you are only familiar with the Disney cartoon, you should read the stories.

My son Michael inspired this book. He was only two years old, riding his little tricycle between gravestones in the summer, and I had a book in my head. Then it just took me twenty-something years to write it.

When I started writing the book (I started with Chapter Four), only my daughter Maddy's request to know what happened next kept me writing beyond the first couple of pages. Holly did nothing specific, but made everything better.

Gardner Dozois and Jack Dann were the first people to publish "The Witch's Headstone." Professor Georgia Grilli helped throw the book's themes into focus for me.

Kendra Stout was there when I saw the first ghoul gate, and was kind enough to walk through several graveyards with me. She was the audience for the first chapters, and her love for Silas was awesome.

Artist and author Audrey Niffenegger is also a graveyard guide, and she showed me around the ivy-covered marvel that is Highgate Cemetery West. A lot of what she told me crept into Chapters Seven and Eight. Former Web Elf Olga Nunes and Scary Goddaughter Hayley Campbell made it happen and walked with me.

Many friends read this book as it was being written, and all of them offered wise suggestions—Dan Johnson, Gary K. Wolfe, John Crowley, Moby, Farah Mendlesohn, and Joe Sanders, among others. They all spotted things I needed to fix. Still, I missed John M. Ford (1957–2006), who was my best critic of all.

Isabel Ford, Elise Howard, Sarah Odedina, and Clarissa Hutton were the book's editors on both sides of the Atlantic. They made me look good. Michael Conroy directed the audiobook version with aplomb. Mr. McKean drew wonderfully. Merrilee Heifetz is the best agent in the world, and Dorie Simmonds made it happen excellently in the UK. Jon Levin offered advice and took care of film rights. The Fabulous Lorraine Garland, the Wonderful Cat Mihos and the Amazing Kelli Bickman all struggled with my hand-writing, mostly successfully.

I wrote this book in many places: among other places, Jonathan and Jane's Florida house, a cottage in Cornwall, a hotel room in New Orleans; and I failed to write in Tori's house in Ireland because I had flu there instead. But she helped and inspired me, nonetheless.

And as I finish these thanks, the only thing I'm certain of is that I have forgotten not just one very important person but dozens of them. Sorry. But thank you all anyway.

—*Neil Gaiman*

I said
she's gone
but I'm alive, I'm alive
I'm coming in the graveyard
to sing you to sleep now
—*Tori Amos*, "GRAVEYARD"

The Graveyard Book

Neil Gaiman's Answers to Readers' Questions

The Newbery Medal Acceptance Speech

Additional Illustration by Dave McKean

Neil Gaiman's Answers to Readers' Questions

Neil Gaiman receives thousands of questions each year from his readers who write to him or see him at personal appearances. Here are his answers to some of the most frequently asked questions on his website for young readers; visit www.mousecircus.com to submit your own questions to Neil Gaiman.

On *The Graveyard Book*:
What is Silas in *The Graveyard Book*?
Silas is a Very Important Character in *The Graveyard Book*. Also, he is Bod's Guardian.

Could you write a sequel to *The Graveyard Book*? I just finished it and I want more!
I will, yes, but it will go to very different places—and it may not get back to the Graveyard.

I think Dave McKean's artwork really complements your stories. Will you continue to work with him (please)?
As long as he'll let me.

On Writing:
How do you keep yourself motivated to finish a story instead of hopping off to a fresher idea?
I quite like having more than one thing on the go. Then when I get stuck on one thing I can go and mess around with something else.

When writing a story, do you prefer to write it first by hand,

then transpose it onto the computer? Or do you write your stories entirely on the computer?

Depends on the story. I often use the computer for the second draft, so that what I type in is slightly better than what I wrote by hand.

During what part of the day do you get most of your ideas?

Teatime.

What is the best advice you have for aspiring writers?

WRITE. FINISH THINGS. KEEP WRITING.

On Neil Gaiman's:

Why does it say "critically acclaimed and award-winning" every time your name is mentioned in your books?

It's a formal title. Like The Honorable, or Mister President. My full title is Critically Acclaimed and Award-Winning Author Neil Gaiman. But because we're friends, you can call me Neil for short.

How do you feel about seeing film or stage adaptations of your stories?

I pretty much always enjoy them. Sometimes I shake my head and wish they had done something a different way, but mostly they just make me happy—it's a wonderful thing to see creative people take an idea of yours and try to make it real.

What is your sign?

It's a painted piece of wood with BEWARE OF THE MONGOOSE on it. . . . Oh, you didn't mean that sign. I was born on November the tenth, 1960, which makes me a Scorpio Rat.

What was your favorite place to explore as child? And now?
As a child I liked to explore the gardens and grounds of old, empty houses in the town I lived in. Now I like exploring stories best.

What is your favorite monkey?
Probably the Colobus. It's something in the eyes.

What was your favorite book when you were a child? What is your favorite children's book now that you're grown up?
When I was growing up . . . probably the Narnia books. Probably *The Voyage of the Dawn Treader*. Now that I'm grown up I've got to read the Narnia books out loud twice, about a decade apart, and I still think they are astonishing, although I'm more aware of the things I don't like about them. As a grown-up, I think Richmal Crompton's William books are better than I thought they were as a kid, and I loved them, most of them, as a kid.

If you had the opportunity to turn into a piece of fruit, what kind would it be?
A pomegranate, I expect. Or a mango.

If you could be any of the characters in your books, which would you most like to be? Which one has been most like you?
Well, there are a lot of them who pretty much are me—lots of narrators of short stories are as me as you can get. But there's bits of me in all of them. I'm not sure I'd want to be any of the ones I've written. But there are a few in books I've not yet written whose shoes I'd like to inhabit for a while.

4

The Newbery Medal Acceptance Speech
Neil Gaiman's Newbery Acceptance Speech for THE GRAVEYARD BOOK
Delivered at the annual conference of the American Library
Association in Chicago on July 12, 2009

1

In case you were wondering what I'm doing up here—and I think it's a safe bet that right now I am, so that makes at least two of us—I'm here because I wrote a book, called *The Graveyard Book*, that was awarded the 2009 Newbery Medal.

This means that I have impressed my daughters by having been awarded the Newbery Medal, and I impressed my son even more by defending the fact that I had won the Newbery Medal from the hilarious attacks of Stephen Colbert on *The Colbert Report*, so the Newbery Medal made me cool to my children. This is as good as it gets.

You are almost never cool to your children.

2

When I was a boy, from the ages of about eight to fourteen, during my school holidays I used to haunt my local library. It was a mile and a half from my house, so I would get my parents to drop me off there on their way to work, and when the library closed I would walk home. I was an awkward child, ill-fitting, uncertain, and I loved my local library with a passion. I loved the card catalogue, particularly the children's library card catalogue: it had subjects, not just titles and authors, which allowed me to pick subjects I thought were likely to give me books I liked—subjects like magic or ghosts or witches or space—and then I would find the books, and I would read.

But I read indiscriminately, delightedly, hungrily. Literally hungrily, although my father would sometimes remember to pack me sandwiches, which I would take reluctantly (you are never cool to your children, and I regarded his insistence that I should take sandwiches as an insidious plot to embarrass me), and when I got too hungry I would gulp my sandwiches as quickly as possible in the library car park before diving back into the world of books and shelves.

I read fine books in there by brilliant and smart authors—many of them now forgotten or unfashionable, like J. P. Martin and Margaret Storey and Nicholas Stuart Gray. I read Victorian authors and Edwardian authors. I discovered books that now I would reread with delight and devoured books that I would probably now find unreadable if I tried to return to them—Alfred Hitchcock and the Three Investigators and the like. I wanted books and made no distinction between good books or bad, only between the ones I loved, the ones that spoke to my soul, and the ones I merely liked. I did not care how a story was written. There were no bad stories: every story was new and glorious. And I sat there, in my school holidays, and I read the children's library, and when I was done, and had read the children's library, I walked out into the dangerous vastness of the adult section.

The librarians responded to my enthusiasm. They found me books. They taught me about interlibrary loans and ordered books for me from all across southern England. They sighed and were implacable about collecting their fines once school started and my borrowed books were inevitably overdue.

I should mention here that librarians tell me never to tell this story, and especially never to paint myself as a feral child who was raised in libraries by patient librarians; they tell me they are worried that people will misinterpret my story and use it as an excuse to use their libraries as free day care for their children.

3

So. I wrote *The Graveyard Book*, starting in December 2005 and all through 2006 and 2007, and I finished it in February 2008.

And then it's January 2009, and I am in a hotel in Santa Monica. I am out there to promote the film of my book *Coraline*. I had spent two long days talking to journalists, and I was glad when that was done. At midnight I climbed into a bubble bath and started to read *The New Yorker*. I talked to a friend in a different time zone. I finished *The New Yorker*. It was three A.M. I set the alarm for eleven, hung up a DO NOT DISTURB sign on the door. For the next two days, I told myself as I drifted off to sleep, I would do nothing but catch up on my sleep and write.

Two hours later I realized the phone was ringing. Actually, I realized, it had been ringing for some time. In fact, I thought as I surfaced, it had already rung and then stopped ringing several times, which meant someone was calling to tell me something. Either the hotel was burning down or someone had died. I picked up the phone. It was my assistant, Lorraine, sleeping over at my place with a convalescent dog.

"Your agent Merrilee called, and she thinks someone is trying to get hold of you," she told me. I told her what time it was (viz and to wit, five thirty in the bloody morning is she out of her mind some of us are trying to sleep here you know). She said she knew what time it was in L.A., and that Merrilee, who is my literary agent and the wisest woman I know, sounded really definite that this was important.

I got out of bed. Checked voice mail. No, no one was trying

to get hold of me. I called home to tell Lorraine that it was all bosh. "It's okay," she said. "They called here. They're on the other line right now. I'm giving them your cell phone number."

I was not yet sure what was going on or who was trying to do what. It was five forty-five in the morning. No one had died, though, I was fairly certain of that. My cell phone rang.

"Hello. This is Rose Treviño. I'm chair of the ALA Newbery committee . . ." Oh, I thought, blearily. Newbery. Right. Cool. I may be an Honor Book or something. That would be nice. "And I have the voting members of the Newbery committee here, and we want to tell you that your book . . ."

"*THE GRAVEYARD BOOK,*" said fourteen loud voices, and I thought, I may be still asleep right now, but they probably don't do this, probably don't call people and sound so amazingly excited, for honor books . . .

". . . just won . . ."

"THE NEWBERY MEDAL," they chorused. They sounded really happy. I checked the hotel room because it seemed very likely that I was still fast asleep. It all looked reassuringly solid.

You are on a speakerphone with at least fifteen teachers and librarians and suchlike great, wise, and good people, I thought. Do not start swearing like you did when you got the Hugo Award. This was a wise thing to think because otherwise huge, mighty, and four-letter swears were gathering. I mean, that's what they're for. I think I said, "You mean it's Monday?" And I fumfed and mumbled and said something of a "thankyouthankyouthankyouokaythiswasworthbeing wokenupfor" nature.

And then the world went mad. Long before my bedside alarm went off I was in a car on my way to the airport, being interviewed by a succession of journalists. "How does it feel to

8

win the Newbery?" they asked me.

Good, I told them. It felt good.

I had loved *A Wrinkle in Time* when I was a boy, even if they had messed up the first sentence in the Puffin edition, and it was a Newbery Medal winner, and even though I was English, the medal had been important to me.

And then they asked if I was familiar with the controversy about popular books and Newbery winners, and how did I think I fitted into it? I admitted I was familiar with the discussion.

If you aren't, there had been some online brouhaha about what kinds of books had been winning the Newbery Award recently, and about what kinds of books should win the Newbery in the future, and whether awards like the Newbery were for children or for adults. I admitted to one interviewer that *The Graveyard Book* winning had been a surprise to me, that I had assumed that awards like the Newbery tend to be used to shine a light onto books that needed help, and that *The Graveyard Book* had not needed help.

I had unwittingly placed myself on the side of populism, and realized afterward that that was not what I had meant at all.

It was as if some people believed there was a divide between the books that you were permitted to enjoy and the books that were good for you, and I was expected to choose sides. We were all expected to choose sides. And I didn't believe it, and I still don't.

I was, and still am, on the side of books you love.

4

I am writing this speech two months before I will deliver it. My father died about a month ago. It was a surprise. He was in good health, happy, fitter than I am, and his heart ruptured without warning. So, numb and heartsick, I crossed the Atlantic, gave my eulogies, was told by relations I had not seen in a decade just how much I resembled my father, and did what had to be done. And I never cried.

It was not that I did not want to cry. It was more that it seemed there was never any time in the maelstrom of events to just stop and touch the grief, to let whatever was inside me escape. That never happened.

Yesterday morning a friend sent me a script to read. It was the story of somebody's lifetime. A fictional person. Three quarters of the way through the script, the fictional character's fictional wife died, and I sat on the sofa and cried like an adult, huge wrenching sobs, my face running with tears. All the unwept tears for my father came out, leaving me exhausted and, like the world after a storm, cleansed and ready to begin anew.

I'm telling you this because it's something that I forget and need to be reminded of. . . . And this was a sharp and salutary reminder.

I've been writing now for a quarter of a century.

When people tell me that my stories helped them through the death of a loved one—a child, perhaps, or a parent—or helped them cope with a disease, or a personal tragedy; or when they tell me that my tales made them become readers, or gave them a career; when they show me images or words from my books tattooed on their skin as monuments or memorials to moments that were so important to them they needed to take them with them everywhere . . . when these things have happened, as they have, over and over, my tendency is to be polite and grateful, but ultimately to dismiss them as irrelevant.

I did not write the stories to get people through the hard places and the difficult times. I didn't write them to make readers of nonreaders. I wrote them because I was interested in the stories, because there was a maggot in my head, a small squirming idea I needed to pin to the paper and inspect, in order to find out what I thought and felt about it. I wrote them because I wanted to find out what happened next to people I had made up. I wrote them to feed my family.

So I felt almost dishonorable accepting people's thanks. I had forgotten what fiction was to me as a boy, forgotten what it was like in the library: fiction was an escape from the intolerable, a doorway into impossibly hospitable worlds where things had rules and could be understood; stories had been a way of learning about life without experiencing it, or perhaps of experiencing it as an eighteenth-century poisoner dealt with poisons, taking them in tiny doses, such that the poisoner could cope with ingesting things that would kill someone who was not inured to them. Sometimes fiction is a way of coping with the poison of the world in a way that lets us survive it.

And I remembered. I would not be the person I am without the authors who made me what I am—the special ones, the wise ones, sometimes just the ones who got there first.

It's not irrelevant, those moments of connection, those places where fiction saves your life. It's the most important thing there is.

5

So I wrote a book about the inhabitants of a graveyard. I was the kind of boy who loved graveyards as much as he feared them. The best thing—the very best, most wonderful possible thing—about the graveyard in the Sussex town in which I grew up was that there was a witch buried in it, who had been burned in the High Street.

My disappointment on reaching teenagehood and realizing, on rereading the inscription, that the "witch" was nothing of the sort (it was the grave of three stake-burned Protestant martyrs, burned by order of a Catholic queen) stayed with me. It would become the starting place, along with a Kipling story about a jeweled elephant goad, for my story "The Witch's Headstone." Although it's chapter four, it was the first chapter I wrote of *The Graveyard Book*, a book I had wanted to write for over twenty years.

The idea had been so simple, to tell the story of a boy raised in a graveyard, inspired by one image: my infant son, Michael—who was two, and is now twenty-five, the age I was then, and is now taller than I am—on his tricycle, pedaling through the graveyard across the road in the sunshine, past the grave I once thought had belonged to a witch.

I was, as I said, twenty-five years old, and I had an idea for a book and I knew it was a real one.

I tried writing it, and realized that it was a better idea than I was a writer. So I kept writing, but I wrote other things, learning my craft. I wrote for twenty years until I thought that I could write *The Graveyard Book*—or at least, that I was getting no better.

I wanted the book to be composed of short stories, because *The Jungle Book* was short stories. And I wanted it to be a novel, because it was a novel in my head. The tension between those two things was both a delight and a heartache as a writer.

I wrote it as best I could. That's the only way I know how

to write something. It doesn't mean it's going to be any good. It just means you try. And, most of all, I wrote the story that I wanted to read.

It took me too long to begin, and it took me too long to finish. And then, one night in February, I was writing the last two pages.

In the first chapter I had written a doggerel poem and left the last two lines unfinished. Now it was time to finish it, to write the last two lines. So I did. The poem, I learned, ended:

Face your life
Its pain, its pleasure,
Leave no path untaken

And my eyes stung, momentarily. It was then, and only then, that I saw clearly for the first time what I was writing. I had set out to write a book about a childhood—it was Bod's childhood, and it was in a graveyard, but still, it was a childhood like any other; I was now writing about being a parent, and the fundamental most comical tragedy of parenthood: that if you do your job properly, if you, as a parent, raise your children well, they won't need you anymore. If you did it properly, they go away. And they have lives and they have families and they have futures.

I sat at the bottom of the garden, and I wrote the last page of my book, and I knew that I had written a book that was better than the one I had set out to write. Possibly a book better than I am.

You cannot plan for that. Sometimes you work as hard as you can on something, and still the cake does not rise. Sometimes the cake is better than you had ever dreamed.

And then, whether the work was good or bad, whether it did what you hoped or it failed, as a writer you shrug, and you go on to the next thing, whatever the next thing is.

That's what we do.

6

In a speech, you are meant to say what you are going to say, and then say it, and then sum up what you have said.

I don't know what I actually said tonight. I know what I meant to say, though:

Reading is important.

Books are important.

Librarians are important. (Also, libraries are not child-care facilities, but sometimes feral children raise themselves among the stacks.)

It is a glorious and unlikely thing to be cool to your children.

Children's fiction is the most important fiction of all.

There. We who make stories know that we tell lies for a living. But they are good lies that say true things, and we owe it to our readers to build them as best we can. Because somewhere out there is someone who needs that story. Someone who will grow up with a different landscape, who without that story will be a different person. And who with that story may have hope, or wisdom, or kindness, or comfort.

And that is why we write.

Additional Illustration by Dave McKean
The Original *Graveyard Book* Cover Art

Dave McKean originally created the above illustration for the cover of *The Graveyard Book*, but nobody, including Neil and Dave, thought it represented the book properly, so Dave took a different approach. The image shown here contains many of the characters from the story. Can you name the ones pictured?

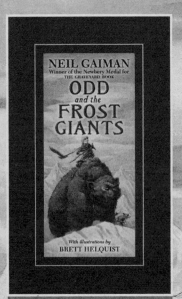